FORBIDDEN IN THE *Falls*

This book is for my Trifecta: Kari and Karen. You two are the Devon Falls of my heart.

Contents

Author's Note

Hello, wonderful reader! Here are a few things to know before you take this trip to Devon Falls, my favorite fictional place.

This book does deal with the topics of past spousal death, grief, and bullying. If any of those are a trigger for you, you may want to step away from this book at this time.

As always, I am deeply grateful for the early readers of my books. Great thanks to Megan, Knox, Katy, Leslie, Rachel, Shantel, Riley, and everyone else who first visited Devon Falls with me. Big thanks to Kari Shafenberg, my editor, who continues to pick up ellipses and em dashes behind me as we walk together on this writing journey.

An important disclaimer: while plenty of research went into writing this book, I chose to alter certain elements of reality to suit the story. Devon Falls is very much a place of my imagination, and I always enjoy suspending some of my own reality while I'm writing for this series.

Huge thanks to all of you for supporting my books and encouraging me to share Malachai and Sam's story after reading *Fauxmance in the Falls.* Malachai and Sam will forever hold a special place in my heart, and I hope they find a special place in yours as well.

Last but not least: no one hates a typo more than me and Sherbert! Should you find a typo in this book, rather than report it to Amazon, please email jebirk@jebirk.com so I can fix it!

Love,

J.E.

Chapter 1

44 Days to the Devon Falls Leaf Festival

A person should never have a boss who makes it impossible for them to speak in complete sentences. —Malachai Flynn

"I can't believe I've let the entire town of Devon Falls take over my wedding. This place is known for exactly two things: an annual festival celebrating a bunch of dead leaves and a statue of a poop emoji."

I choke back a laugh while Dr. Jack Lancer, my boss at Lancer Family Medicine, rubs his fiancé's back. He looks like he's trying to hold back a smile himself. "I hate to say it, hon, but we both knew what we were getting into when we decided to hold our wedding as the launch event for the Devon Falls Leaf Festival this year."

Benson jerks his head out of his hands and glares at Jack as he sinks lower into his chair. "You should have talked me out of this idea the second I suggested it," he growls. "What the hell was I thinking letting this place plan my *wedding*? Bringing in the high school band to play at the ceremony was bad enough. Adding a dance troupe to the cake-cutting is the last straw. We're canceling the whole thing and eloping. Tell Henri to call off the goats and the maple syrup fountain. We're getting married in Aruba. I'm ending all of this before the poop emoji statue ends up taking center stage during our vows."

"Babe, you know very well that the statue isn't supposed to look like a poop emoji. That was an accident."

"And you hate hot weather," Dr. Marie Lancer, Jack's mother and my other boss, reminds him from where she's standing next to my desk studying something on her tablet. "Plus, Jack's father doesn't fly well. Are you going to tell Alan he has to miss your wedding, sweetie?"

Benson drops his head back into his hands again as he sinks even further into his seat across from me in the office's waiting room. "Save me, Malachai," he mutters.

I try to give him my best sympathetic look from where I'm sitting behind my desk, but the effort creates a strange squeezing sensation in my chest. Am I sometimes jealous of Benson? Maybe. When he first moved to Devon Falls, he was essentially the town pariah: the guy who came here to destroy Devon Falls' beloved annual leaf festival. A year later, the festival is more popular than ever and he's so well-liked that the entire town has turned his wedding celebration, which is taking place on the leaf festival grounds the night before the festival fully opens, into an actual festival *event.* There are rumors that Vermont's beloved state cow, Vermonica, might even make an appearance.

"Great," Benson grumbled when he heard the news. "Because more manure is just what this wedding needs."

He may be prickly and complain constantly about how the Devon Falls festival planning committee has taken over his wedding, but I think somewhere deep down Benson loves just how much this community has embraced him and made him one of their own. I swear I saw him blush when Henri Fontaine, our town's matriarch and the festival manager, patted his cheek the other day and told him she couldn't imagine a better opening to the festival than his wedding.

Meanwhile, I can't even walk into Falling All Beans, our town's coffee shop, without someone taking a not-so-subtle step away from me. I'm not a complete town pariah like Benson was; the Lancers and Benson and the Fontaines have never been anything but kind to me since I arrived here. Everyone else? Their reactions are a lot more hit-or-miss. Avon Loseff, the son of the town's former mayor, whispered the word "criminal" under his breath when I ran into him at the Farm-Acy last week.

Things like that tend to happen when you end up homeless and squatting in a barn with a meth lab in it, fail to tell the authorities about said meth lab, and then nearly get people killed because of your silence. That all happened a year ago, right after Benson arrived in town. I was so certain I'd be fired after the town discovered what I'd done that I showed up to work the next day with my letter of resignation.

Dr. Lancer (or Jack, as he keeps telling me to call him) barely glanced at it. "Do you want to leave?" he asked me.

"Uh, no," I stuttered. "But I really screwed up, and—"

He ripped the letter up. Right on the spot. No one at the office has ever mentioned it since.

If only the rest of the town shared the Lancers' level of forgiveness. No one in Devon Falls is exactly *mean* to me—that's just not the vibe of this place, unlike the town I grew up in. It's more like they're *wary*. And I really can't blame them for that wariness after what I did last year.

If only I could manage to live in just one town in Vermont without somehow becoming a complete and utter outcast. When I first left Alcott, the town I was born in about eighty miles northwest of here, I was sure that leaving my county and finding a new home would give me a whole fresh start.

Unfortunately, things haven't worked that way.

This is why you're leaving Vermont, I remind myself. *This is why you can't stay in this state.*

My eyes drift toward the screen door of the office that shows a wide view of the front porch, where I've been watching the office mailbox with at least one eye for days now. In this age of electronic communication, who even sends snail mail anymore? I couldn't believe it when I read that this acceptance or denial notice would be coming by post. I swear, it's been actual torture waiting for this letter to arrive. My heart skips in my chest as my eyes brush past the box, with its red flag still raised high in the air. The flag that clearly means mail needs to be picked up and no new letters have been dropped off yet.

It's the first day of September. The news is supposed to arrive this week. How long am I going to have to wait? Does news coming later mean I didn't get in? Does it mean I've been waitlisted? Does it mean that I—

"Malachai? Are you okay?" I force myself to look away from the porch and find Marie staring at me. "You seem distracted today. Are you feeling alright?" She leans over like she might put a hand on my forehead, but I duck away, shaking my head.

"I'm fine. Just a little tired," I tell her, forcing a smile onto my face. Tired and a nervous wreck, actually, but there's no way I'm telling Marie, Jack, and Benson that the Devon Falls letter carrier, who delivers the mail from a purple zebra print bag, could either make or break my entire future today. After all, what if I don't get in? The last thing I need is the only people in town who still regularly speak to me seeing me as a complete and total failure.

"You work too hard." Jack frowns. "Are you still taking all those credits you said you were signing up for this fall?"

I swallow hard and nod. I don't need any reminders that my daily schedule is basically untenable. I've got a full course load at the nearby community college campus and I work as the Lancer Family Medicine office manager and general all-around assistant to everyone else who works here full time, not to mention all the side jobs I often pick up around town for extra cash. I think the last time I got a full night's sleep was when I was fifteen years old. Did I mention that I recently turned twenty-one? So yeah, it's been a few years since I fully understood the term "rest."

"And here I thought he was just dreaming about Sam." Benson sits up slightly in his chair and sends me a characteristic smirk.

"I don't *dream* about Dr. Evers," I answer testily, but I can feel the heat rising in my cheeks. Benson's a little too observant sometimes, and the moment Dr. Sam Evers, Jack's best friend, arrived in town to work at our office, Benson seemed to figure out that I was more than a little obsessed with the guy. I'm not sure how, exactly. I don't think I'm *that* obvious. Maybe lawyers have strong investigative skills or something.

Marie sighs and shakes her head. "Benson, please stop teasing him like this. Malachai and Sam both work here. You're a lawyer, for goodness sake. Don't create HR nightmares inside my medical practice."

Benson scoffs. "No problem. I can whip up some paperwork anytime the two of them want to get it on. There's a clause in your office contracts that—"

"I'm not getting it on with anyone!" I nearly shout. I suck in a deep breath and let it out slowly, the way my high school guidance counselor used to make me do whenever I had a panic attack. "Especially not Dr. Evers. He's leaving in like six weeks, anyway!"

Not to mention that me getting it on with *anyone* is a hurdle I don't have the time or energy to get over right now. But there's no way I'm sharing that story in the middle of my workplace.

Jack frowns and lets out a long breath of his own. It's no secret that Dr. Evers only came to Lancer Family Medicine to help out during this busy period while Jack and Benson are getting ready for their wedding. He's made it very clear that he plans to go back to New York, where he and Jack both used to live, the second the wedding and the leaf festival are over.

It's also no secret that Jack doesn't want Dr. Evers to leave. I'm not exactly sure what Dr. Evers' background is, but I know his husband passed away a few years ago, and all the town gossip says he hasn't handled it well.

The only other thing I know about him is that I somehow manage to lose the ability to speak whenever he walks into the same room as me, which is definitely *not* working out well. A person should never have a boss who makes it impossible for them to speak in complete sentences. I enjoy and need my job. And my job requires that I have regular, meaningful conversations with my new boss, who also happens to be the biggest crush I've ever had in my life, without forgetting how to speak English.

So. I'm working on that.

Jack leans over to kiss the top of Benson's head. "Babe, we all know that subtlety isn't your strong suit, but Malachai's feelings are his own business. And Malachai, regarding Sam—"

"What about me?" A deep voice I know all too well rolls into the room. That voice *glides,* I swear, like a rolling chair moving across a long, smooth wood floor. Behind it comes Dr. Sam Evers, who steps into the office doorway from the front porch. He must be just coming back from lunch.

And, once again, I immediately lose all ability to speak.

I really, really, *really* hate what my body starts doing whenever Dr. Sam Evers steps inside my line of sight. It's like each one of my nerves begins screaming *alert alert alert* while my heart beat starts racing a little faster with every step he takes anywhere near me. Human beings just shouldn't be allowed to be as good looking as he is. Jack is pretty hot, but his friends all seem to be movie star handsome, and Dr. Evers is *blockbuster* movie star handsome. He's broad and tall, with shoulders that stack widely over a long torso. He's around Jack's age, thirty-five, I think, and he walks with the kind of confidence and self-assuredness I can't imagine walking with when I'm sixty-five, for crying out loud. His dirty blond hair is cut short and always looks effortlessly styled, and of course it matches perfectly with his golden-beige skin and green eyes. Today he's wearing a green polo that hugs every muscle of his upper body perfectly, and his pressed khaki pants somehow manage to look exceptionally professional and easily casual all at the same time.

I glance down at my fading black button-up shirt, with the hole in the hem that I've hidden by tucking it in, and the khaki pants I'm wearing that are almost a size too small for me because I've had them since junior high school, and I fight the urge to run and hide in the supply closet.

"Hello, all," Dr. Evers growls.

Yup. *Growls.* He growls the words, I swear. A growl shouldn't be sexy as fuck, right? It should be scary or intimidating or terrifying... something like that, shouldn't it? But Dr. Evers speaks in this voice that's low and rumbly and almost dark and seems to sit inside of my body for hours after any conversation we have. And I've never seen him smile—he's basically the opposite of Jack, that way—which makes his presence even larger somehow.

When I was a kid, I'd sit on my mom's thread-bare couch and dream of getting the fuck out of Alcott, Vermont. Back then, I'd often see people who looked like Dr. Evers on our television screen. I'd imagine what it would be like to be in the presence of someone so in control and perfectly put together that they were almost otherworldly. The men and women who looked like that seemed a million miles away from the men and women my mother and I were surrounded by: everyone we knew who lived in Alcott always seemed so small, so lacking, so destined for failure. And fail they did, one after the other, at everything from holding down a job to staying out of jail.

But the people on the screen? The ones who looked like Dr. Evers? They were reliable. They were dependable. They were strong, and they always succeeded.

I used to dream of meeting someone like that in real life.

"Hey, Sammy." Benson waves, and Dr. Evers rolls his eyes.

"I thought we agreed you wouldn't use that nickname anymore."

Benson looks back and forth between Jack and Sam innocently. "Did we agree to that? Huh. Must've forgotten."

Sam shakes his head, but he's got a kind of fond expression on his face that wrings another drop of jealousy out of me. I understand the feeling, though. It's weird how Benson Lewis grows on you even as he's bugging the crap out of you. I can't figure out exactly how he does it. Maybe it's because he does things like leave sandwiches on my desk when he knows I don't have any time between classes and work—and he probably knows I don't have money for the maple turkey sandwich from Luis' cafe, which I love—in between making snarky remarks about Devon Falls' obsession with textile arts and teasing me about my not-so-secret crush on Dr. Evers. I can't even imagine what Benson's done to win over Dr. Evers himself.

"Hello, Sam." Marie sends Dr. Evers a bright smile. "We were just wondering if you'd reconsider our offer to stay at the office permanently? Rather than leave in October?"

The question seems to roll through the small office space, creating a wave of silence with it, and for a moment it feels like everyone's holding their breath while we wait for an answer.

"No," Dr. Evers finally says. His voice is succinct. Direct. "I believe I was clear about when I'd be departing Devon Falls to return to New York."

"Of course," Jack says quickly. "We don't want to pressure you, buddy." He shakes his head. "We could just use the help around here, and the patients really like you. That's all."

Dr. Evers nods. "That's very good to hear. I ran into Donna Brightly as she was dropping off the mail, so I took it from her." He steps across the room and passes a pile of letters to me, and I do my best to ignore the slight tingling in my hand that seems to linger there after our fingers brush together.

Then I spot the envelope on top of the pile, and I almost choke on my next breath as I see the lettering printed on the front.

BILLINGTON UNIVERSITY, BOSTON, MASSACHUSETTS

I try to thank Dr. Evers, but I can't make the words come out. I've lost the ability to speak again, and for once my boss has nothing to do with my frozen vocal chords.

Dr. Evers frowns at me. "Malachai," he asks in that horrifyingly perfect grumble of his, "how are you feeling? You suddenly look awfully pale."

"I'm. Uh. I'm." Oh, great *fuck.* I take a deep breath and burst out a word. "Fine!" I send him and everyone else in the office a weak smile as I do my best not to clutch the envelope so hard in my hands that it crumples.

"If you're sure." He waves as he heads out of the lobby and down the hall toward the patient exam rooms. "Jack, Benson, I'll see you for dinner tonight."

"Bring some of that excellent chocolate pie you make," Benson calls after him. He stands up and stretches. "I've got to head back to work for a few hours. Malachai," he asks, "are you really sure you're okay? You've turned like four different colors in the last few minutes. I'll stop teasing you, okay? I know I'm an ass, but I mostly don't mean to be, and—"

I shake my head. "I'm okay, Benson," I tell him. "I, um, just need some air, I think. Can someone watch the phones for a minute?"

"Of course, love," Marie says. "Take as much time as you need." She and Jack share a quick glance, but I barely notice it as I hold onto the envelope and basically make a run for the front door of the old Victorian house that Lancer Family Medicine resides in.

I get to the porch before I realize I'm holding my breath. This is it. This is the moment I've been waiting for: the chance to achieve every dream I've ever had in my life.

My dream to get into a nursing school I've always wanted to attend.

My dream to get out of Vermont, a place that's never accepted me.

My dream to find the kind of life I've only imagined could ever be possible.

I swallow down a gulp of fear and make my first tear into that envelope. I tug the piece of paper inside from its confines, and at first, the whole world seems light and real and perfect.

And then that same world begins to go dark around the edges.

Back when I was growing up, after she'd had a particularly bad day at work, my mother used to sit on the couch with me sometimes. I remember her blowing cigarette smoke rings at the ceiling as she told me everything that had gone wrong that day. "Malachai," she said once, "I swear, some people just aren't meant to be happy."

In moments like these, I'm sure she must have been right.

Chapter 2
43 Days to the Devon Falls Leaf Festival

The knitting club would probably not approve of me kidnapping my underling. —Sam Evers

"You dropped your purl stitch."

I glare at the row of knitting in front of me while I try to figure out exactly what Amelia Shiner, town mayor and president of the Devon Falls Knitting Association, is talking about. "What? Where?"

I do my best to speak the words in an even tone. Recently, my friend and colleague Jack sat me down and asked me if I could stop grumbling at all of our patients; apparently I have a *presence* to my voice that's a bit more foreboding than what they're going for at a family practice catering largely to local farmers and elementary school students. "Watching your tone is more for the farmers," he told me. "They're not used to seeing so much scowling. The children seem to think you're just funny."

He also casually asked again if I've possibly been watching too much *Downton Abbey*. Every single day, he said, I was starting to sound more like I'd stepped out of a period drama. I gave him the same answer I shared the last time he brought up my speaking patterns and compared them to BBC television shows: that I've always spoken formally, and he should know that better than anyone. We've been friends for years, after all.

My answer was not entirely true, of course. Naturally, I've realized that my vocal patterns have shifted slightly since I temporarily moved to Vermont to help out at the Lancer Family Medicine practice. While both my brother and I did attend some rather prestigious private schools growing up, it's always been very easy for both Tom and me to turn the highly formal speech patterns those schools often encouraged on and off.

No, I can never tell Jack why my speech and behaviors, particularly my interactions with others, have become so very stilted and formal since I came to live in Devon Falls. That's a secret I can't possibly share with him.

Or with anyone else.

"There's the dropped stitch," says Amelia. Her once white hair, which she's recently dyed in rainbow hues, dances as she jabs a pale, wrinkly index finger cheerfully at a row of the dark green beanie I've been working on for two weeks. The beanie is for the charity clothing drive that all of us are knitting items for right now. I'm choosing to ignore the fact that Amelia's already finished two sweaters, a scarf, a pair of socks and half a mitten in the same amount of time it's taken me to create half of a hat.

To be fair, I imagine being mayor of a town the size of a postage stamp isn't that taxing of a job; she must have plenty of time for knitting outside of this group. Of course, she is also the pastor at the local community-inclusive church, but I can't imagine her congregation is big enough to be spilling out of the pews. I wouldn't know, of course. Jack and his fiancé, Benson, keep inviting me to attend a service with them, but I keep turning them down.

I appreciate that Amelia's church is covered in rainbow flags and invitations to the LGBTQIA2S+ community. I came out as bisexual at a rather young age, and it's refreshing to live in a town that's so inclusive and welcoming throughout its spaces and places. But I don't do church. Any church. I tried after Christian died. It never helped.

Knitting. Knitting helps.

Well. It helps when my self-assigned knitting buddy at the Devon Falls Knitting Association (trademark pending, I'm told), isn't side-eyeing me and waiting to watch me rip out an entire row of stitches.

I inwardly groan. I hate ripping out stitches. It leaves an ugly taste in my mouth: the taste of failure. Plus, half the time I accidentally take out too many and end up ripping apart the entire project.

"Maybe I meant to drop that stitch," I tell Amelia. "Maybe I did it on purpose."

She snorts. "Only if that pattern was made by half-deranged fairy elves on a quest for small and extremely ugly hats. You'll probably need a crochet hook. You can borrow mine." She starts rummaging in the large duffel bag she brings to every one of our meetings. "So, how are you liking it here in Vermont, Sam? Marie tells me things are going well over at the doctor's office."

"Devon Falls is perfectly fine," I tell her, still keeping my voice as even as possible. This is mostly true. After living in New York city for the majority of my life, I've found it difficult to adjust to the Devon Falls custom of inserting yourself into everyone else's business. I expected Jack and his mother to nose their way into every part of my existence once I moved here; they've both known me for a large portion of my adulthood. I did not expect perfect strangers to stop me on the street and ask me if I'm pleased with the original hardwood floors in the old farmhouse I'm renting for the duration of my stay here.

It's a ridiculous question anyway. Those floors are original to the house. Only a sadist would prefer carpet.

"Very glad to hear it," Amelia responds crisply as she passes me some kind of metal stick that I have no earthly idea how to use. "I know you're only staying through the wedding and the festival, but we like to make sure people feel welcome."

Janice Ryker's nose pops up from behind the large blanket she's working on. "How are things going for that office worker of yours? Malachai Flynn? I worry about him. My Tom says Avon Loseff's been spreading some nasty rumors about him around town and that people still won't sit with him at the coffee shop sometimes."

"Poor Malachai." Marion Stevenson, the local bakery owner, shakes her head as she peers through the stitches of a large shawl. "I'll make sure he gets an extra muffin the next time he comes in. I'm trying to fatten that boy up. He's far too skinny. What's Avon going on about? I swear, the man has a chip on his shoulder the size of Maine. Maybe it's true that money can't make people happy. He certainly has more of it than almost anyone else around here. Imagine, being the great-grandson of the family that started one of the most beloved ice cream plants in Vermont and still being as miserable as he is!"

"Oh, Avon's got it in his head that Malachai's still involved with those drug dealers he got caught up with last year," Luis Morales informs Marion as he carefully works some bright blue yarn into the snowflake pattern on a scarf. "It's all bullshit. But everyone here's been so jumpy about what happened back then that some people still get worried. And nerves and bullshit don't go together well."

"My heavens." Marion frowns. "Is this why I need to join this Insta-place Janice's children are always telling me about? They keep saying it would help me stay up on the happenings around town. Would I be able to keep up on this new-fangled slang there too? Would I know who's going steady?"

"If you still think people are using the phrase 'go steady,' then I don't think Instagram is going to save you," Amelia tells her. "Let's not get off the topic, though. Sam, do you think we should be worried about Malachai? Spill the tea."

"Not near my project!" Marion looks horrified.

"That means 'tell us everything,'" Janice interjects. "Yes, tell us, Sam. Is Malachai okay?"

"I'm afraid I wouldn't know," I tell them sharply, as I work to ignore the bass drum thwacking loudly inside of my heart. Every cell in my body screams to demand more information from them: who's this Avon, and what exactly is he saying about Malachai? How do I immediately ensure he never causes Malachai any further harm in the future? How do I make sure *no one ever* causes Malachai any harm at all?

But those are questions I can never allow myself to ask, and I've been working so hard *not* to pay attention to Malachai Flynn that I have no answer in response to their concerns. I'm careful to keep my voice even enough that I'm sure I couldn't be accused of growling, even by the most sensitive of farmers. "I haven't noticed anything about Malachai's demeanor," I tell Janice. "We're simply colleagues."

"Hmm, too bad," Marion adds. "That Malachai's such a nice boy, and he always looks so... sad? Lonely, maybe. I'd like to see him find a friend like you, Sam."

"I'm almost fifteen years older than him," I remind her. Moments like these are when I wish I'd kept my newly developed knitting habit inside the comfort of my own home instead of letting Amelia talk me into joining this absurd gossip circle. If I didn't need Janice to teach me slip stitch for my next pattern, I'd quit the group right now.

"Age is just a number," Janice replies. "I'm ten years older than Tom, and he's the love of my life. My boy Ellis is the same age as Malachai, and he's friends with Luis. And Luis is his boss at the diner!"

Luis nods as he focuses on his scarf. I, meanwhile, struggle to remember which one of Janice's fourteen children Ellis is. Ryker children are everywhere in Devon Falls. They're the equivalent of hot dog vendors in New York City, but far more polite and much more likely to have Janice's orange hair.

"We know you won't be here in town long, Sam," Amelia says, "but personally, I would like to see you make a few more friends. We can only imagine how much you must miss Christian, and—"

"I'll be leaving now." I stand abruptly, grabbing for the reusable grocery bag I use to cart around my needles and wool. "See you all next week." I head for the large front door of the town hall, the spot where our group regularly meets, ignoring the round of loud protests ringing behind me.

The members of my knitting group may cross constant lines of propriety in regards to their topics of discussion, but they certainly know better than to cross the line they just stepped over. They, like everyone else in this town, know better than to *ever* bring up Christian in front of me without my express permission.

I step out the front doors of the building into the cooling fall air of an early evening in Devon Falls. The sun's setting in soft pink and orange hues over the darkening buildings of Main Street. The street is fully empty, quiet in its respite, and I pause briefly while I take a moment to let the stillness of the street and the soft scent of sweet grass wash through me. For so long I ignored Jack's pleas to come to Devon Falls to work with him, sure that I'd miss the volume and sights and speed of New York City.

The city had been home for so long. Home with Christian. The apartment we shared, the one that brought so much routine to my life for so many years, felt nearly impossible to leave. However, I must admit that coming to Devon Falls has offered a tremendous reprieve from the ghosts haunting that apartment. From the guilt and shame that followed me, trailing my steps between the living room and the kitchen and bedroom every morning, noon, and night.

If only that same guilt wasn't currently taking up space in the very doctor's office I'm working in.

I sigh as I take a step forward and begin the walk up Main Street toward Lancer Family Medicine, where I left my car parked after work today. That guilt is now apparently spreading into my own knitting group; it seems there are no steps I can take to avoid it.

What's a person supposed to do when they find themselves obsessed with their office assistant and discover that obsession to be much more intense than anything they ever felt for their own late husband? When Christian died, his death weighed so very heavily on me. We'd known each other since childhood, and he was rooted in every part of my life. But my grief went deeper than that. It spiraled down into a much larger problem: I knew I didn't miss Christian in the way a spouse probably ought to miss the great love of their life. And I knew that Christian likely would never have died that day had I loved him the way a husband should love their spouse.

Those ghosts of guilt, those whispers of *what if...* I thought saying yes to Jack and coming to Devon Falls, even for a short time, might chase them away. But then I began working with Malachai.

And now those ghosts haunt me by the hour.

My feelings toward Malachai are entirely illogical. They're rooted in chaos. I never imagined when I came to this town to help Jack and Marie during this period of their lives that I would find myself inexplicably drawn to the quiet, shy young man who spends far too much time sinking into himself and seems to panic over every word he's forced to utter. The urge I have to step in front of him and protect him from anyone who may cause him harm, the instinct within me to draw him out of his shell and let the world see the kind, caring, strong, brilliant person hiding inside—those urges and instincts threaten to overwhelm me at least once a day.

Those urges are a constant, pounding reminder of what a failure I was in my marriage.

So far, I've managed to resist my highly inappropriate and dangerous feelings. I've done my best to maintain distance and decorum in my interactions with everyone here, particularly Malachai. There's no denying that my attempts at distance are what's pushed me back into the formal speech patterns Jack likes to tease me about, and I'm quite comfortable with that. There are only six weeks left until Jack's wedding, and if I can just hold this same level of distance until then, I will be safe. Safe to return to New York and exchange this set of ghosts for another.

I step slowly down the street, where dusk is punctuated by fairy lights in windows and street lights are beginning to click on for the night. There are so few surprises here. At this time of night, everyone in the town has their place: at knitting club, or eating dinner in Luis' café, or at home with their family, or—

Sleeping in the backseat of their car?

I rush to the side of the ancient, tiny Mazda parked behind the medical office before I can stop myself, and I jerk open the back door. Malachai pops up from where he's awkwardly wrapped in a sleeping bag at an unnatural angle, head banging into the cloudy car window as his wrapped feet hit the back of the front passenger seat. His wavy, brown hair is standing up in an odd pattern away from his forehead and ears, his tawny, lightly tanned skin looks flushed, and his dark brown eyes are wide. Not for the first time, I fight the desire to gather him in my arms so I might bring him home and wrap him up in the warm, layered quilts that cover my bed.

He always looks cold, Malachai. Even when it's seventy degrees out. This bothers me.

Right now it's not seventy degrees; the temperature's dropped to the low fifties. We're having a very chilly entry into fall here, and the first frost could be coming soon, Benson told me recently as he frowned and studied the tomatoes planted in his and Jack's backyard. *What the hell is Malachai doing in his car tonight, wrapped up in a sleeping bag? Is he spending the night here?*

"What's going on?" I demand.

That was definitely a growl. Jack would not approve, but I don't regret it. Malachai responds immediately. "I'm so sorry, sir," he says, stammering in the way he does that often has me ordering myself not to draw him into my arms and ward the rest of the world away from him. "I didn't mean—I'll leave—I wasn't trying to—"

I hate how pink and full his lips are when he goes on nervously like this; they're featured in far too many of the ill-begotten fantasies I've had of the two of us alone in my office. No one else around, him pushing at my lab coat while he licks those two lips in quiet rhythm—

No, I order my dick. We're not succumbing to that fantasy now, I remind it. Or ever.

Off-limits. Forbidden.

I know what I owe to the universe. To Christian. I know what boundaries I must maintain.

"What are you doing here?" I demand. "Shouldn't you be at home?" Malachai, I know, has an apartment on the edge of Devon Falls in an old part of town known as Dairy Corners. I hear it was once the place to rent an apartment in Devon Falls, but that time was forty years ago. Now the Dairy Corners complex is in terrible disrepair and reputation; more than once Jack has anxiously worried about Malachai living there. When I finally drove by and caught a peek at its sagging roof and trash-covered parking lot, I was tempted to storm inside and steal Malachai away on the spot. But sanity prevailed, and I kept driving.

"Well." Malachai scratches at the loose hairs on his forehead as his cheeks go pinker. "Uh, I was. But I had to leave kind of suddenly, and I haven't found a new place yet. So..."

That's all I need to hear. I pull the car door open wider. "You're coming to stay with me," I order him.

"Excuse me?" Malachai blinks at me once, and then twice. I inwardly wince at the words I've just said.

Am I really doing this? Did I really just invite the young man I keep inadvertently imagining bent over my office desk to stay at my house? It's a terrible idea, that's certain. I have very specific rules and boundaries I've set for working with Malachai. This invitation will violate all of them. Not to mention that Jack lives right down the road from here. I could easily deliver Malachai to him; he and Benson would be happy to take Malachai in.

And yet.

And yet.

"You're coming to stay with me." I say, or possibly growl, the words again.

Malachai blushes pink once more, and once again I regret nothing.

"Sir, thank you for the offer," he says. "But really, I'm okay. The car is fine just for sleeping, and I'm sure I can find another place soon. I'll be—"

"Malachai," I interrupt. "You're coming home with me. Right now."

Is it my imagination, or does he shiver?

It's getting colder out. That's the only explanation.

He sighs. He has a stubborn, independent streak about him; I see it in the office sometimes, when Jack or Marie offer him help he's sure he doesn't need. Like a young deer determined to stand up by himself, he always lifts his chin upward, and then stammers out the most polite denial of their assistance anyone could imagine.

It's adorable. But there's no way I'm standing for it now. I'll kidnap him from this car if I have to.

The knitting club would probably not approve of me kidnapping my underling. Then again... I imagine Amelia's expression as she discussed Malachai tonight.

There's a strong chance they would highly approve.

"Malachai," I tell him again. "You can't stay here, in your vehicle. It isn't safe. Please. Come home with me."

The words echo across my tongue with a tingling danger as they remind me of the risks I'm taking here. I've worked so hard to ignore my feelings for Malachai, to distance myself from him, and now I've invited him into the safe space of my home here in Devon Falls. A space where I may not be able to hide from him. From myself.

A space where I may never be able to hide from my past.

And yet, when Malachai opens up his mouth and softly replies, I only feel relief.

"Okay," he says. "I'll come home with you."

Chapter 3
42 Days to the Devon Falls Leaf Festival

Normally I try not to end up half-naked on the floor of my boss' kitchen. —Malachai Flynn

I wake up in a strange place, which isn't necessarily unusual for me. I've woken up in a lot of strange places in my life. That list includes my car, on more than one occasion; a barn run by the Norton brothers, who turned out to be meth dealers and would-be murderers; public library floors; and once a table in a shed behind my high school's automotive school.

My neighbors in the trailer park were having a party, and it got very, very loud. I had a test the next day, and I knew the automotive teacher never bothered to lock that shed.

It's amazing how many places and spaces I've been able to sleep in when I had to find someplace to go. That's probably why I didn't bat an eyelash when I found myself homeless again just a few nights ago. It wasn't like that was the first time I'd been in that position, so I didn't worry too much about it. I just moved into my car and resolved to stay there and shower at the Devon Falls gym until I figured things out. The truth is that I have much bigger problems on my mind right now than where I sleep.

And those problems are all thanks to that letter I got from Billington University: a letter that turned out to be one of the best and worst things I've ever received in my life.

Learning that I was accepted into Billington's nursing school for this coming spring semester was honestly the most shocking and exciting news I could have gotten. Billington's picky, and I knew when I applied that getting in would be a long-shot.

But then came the side of the news which wasn't all that great. The financial aid package they offered was decent but not earth-shattering, and I knew right away that I was going to have to tighten my budget significantly and start looking for new sources of income in order to afford the tuition bill that's due to them in late October if I want to start school there as soon as possible. Which I very, very definitely do.

Three seconds after I read that letter I started pouring over my budget. It didn't take me long to realize that rent is what sucks most of my money down the drain every month, and my apartment at Dairy Corners was barely habitable anyway. The roaches and rats weren't going to miss me if I left, I was certain of that. Sleeping in my car and looking for a cheaper living option while I saved my cash seemed like an easy enough decision. After all, I've lived in my car before. I survived then, and I knew I could do it again.

But then Dr. Evers found me in the Lancer Family Medicine parking lot.

"I still can't believe he basically dragged me home with him," I whisper to myself as I get a handle on my new surroundings. I also very definitely can't believe what a fucking dream his guest bed is. The mattress underneath me is like a cloud beneath my back, cushioning and working out all the tension that I've spent weeks trying to move with useless stretches. The pillow below my head is the softest one I've ever touched. Can pillows feel like cotton candy? Because this one definitely does. The duvet on top of me has to be made out of feathers; it's another cloud wrapped around my body. I snuggle inside of it, savoring the moment, letting warmth and comfort wash over me.

I imagine the trailer I grew up in, my tiny bedroom with the ancient mattress on the floor, the one I could always feel the springs poking out of. This room might just be *heaven* compared to that trailer and every other place I've ever slept.

And then I remember again exactly where I am.

Holy fuck. *I am in Dr. Sam Evers' house.*

I sit up in bed as more memories of last night settle themselves back into my brain. One moment I was doing my best to nod off in my car, and the next thing I knew, Dr. Evers was insisting I follow him back to the updated farmhouse he's renting, where he practically ordered me into his guest room.

The whole thing feels like a hazy dream, honestly. I kept insisting that I didn't need to go home with him; I told him more than once that I was perfectly fine sleeping where I was and that he didn't need to help me. All he did was narrow his eyes and stare at me, and the next thing I knew I was following right behind him.

The spell Dr. Evers has over me would be terrifying if it wasn't so fucking *hot*.

I force myself to push the best covers I've ever been under off my legs as I check my watch against the rising light in the sky. It's still early, early enough that I'm guessing Dr. Evers isn't awake yet. It's time to face what I've discovered to be the most difficult thing about waking up in a strange place: deciding how to approach my next action. What should I do? Who do I speak or not speak to? Where do I go? And there's even more pressure on this moment than there was when I woke up on the floor of a barn owned by local criminals. At least the criminals weren't entangled in my complicated romantic fantasies.

Waking up in the guest room of your boss/long-standing crush doesn't exactly come with an instruction manual. Still, I've got an idea of what I should probably do next.

I slip out of bed, stopping for a moment to study more of the room surrounding me. The walls are a light, soft denim blue, and the green-and-white bedding contrasts with the paint color perfectly. There's a gray wooden desk that matches with the bed frame and dresser standing solidly off to the side of the room. The entire space is tranquil, almost forgiving, and peaceful. It's the kind of room that's perfect for studying; the kind of room I could spend hours and hours in. It's the exact opposite of the dank, dark apartment I recently left behind.

It all reminds me of those perfect houses and people I used to watch on TV when I was a kid. I always figured Dr. Evers had to have money; he's a doctor, after all. Now I'm starting to wonder if he has a *whole lot* of money. Because renting a place like this, even in a town like Devon Falls, can't come cheap.

I rummage through my backpack until I find a pair of basketball shorts and a t-shirt that are closer to clean than dirty. I pull them on and push open the door of the room, wincing slightly at the quiet creaking noise it makes.

The rest of the house stands silently around me. Good. Hopefully that means I haven't woken up Dr. Evers.

I tiptoe my way down the stairs of the house, admiring how homey the place feels in the rising light of sunrise. I come to a stop in the kitchen and flip the nearest light switch. Immediately the space is awash in soft lighting that highlights cream cabinets, an industrial sink, a six-burner stove, and a large, black marble island.

Holy shit. My dream kitchen is in my dream lover's house. Wait, scratch that: my boss' house. Talk about standing in the middle of a fantasy that's far out of reach.

But it's in reach this morning, I remind myself. That kitchen is right in front of me, resplendent and ready for cooking. And I'm determined to use it to make Dr. Evers the best thank-you breakfast he's ever had in his life.

Then I've got to get the fuck out of here and find a new place to live—because no way is it a good idea to stay in the guest bedroom of the off-limits boss who haunts my dreams.

I raid Dr. Evers' fridge, pulling out farm-fresh eggs, locally sourced bacon, and fresh vegetables I recognize from the Devon Falls' Farmers Market. I get to work chopping and prepping, pulling spices from cabinets and pots and pans from drawers. The kitchen is definitely set up like someone uses it often. I wonder what Dr. Evers likes to cook, and I almost wish I could stay here long enough to find out.

I turn the knob to start the gas stove, but no flame appears. Huh. Is the pilot light out? I bend over the stove, studying the burner as the stove ticks steadily beneath me, attempting to light. I'm trying to figure out if there's another button I need to hit somewhere or if I need to find a lighter to get this breakfast going, when a sharp, low voice interrupts me.

"What the hell are you doing?"

I pull my hand back in an automatic reaction, triggering something in the stove. The flame lights high and bright, and the hem of my t-shirt meets the edge of that flame.

The cheap cotton immediately goes up in a flame of its own, and it takes the flimsy material of my basketball shorts with it.

"Fuck!" I rear back. I'm supposed to stop, right? Drop? Roll? Something like that? My brain's focused on the orange flames inches from my body, and I know I should be panicking, but it's more like I'm frozen in place, unable to react. I'm in the process of begging my body to move, to do anything useful at all, when I see Dr. Evers quickly flick a button on the stove and then tackle me from behind.

He tucks his body around me as he rolls me over the floor, suffocating the fire in a blanket he's conjured from who knows where. A moment later we're both panting into silence. I'm vaguely aware that *Dr. Fucking Sam Evers* has his body wrapped around me, that my clothes are in tatters, and that there's a stinging pain on the right side of my abdomen which suggests I haven't escaped this fiasco completely unscathed.

Dr. Evers is breathing heavily into the space next to my ear, but he isn't saying anything. Good thing I was planning to leave right after breakfast. Nothing makes sleeping in your boss' house more awkward than nearly catching his kitchen and yourself on fire.

"Uh," I finally manage to say. "Sorry about that. I was trying to make you eggs."

Dr. Evers lets out a strangled cough. "I guessed that," he finally says.

He still hasn't moved. His arms are tight around my torso, his legs heavy against mine. This tableau we're in is basically every wet dream I've ever had, and I'm fighting to keep my low-key chub from expanding into something much higher-key.

"Well," he finally says. "I suppose next time someone stays the night, I'll be sure to leave a note for them about my finicky pilot light."

"Um, yeah," I answer. "That might be a good idea. I mean, normally I try not to end up half-naked on the floor of my boss' kitchen."

I choke out a laugh that's a lot more nerves and quick-releasing adrenaline, and the next thing I know, I'm howling with laughter into his shoulder while smoke settles across the kitchen. He lets out his own bark of loud laughter, and pretty soon we're snorting and giggling together on the floor, choking back chortles of post-adrenaline panic into each other's skin.

It isn't until we've both calmed down slightly, and Dr. Evers is slowly pulling away from me, that I realize this is the very first time I've ever seen Dr. Evers *smile*, let alone laugh. At that moment, he seemed so carefree, so relaxed. His entire face went slack as his lips tilted up, and the skin around his eyes wrinkled with a softness

I've never seen in him before. I wish I'd paid closer attention—I'm not sure I'll ever see that expression on his face again.

I wonder if he smiled and laughed all the time when his husband was alive.

Eventually we end up on one of the stools next to the island, with Dr. Evers dabbing burn cream against the pink, stinging skin of my stomach where the fire managed to singe me through my shirt. I'm in my boxers and he's still in a bathrobe, and mostly at this point I'm just glad this burn isn't too painful but is just painful enough to keep me from getting hard in front of him again.

He frowns. "You got very lucky; this injury could have been so much worse. Still, we'll need to keep a close eye on it and watch for infection." He rummages through a large first-aid kit and starts pulling out bandages and other tiny bottles.

I once accidentally set my hand down on a live burner, and I took care of myself with band-aids and cold water. My mother was at work, and there was no way I was calling her away from a shift just because I'd been an idiot. Every shift she lost meant more of a chance that we wouldn't have food the next week. I didn't even have burn cream then, let alone someone to dab it on me and check me for infection. "I'll be fine," I tell him.

"I'm sure you will," he agrees. "As long as we keep a close eye on your injury and ensure you have proper medical care." He dabs something else against my skin that instantly removes most of the burn's sting, and then he starts carefully placing bandages over the spot. "Why were you sleeping in your car?" he asks abruptly.

I reach for anything I can say that isn't a lie but also doesn't require me to tell the full story. A guy like Dr. Evers has probably never had to worry about something like a tuition deposit in his life, and if there's one thing I learned growing up in Alcott, it's that being poor isn't something you want to advertise to the world. I swallow hard and find a sentence that isn't completely untrue. "Uh, my apartment wasn't the most secure location. I decided I shouldn't stay there anymore, but I haven't found a new place yet."

All of that is true. Dairy Corners averages three break-ins a week, and I decided a while ago I needed to get out of there. I just left a little faster than I planned to.

Dr. Evers nods. "Well, it's settled then. Fetch whatever items you have and move them into my guest room. You'll stay here as long as you need to find better, safer lodgings." He stands up and starts washing his hands in the sink.

I nearly spit out the sip of orange juice he handed me a few minutes ago—for shock, he said. "I can't impose on you like that, sir," I say carefully. "After breakfast I was going to tell you that I'll get out of your hair right away. I appreciate you letting me stay here, but I can take care of myself."

There's no way I can stay here. I'm barely coherent and functioning around Dr. Evers as it is. Living down the hall from him is *not* going to help the problem. Seeing one glimpse of him out of a shirt or in boxers would have me melting into a puddle of goo on the floor. Best if I get the fuck out of here before I manage to get myself fired on top of all my other problems.

Then again: I do need a place to stay, and I do need to start saving as much cash as I can right away. I'm going to have to pick up so much extra money with odd jobs if I'm going to make that tuition bill deadline. "How much would rent here cost?" I blurt out.

Dr. Evers looks up at me, his eyes wide. "Nothing, of course. Just stay here as long as you need." He goes back to studying my torso.

"No way," I say, shaking my head. "I can't stay here for free. That's not fair to you."

Dr. Evers stands up fully and matches his gaze with mine. "Malachai," he says. "I don't generally share this with people, but you should know that my parents were very well-off. My brother and I have never wanted for anything, especially money. I never mind sharing my financial privilege with others. You need a place to stay, and I have one. You're more than welcome to stay here, and I'll accept no rent monies in return."

Dammit. His voice goes straight to my dick, rushing blood to every sensitive point in my body. Does he even realize how attractive he is when he talks like that? Painful burn be damned—I just want to throw myself against him and climb him like some kind of tree.

Not to mention what he's offering... a free place to stay? Taking him up on this would be *huge* in helping me get that tuition bill paid on time.

"I'll think about it," I tell him, because saying either yes or no feels almost impossible right now. "Thank you, sir. That's incredibly generous of you."

"You're welcome to call me Sam," he says. "Now. I can tell you put a great deal of thought into preparing these breakfast ingredients. Are you feeling well enough to cook breakfast with me? I'll be in charge of lighting the stove," he adds, and he almost smiles as he says that, the left corner of his lip tilting upward as his right eye sinks into something like a *twinkle*. If eyes actually can twinkle.

Wow. Nearly a second smile in the same morning. I try not to lean into disappointment that I didn't just get another chance to see the fully relaxed and chortling Sam I saw earlier when we were rolling on the floor together.

"I feel well enough," I tell him, carefully hiding the slight twinge of pain in my side as I hop off the island stool. "After I put on some clothes," I add jokingly.

He nods, and I swear his eyes flash slightly in the light. "I want you to be comfortable here, Malachai. There's a shower down the hall from your room. After we eat, I'll explain the best way for you to wash while keeping that wound safe and protected. If you need anything while you stay here, please just let me know. I'm happy to pick things up for you as I run errands today."

I swallow hard. Never before has this kitchen felt more dangerous than it does when the man of my dreams, a man I can never, ever have, stands in it promising me care and comfort and company—all things I haven't had in so very, very long.

Honestly, this kitchen felt less dangerous when it was trying to burn me alive.

Chapter 4
40 Days to the Devon Falls Leaf Festival

It's clear I need to create a house rule stating no shirt may ride up above the hip line. That tight cotton is simply too dangerous.
—Sam Evers

"Sir," Malachai whispers into the cool air of my office. His breath is harsh with need—no, desperation—and I can feel that desperation as it shudders through his entire body. His cock is hard against the palm of my hand, the tip of it wet with unspoken desire. He shudders against me again as I stroke him gently. "Sir, I don't know how much longer I can last..."

"You'll last until I tell you, darling," I murmur into his ear. "Until I'm ready to enter you." He shudders one more time, and it's as if I can feel my words running through him. He's so very attractive when he's coming apart in my hands like this, his clothing askew on my office floor, every inch of his skin mine for the taking as he leans heavily against my desk, his weight balanced between the large piece of polished wood and my own arms, which support him from behind. I'm still fully clothed, and I enjoy knowing how impatiently he's waiting for me to push down my own trousers and underwear. It's heady how much he craves having me inside of him. "Did you prep yourself like I told you to?"

He whimpers in response, his neck falling against mine in a heavy movement. "Yes, sir."

How those words make me crave him even more. I slip a finger up against the pucker of pink skin I think about so often, swirling and tickling it with a finger while he nearly mewls in demand. "Please, sir!" he yelps. Thank goodness we're alone in the office tonight, or there's no doubt Jack would have heard that cry next door.

"I love when you beg me," I say softly as I nibble at his earlobe. I push my finger in, just slightly, relishing in the give of his body against mine. And then—

I jerk awake in bed, hard as a rock, panting loudly in the dead-silent room. A photo of a smiling Christian beams cruelly at me from the bedside table.

I flip the photo over quickly, smacking the frame into the table harshly as his face disappears from view.

I fall back against the covers, groaning as I reach down to take hold of my cock. Fuck. That dream... I haven't had one that vivid in a very, very long time. I can't remember the last time I woke up this hard, this desperate. Fuck fuck fuck. I jump from the bed and quickly throw on the bathrobe that lives attached to my closet door. I need a cold shower.

I shove open the bedroom door as quickly as I can, only to find Malachai standing in the hallway, arms above his head, deep in an early-morning stretch as he also walks to the bathroom. His back is to me as he moves, the white cotton of his t-shirt easily riding up his torso away from the slim exercise shorts he's wearing. Miles of golden skin stretch between the two pieces of cloth. His sinewy body is laid out before me, and his soft, taut bottom is on full display in those shorts. His back is a perfect expanse of untouched space meant for me to explore, just like in my dream.

I step back into my bedroom before he can notice me, falling onto the bed, grabbing for my cock again and squeezing it so tightly in my hand that I feel like I might be punishing myself as I stroke back and forth with dry, hot pulls until I finally bring myself to completion. I bite my tongue against the shout that nearly moves against my lips to make sure Malachai hears nothing in the hallway.

I collapse into the warm sheets of the bed as some of the tension that's consumed me since I awoke finally leaves my body. That running line of energy that seems to wave through me whenever I think of Malachai stays behind, though. What on earth is wrong with me? I never should have invited him here to stay with me. It's clear to me now that I don't have nearly the self-control I thought I did; not if I'm having dreams of fucking my office manager across my desk and then rushing back to my room to jerk myself off after I see him in the hallway.

It's clear I need to create a house rule stating no shirt may ride up above the hip line. That tight cotton is simply too dangerous.

It's even clearer that I need to get my head out of my ass and Malachai out of my nighttime fantasies. It's been easy enough to avoid him for the past two days: his schedule is extremely full, and he's so busy with studying and work that we've hardly spent five minutes alone in the house together. Yesterday I had to hunt him down at the office to make sure he'd seen Jack about his burn. He had, thank goodness, and I looked at it myself to ensure it was healing properly.

I also made sure we stepped into an exam room together before he pulled up his shirt, as I clearly struggle with seeing any part of Malachai's exposed body without reacting in highly inappropriate ways.

I sit up in bed, reaching for the photo I so cruelly struck against the table a moment ago. I steel myself to pick it up, flip it back over, and study it. It's a photo of me and Christian, laughing and smiling by the very pool that spelled the end of our lives together.

"Look at us," I murmur to my dead lover. "That fucking pool. You loved it so much. I hated the damn thing. I never even wanted to buy an apartment with a rooftop pool. You insisted."

Christian doesn't answer. Neither does younger Sam.

I sigh. "Of course, you always got your way when we fought. I used to tell myself I just liked seeing you happy. Now I wonder if I just didn't care enough to argue with you."

Still no response.

"You know," I tell the photo, "my therapist in New York and I talked about you at length. She insisted I should tell more of our friends about exactly why I was so upset after you died. She said I needed to explain to them that I felt guilty about refusing to go to your pool party that day, and that so much of my guilt came from the fact that I hated going to your parties when we were married. She kept prodding me to open up about how I worked so much because I never minded being away from you as much as I now realize I probably should have. And you were always so busy spending time with other friends I didn't know. It all seems so obvious now, that something was clearly missing between the two of us."

Christian's face remains frozen in a smile, his younger eyes peering into the eyes of my former self. It's a cruel reminder that we always got along well, particularly when we were first engaged and then married. But then, we'd known each other since we were six years old. Our worlds were perpetually linked, our camaraderie easy, our relationship simple but firm. Our marriage felt like a foregone conclusion in a world where adults rising in their professional lives are simply expected to permanently partner at some point, especially when they've been dating for as long as Christian and I dated.

But our marriage never grew beyond that steady camaraderie, and I don't think I ever realized that fact until Christian was gone.

I know I became a catatonic version of myself after Christian died, as I mourned the loss of a relationship I'd had my entire life and secretly wondered if my husband's death was my punishment. My penance for not going to my own husband's pool party when I couldn't be bothered. For not bothering to care.

"Whatever was wrong with our marriage," I whisper to the picture. "You were my best friend. I hope you know that. And I'll never forgive myself for not being there when you slipped on the tile that day and fell."

I've wished so many times since I arrived in Vermont that younger Sam had responded to Christian the way I respond to Malachai now. If Malachai and I were together, I can't possibly imagine outwardly ignoring any party he planned to throw, not that Malachai seems the type to throw many parties. But this urge I have, to protect Malachai at all costs, to support him and make him mine in every possible way... I never had this level of intense feeling for Christian.

And it's all too clear to me now that my own lack of passion for Christian may have cost him his life. Christian was a good man. An honest and kind man. He deserved so much more than an incomplete marriage and an early death that could have so easily been prevented, and I'm quite certain I could have prevented the accident at the party that day had I been there. His party friends were irresponsible miscreants who took no kind of safety precautions in anything they did. There was so much alcohol by the pool when the ambulance arrived that they might as well have been running their own speakeasy. One of them had actually made an entire bucket of fruit juice laced with rum. Who makes beverages in buckets after they've graduated college?

"I'm sorry," I whisper to the photo. "I'm sorry I didn't go to the party that day. I'm sorry I let you die such a stupid and meaningless death. You didn't deserve that, Christian."

Photo Christian still says nothing.

"I'm honoring you the best way I know how," I tell him. "Staying true to you as though you were still here. And I'll keep doing that, I promise. I owe you at least that much."

I won't give into these feelings, strange and foreign, that I have for Malachai. The shame of what I just did a moment ago washes through me like water as I shudder slightly—I never once jacked off to the image of my dead husband. I'm certain I never dreamed about him. How dare I offer that to someone else? Someone I hardly know? It's horrific.

And now I've invited Malachai to live in my house.

I groan aloud as I force myself up off the bed so I can finally start my day. No, I tell myself. Inviting Malachai to stay here was the correct choice. He deserves safety and comfort. He should not be denied those things simply because I have so many inappropriate feelings for him.

I'll be in Devon Falls for less than six more weeks. Surely that's enough time to help ensure Malachai has proper housing, and surely I can hold myself together in Malachai's presence for that long.

I simply have to keep reminding myself that he's off-limits to me. Forbidden.

I flip the photo upside down again as I get dressed.

Chapter 5

39 Days to the Devon Falls Leaf Festival

He's the powerful, rich doctor who's basically letting me squat in his guest room. I'm the criminal loser who can't even walk through a barn without hurting himself. —Malachai Flynn

"Okay," I murmur to the glaring creature in front of me. "I've got a little over a month before this deposit is due. A little over a month to come up with this money. And you're going to help me do it."

Sherbert the goat tilts his head up at me slightly. I'm still not totally sure how a goat can spend so much of his time standing up on his hind legs. Doesn't that stance get tiring after a while?

"I'm going to feed you and the other animals in this barn," I tell him, determined to hide my nerves. So what if I'm not exactly an animal husbandry expert? So what if I never even had a cat or a dog growing up? The Stock Tree Farm, also sometimes known around here as the 3Way Farm, was hiring seasonal help for their animals and pumpkin patch operation. And I need money badly right now.

So here I am, in the short hours between a day of office work and a night filled up with a chemistry class, standing in a barn staring down an angry goat while I hold a bucket of feed in one hand.

It could be worse. I could have offered to work with the Clydesdales. That job paid more per hour, but even I'm not desperate enough to lie and say I have experience driving a cart pulled by large horses when I definitely, absolutely, do not.

"The trick is to give him an apple."

I whirl around to find someone about my age watching me. He's got a round, golden brown baby face that matches the bright flash of dark hair which is hanging down into his brown eyes. He's wearing overalls on top of a flannel shirt and rubber boots, and he's definitely better dressed for this job than I am; all I had to wear today was sneakers with my old sweatshirt and jeans. Luckily, Jeb Stock, who runs this farm with his partners Embry and Adam, is a really nice guy. He lent me some boots when I got here and he saw my footwear, and those boots have already come in handy as I slogged through mud and literal crap to get to this building.

"An apple?" I ask.

The guy shrugs. "Sherbert loves apples. If you give him one he'll leave you alone and let you be so you can take care of the other animals. Also, he actually kind of loves little kids, even though he pretends he doesn't. But since we don't have any four-year-olds nearby at the moment, I recommend apples. Jeb keeps them in the bucket next to the door."

"Apples," I murmur. "Um, cool. Thanks."

"I'm Gabe Gomez." He thrusts out a gloved hand, which I shake. "I work here sometimes for extra cash. Actually, I sort of work everywhere in town for extra cash."

My lips tip up in a smile. "Me too these days. I'm Malachai Flynn."

His eyes immediately go wide. "Malachai Flynn? Are you that guy who—" Gabe cuts himself off, but his mouth stays open in a circle. "Uh, never mind," he says quickly.

Too late for that. It's pretty clear exactly what he was about to say: *Are you that guy who accidentally ended up sleeping in a drug den and nearly got people killed last year?*

Fuck my life. Gabe's still swallowing his surprise, and I'm trying to figure out how to answer him, when my phone rings. Saved by the bell from total awkwardness. "I'll just take this really quickly," I tell him. "Be right back." I drop the bucket I'm holding and quickly step outside of the barn's side door into the Vermont fall air as I slide the button on my cheap, off-brand phone. "Hi, Mom."

"Hi, Mal!" She smacks a piece of gum when she says the word, which means she's trying to quit smoking again. She usually makes it about three months. Then she gets put on too many all-night shifts back-to-back and starts smoking again to stay awake. It's a vicious cycle. "I just wanted to check in. How are you?"

This is also a cycle I know all too well, too: not talking to my own mother for weeks or months at a time before she feels guilty about not calling me and reaches out. It's been our pattern since third grade, when my grandma died and she started working graveyard shifts to keep us afloat. I took care of myself, hardly seeing her for weeks at a time, and then she'd show up randomly at school to pick me up and take me out for a picnic to "check in" with me.

It's not her fault. She's always done her best. It's hard being a single mom in a town where the minimum wage is a joke and you don't even have a high school diploma.

"I'm okay." I can imagine her sitting on the couch in our old trailer, the one with the spring sticking out on the side, twirling a strand of her hair and she tries to come up with topics of conversation to discuss with me. We don't know each other very well, Mom and I. That's what happens when you grow up in a house with someone you never see. "How are you? What's new?"

She sighs. "Not much. Ken Davidson came into the diner the other day. Said to say hi to you."

My stomach twists around itself. "Oh he did, huh?" I reply stiffly.

"Sure. He was with Emily Getterson. Think they've got a few kids now."

"Sure, of course they do." Never mind that Ken and Emily, like me, are both barely in their early twenties. It was pretty clear from our junior high days that the two of them were going to end up together, at least in the short term. I'm betting they won't make it out of their thirties together, though.

You end up with a lot of time to observe the habits of people who torture you on a near-daily basis, and I saw Ken and Emily an awful lot in my early years. Ken hung out at the bus stop next to our trailer park, and he never tired of making my life miserable.

"Doesn't your mom have money to get you anything that isn't from the Goodwill? You ever seen the inside of a mall, loser?"

"What do you mean you don't even have a computer at home? Don't they let you own computers in trailer parks?"

"Oh my God, look at Malachai! He's wearing sneakers from that store that doesn't even sell Nikes!"

I shudder at the memory of the snickers and the laughter, which rings so clearly it might as well sit in my soul. Ken and Emily were both young basketball stars in our town, all the way from elementary school through high school graduation, and people listened to what they said. I grew up with very few friends who were actually willing to be seen with me in public thanks to Ken and Emily.

"Tell Ken I said hi," I tell Mom, even though the words are like bile moving through my body and out of my mouth. Mom never knew how miserable I was in Alcott. She had plenty to worry about, and I sure never wanted her to find out that her son was the town outcast.

"Anything new with you?" she asks me, jolting me back into the conversation. I let out a long breath. "Any news?"

I got into nursing school! I'm finally getting out of Vermont!

I fight the urge to shout the words through the phone line. I haven't told anyone yet. I mentioned to Marie and Jack that I wasn't sure what my next semester at school was going to look like and that they might have to hire someone else for the office, but I didn't give them any details. Celebrating getting into my dream school and then not being able to go would be like twisting a knife deep into my own chest. I'm not telling a single soul about Billington until I've paid that tuition deposit.

Not even Dr. Evers, and believe me, I've wanted to say something to him so many times. I've wanted to scream to him from a rooftop that I'm not the loser I appear to be, that I'm more than just an idiot who can't even manage to find a place to live long-term or cook breakfast without catching something on fire. But telling him would also mean actually speaking in several complete sentences to him, so I've managed to keep the news to myself. Maybe, I think, I should tell my mom. There's no way she could help me with the money I need, but maybe she'd be excited for me. Even if I don't get to actually go to school, a reality that seems more and more likely given that I can't even figure out how to feed a goat right now. "Well," I start to say, "I—"

"Oh, I forgot to mention! Ken and Emily are having another little one. I bet this one's a real cutie. The last one looked just like Ken! Such a darling face."

I let the words that never lived die inside of me as I go silent again.

The apple trick does work, luckily, and I manage to get the animals fed easily with Gabe's help. He doesn't say much to me, of course.

Just keeps glancing over at me every once in a while. Like he's trying to figure out if he should say something to me. Like I'm some kind of sideshow in a carnival.

And in this town—this entire state, apparently—I guess I might as well be exactly that.

"Great work today," Jeb says, slapping me lightly against the shoulder when I tell him I've finished up. He's a big guy, with a definite farmer's build, and the hit nearly knocks me over. "Whoops!" he says as he grabs for my arm to hold me up. "We've got to invite you over for dinner sometime. Embry's going to want to put some meat on your bones if you're going to keep working for us." There's nothing but kindness in his eyes, and that's a soothing balm to my nerves right now. The Stock Tree Farm is in La Fierte, one town over from Devon Falls. Maybe there's just enough miles between us that Jeb hasn't heard the stories about me yet. Too bad he eventually will. This county has zero ability to keep secrets.

I get back to Dr. Evers' house after class and kick my sneakers off in the front hall, sniffing at my sweatshirt again to make sure that it doesn't smell too badly of horse, goat, and sheep manure. Luckily the jacket Jeb lent me seems to have saved it, as this is one of two sweatshirts I own and I don't have time to do laundry this week. My stomach growls, reminding me that I haven't eaten anything all day. Maybe I have some ramen packets in the car somewhere? Or at least a granola bar, I hope. Then, I'm so tired that—

"Malachai? Are you home? Dinner's ready in the kitchen if you'd like to join me."

There's the voice I know all too well: Dr. Evers.

I tug at my sweatshirt and make my way up the front hallway, and then I manage not to gasp out loud when I step into the kitchen.

The table is dressed and set, complete with tablecloth and cloth napkins—and I honestly didn't realize cloth napkins were something actual people used outside of television shows set in the 1950s—with tall candles in the middle of the set-up and a hefty-looking lasagna laid out across the farmhouse wood. There's a large bowl of salad next to it and a fancy platter covered with what looks like garlic bread on the other side.

"Holy—what's this?" I whisper.

Dr. Evers looks up from the book he's reading. "Dinner," he says simply. "Benson mentioned when your class ended tonight, so I thought I'd keep it warm for you."

Every part of my brain scrambles to catch up to that sentence. No one's ever cooked for me before, let alone bothered to keep food warm for me. No one's ever set a table for me before or lit candles with me in mind before.

"Is there a problem?" he asks. "I hope you don't mind, but I like to sit down formally when I eat. It's a habit from when I was younger."

His words take the air out of me; they're a firm reminder that none of this is actually for me or even has anything to do with me. Dr. Evers is just a nice guy. I already knew that, of course. I mean, he offered to let me stay for free at his house, for fuck's sake.

Calm down, I order myself. *It's just lasagna. Just sit down and eat the damn lasagna, Malachai.*

I sink into my chair and do my best to avoid staring at Dr. Evers as he starts eating. He looks perfect, like he always does, in jeans and a blue sweater that probably cost more than my car. I tug my ratty sweatshirt up over my shoulder blade.

"How was your day?" he asks as he scoops a massive portion of lasagna onto my plate. I do my best to avoid looking like a total animal as I dive into it, but it's hard. Dr. Evers' lasagna is *good.* Cheesy and melty and full of some kind of meat that's just a little spicy but not too spicy. "Oh, it was fine," I tell him. "I helped out a little bit at the Stock Tree Farm out in La Fierte before class. Just seasonal work, of course. I mean, I'm not doing it permanently or anything. Because I work at the doctor's office. With you. As you know." I smile meekly and force myself to stop talking by taking a giant gulp of milk from my glass. At least this time my problem was talking too much, rather than completely going mute in front of him. That's progress, right? "Um, what about you?

"Oh, not much. Dealt with a minor case of the flu, then some tonsillitis. Is that a bruise?" He leans across the table and runs a hand lightly over the side of my cheek and it's as though my skin ignites in a small, slight burst of flame the moment his hand reaches it.

I gulp. "I ran into the side of a pipe in Jeb Stock's barn. Not a big deal. It didn't even really hurt." It didn't, really. I hardly felt it at the time. But right now that spot is all I can feel as Dr. Evers brushes his hand gently over it, caressing my skin carefully and narrowing his vision against it. "We'll put some cream on it after—" he stops and shakes his head, quickly pulling away from me. "Never mind. I meant to say that I'll leave some cream for that on the table in the living room. You should put it on later."

The sudden space between us feels like an all too important reminder of what I am to him and what I am in this town. He's the powerful, rich doctor who's basically letting me squat in his guest room. I'm the criminal loser who can't even walk through a barn without hurting himself. The guy who ran from bullies his entire childhood and now walks out of a store if he sees Avon Loseff got there first.

But as I sit here, in Dr. Evers' perfect house with his clothes and perfect table setting and perfect food, I realize something: I'm tired of being that person. It's time for a change. It's time to prove people like Ken Davidson and Avon Loseff wrong. It's time to prove *everyone* wrong. It's time for a brand-new start.

"Thanks, but you don't need to worry about me," I finally tell him. "I can take care of myself. I always have."

He raises an eyebrow like he's thinking about arguing with me. Then he frowns, nods, and turns back to his food.

I tell myself that I'm glad he's silent for the rest of the meal.

Chapter 6
37 Days to the Devon Falls Leaf Festival

I'm starting to worry that Jack's father might be putting some of the herbs from the "special" section of his garden into the tomato sauce he sends me every week. —Sam Evers

"I still don't understand," I tell Jack as I follow him through the throng of Devon Falls residents and into the town hall. "The entire town of Devon Falls gathers for a meeting once a week?"

"It's not always that often," Benson says from the other side of Jack. He points to a set of three chairs available in the corner and guides us over to them. "But sometimes it's more often if there's an issue the town can't agree on. Like the time no one could decide if we should go with neon Easter decor in the town square and everyone kept bringing in new samples."

"I bowed out of that conversation after the third meeting," Jack says. "I hadn't seen that much hot pink in one place since my mother used to host eighties nights at our house." He sits down and Benson drops into the seat next to him. "You get used to them," Benson says as I dust off the seat next to him with a kleenex and then drop into it. "Or at least you do until every single fucking one of them is about your wedding."

"Henri promised that this meeting isn't about our wedding," Jack reminds him. "It's about the entire festival."

"Which means one fourth of it will be about our wedding. Are you sure we can't elope? I was thinking of maybe a nice coastal region in Italy. You like pasta."

Jack grins and leans over to kiss his cheek. "Babe, if I thought for one second that you didn't really want to get married here, you know I'd have already canceled this whole thing."

Benson mumbles something under his breath about Devon Falls brainwashing him, and I sit back while I study the way the two of them slowly nudge closer to one another on their chairs. How did I never notice that Christian and I never once nudged toward one another like that, sliding our hands together as though we couldn't possibly live without skin-to-skin contact?

Jack clears his throat. "So, Sam," he says. "Mom and I thought one of us should talk to you about, well, your living situation."

I raise an eyebrow. "You mean the fact that our office manager is currently residing in my guest room," I say evenly.

"Yup, that," Benson says. He reaches down into the satchel at his feet and pulls out a small stack of papers. "You should sign this."

"What the earthly hell is this?"

"Just a disclaimer that if you and Malachai enter into a relationship of any kind that you'll alert Jack and Marie," Benson says evenly.

It never ceases to amaze me how Benson manages to have his hands in almost every single operating business in Devon Falls. That's what happens, I suppose, when your town only has two lawyers. I shake my head as I wave at the papers. "There's no need for me or Malachai to sign anything," I tell them quickly. "Malachai and I will not be entering into any kind of relationship. I would never allow that to happen."

Benson snorts. "Just because you've basically become a robot since you got here doesn't mean you're actually made out of metal," he says. "And let's be honest, right now your house is one giant boning waiting to happen."

I sit upright in my chair. "Excuse me?" I ask carefully. I thought I had done a fairly strong job of keeping my inappropriate attractions to myself. Have Jack and Benson noticed my feelings for Malachai? An icy sensation begins to spread through my extremities.

Jack sends Benson one of those quick, coded glances they so like to share before he looks at me. "Sam," he says, "this paperwork is about our concerns that Malachai has feelings for *you*. He's clearly in a vulnerable spot right now."

"I would never do anything to take advantage of him." I bark the words more than say them, and Jack holds up his hands in a gesture of surrender.

"I know that," he says. "Everyone in our office knows that. It's just... listen, Sam. If you were interested in Malachai, that would be okay. You know that, right?"

"Technically it does create some further paperwork, from an HR perspective," Benson says. Jack sends him a narrowed look that's far less coded. "But hey, what's a little more paperwork?" he adds quickly. "Billable hours are my best friend."

"It would certainly *not* be okay. Malachai works for us. Not to mention that—"

I can't bring myself to finish the sentence. As far as I know, Jack has no idea that I've been questioning my feelings for Christian ever since his death. I don't exactly feel like starting that conversation in the middle of a large and very crowded room.

Jack sighs. "I know this is a tough subject for you, Sam, and believe me when I say that I'd rather swim in the Rykers' cow pond than make you keep talking about this, and you know how seriously I take the potential dangers of swimming in standing water. But we have to discuss this. Christian's been gone for a long time now, and you're still not moving on. You don't date.

You barely talk to anyone besides us and Milo. You're insisting on moving back to New York to live in that giant echo chamber of an apartment once our wedding is over. You can't be a monk for the rest of your life, okay? Milo and I are worried about you."

I close my eyes against the push of pain building between my temples. I'm contemplating making a complete escape from this conversation by mentioning the headache that's currently building in my skull, but a smack of a gavel at the front of the town hall grabs my attention first.

"Okay, folks! Time to get started!" Amelia appears at the lectern at the front of the room, and I've never been so excited to see hair the color of an Easter egg basket. I sink back down into my chair, only because leaving the room would attract a great deal of attention right now. "Listen, I called this meeting because the town's moving up manure creek and we need your help."

Henri Fontaine, who once ran the office at Lancer Family Medicine before she trained Malachai to take over and then retired, rolls her eyes as she steps in front of Amelia at the lectern. Her brown braids with their graying ends sway behind her head, brushing up against her dark brown skin. "Let's not be melodramatic," she tells Amelia. "But here's the scoop, friends. As you all know, I've been in charge of managing the festival for years now. I love this town and I love this festival. But Harry and I have some exciting news: our daughter in California is having a baby!" Everyone in the room bursts into applause, and Henri curtsies slightly.

"Thanks, loves. We couldn't be more thrilled. The downside to this wonderful news is that the pregnancy has had some rough patches, and Melody's on bed rest. She's asked me to come out to California to help her out, and of course I can't say no. Which means that we need to hire someone to take care of managing the rest of the festival."

A small gasp runs through the room. "But no one can replace you, Hen!" Burt Busby calls out.

"Thanks, Burt." Henri nods in his direction. "But listen, most of the hard work is done at this point. Everything is all planned out, including the Lewis-Lancer wedding."

Benson makes a choked noise as the entire room turns to look at him and Jack. A smattering of people applaud.

"And now the job's really just about keeping the train on the tracks. Not a ton of hours of work each week, I don't think, mostly just managing some lead-up events here and there, and then coordinating things through the festival itself. The job pays a stipend, so the person wouldn't be working for free, and—"

"I'll do it!"

The entire room seems to turn again as a voice I know all too well sounds from the back row of chairs.

Malachai's standing there, his face flushed and his arms crossed in front of him. He takes a long gulp of air, and my heart clenches at the nervous expression on his face. It's clearly costing him a great deal to make this announcement in front of such a large group, to put himself out there in front of the town like this, and yet he does it anyway.

Emotions that seem to linger in the area of *pride* swirl within me. The urge to protect Malachai from anyone who might make this moment difficult for him has me nearly jumping from my seat.

Henri beams. This entire town knows she adores Malachai, her protege at our office, and my nerves relax for a moment. Certainly there's no danger to Malachai's ego here. "Wonderful! Malachai, you're the perfect choice. Everyone, looks like our problem is solved! Sweetie, let's meet tomorrow morning and we can—"

"I don't think this is a good idea."

A man with black hair cut into an absurd bowl cut and pale skin perfectly at odds with said hair shouts loudly from the other side of the room, and immediately I see Malachai sink into himself.

My nerves stand on edge again.

"Who the hell is that?" I ask—okay, possibly growl—Jack and Benson.

Benson looks slightly murderous. "Avon Loseff." He and Jack share one of their patented looks. "This isn't good," Benson adds.

I clutch the edge of my seat and will myself not to stand. I can't step in for Malachai here. Such an action would go against all the promises I've made to myself.

If only he wasn't lowering himself back toward his chair right now, his face reddening, as though he wishes to disappear into the floor.

"Avon," Henri says cooly, "Malachai's an excellent choice. I've worked with him before, and I know I can easily train him before I leave."

"He's a criminal." Avon nearly sneers the words, and whispered gasps run through the crowd in the hall. "A lot of money goes through that festival. We can't trust him."

A heat is running through my blood now—a kind of heat I'm not sure I've ever felt before, not even in the most frantic, panicked moments of my early days as a doctor, working hard rotations in emergency departments. A kind of heat I don't remember ever feeling on behalf of anyone before, but there's no time to think of that right now. Despite the fact that both Jack and Benson look as though they're on the verge of intervening in this disaster of a meeting, I'm on my feet before I can second guess myself. "He's not a criminal," I bark out. "He's a hard worker, a good soul, and this town would be incredibly lucky to have him managing your festival." I cross my own arms and ensure that the glare I've carefully fixed on this Avon Loseff character lands squarely and surely.

The asshole just tilts his lip in derision. I'm not generally a violent man, but I find myself wondering how many ways I could take him in a physical fight.

"Easy for you to say, you're not even from there." Avon-Terrible-Bowl-Cut scoffs. He tosses his head in Malachai's direction. "Listen, kid, this is nothing personal. But you've proven that we can't trust you. And everyone here knows it, even if they don't want to say it."

Murmurs move through the crowd around me, and it's now the heat that's been building in my blood suddenly reaches a rolling boil. Jack opens his mouth to say something, but once again I beat him to it. "I'll vouch for him," I bark out. Loudly.

The crowd goes silent, and in my peripheral vision I see Malachai's eyes go very wide. I can't look directly at him right now, and instead I keep my eyes fixed on Avon.

"What?" I can't tell if Avon's response is outraged or incredulous, and frankly I don't care.

"I'll vouch for him. If any funds go missing or anything else goes awry, I'll take responsibility. I'll even help with overseeing the upcoming festival activities if that will put your mind at ease. I'm only supporting the medical practice part-time right now, so I can support Malachai with the extra hours in my day. I'm quite certain he doesn't need my supervision or my backing, but I'll provide it if that's what you want." My fists are curling in on each other as I imagine the many more hours of time with Malachai I've possibly just added to my schedule. Great hell, what am I doing? I'm starting to worry that Jack's father might be putting some of the herbs from the "special" section of his garden into the tomato sauce he sends me every week.

But I could never stop what I've started now. Malachai's looking at me with an expression that's something akin to awe, and the way that look spreads more heat through my body is, well—

That feeling is as utterly addicting as Malachai himself, I'm sure of that.

"Wonderful!" says Henri. "I think we've got our solution, folks! Now, I'm sure that—"

Avon glares and Henri gushes on about what a wonderful team she's certain Malachai and I will make. But I hardly notice either of them. All my attention, now, is on one person in the corner of the room, whose expression remains possibly awe-filled. Or maybe he's confused? Distraught? I can't begin to unwind or fully understand the look on Malachai's face right now.

But I do know this is likely the worst decision I've made since the day I chose not to attend Christian's pool party. And yet, if time were turned back right now, I can say with all certainty I'd make the exact same decision I just made; I'd stand up and offer my help to Malachai over and over again.

Malachai needed me today. And it's becoming increasingly clear to me that any ounce of willpower I ever possessed trickles farther from my grasp with every moment I spend with him.

Chapter 7
32 Days to the Devon Falls Leaf Festival

I'm not even sure what Dr. Evers is to me now. Is he my boss? My babysitter? My landlord? My spank-bank material? All of the above, apparently. —Malachai Flynn

"Malachai? Could you help out Penelope for me?"

Mrs. Shoalski, one of the third-grade teachers at Devon Falls Elementary, guides a sobbing short-haired little girl wearing a giant crown of red and orange leaves around the corner of the soccer field over to where Dr. Evers and I are sitting under a small white canopy tent in front of a folding table. I mentally breathe a sigh of relief at the sight of them. The two of us have been sitting in silence for nearly an hour now, and I was starting to worry that the tension in the September air was actually going to get so tight it would crack and create some sort of rift in the space-time continuum. Although lately I'm starting to think I might enjoy a nice break in the space-time continuum. There are a whole lot of do-overs I'd like in my life right now, that's for sure.

The most recent do-over I'd like would be taking back my stupid impulse to volunteer for Henri's job as Devon Falls Leaf Festival manager. Unfortunately, I knew what the stipend for that position is, thanks to how much time I've spent with Henri. The minute she announced that she needed a replacement, I saw dollar signs. I had instant dreams of no longer having to hunt around town for odd jobs: one festival, one paycheck at the end of it, and *boom*, my tuition would be paid. I could send Billington the money they wanted and get out of Vermont for good.

Then Avon Loseff stepped in, which I absolutely should have seen coming—no one else in town seems to resent what I did last year quite like that dude does—and the next thing I knew, Dr. Evers was coming to my rescue all knight-and-shining-armor style. Except he was wearing cashmere and leather loafers instead of chainmail.

I'll admit I was a little mortified when he stepped in on my behalf like that, but I was also deeply, deeply grateful. I don't think anyone's ever stood up for me like that in my entire life. He basically saved me from total humiliation in that room, and he's the reason I get to keep the gig as festival manager, a gig that really might just change my life.

"I promise you won't have to watch over me or do anything for the festival," I told him the second we got home. "I'll take care of everything, and I promise I won't let you down."

He just cocked his head at me like I was speaking some kind of foreign language. "Of course you won't," he murmured. "You couldn't possibly ever disappoint me, Malachai."

I'm not even sure what Dr. Evers is to me now. Is he my boss? My babysitter? My landlord? My spank-bank material? All of the above, apparently.

I didn't think it was possible for me to get any more nervous around him, but it turns out I was wrong. Ever since the town hall meeting, I've been even more of a wreck than usual around him. I can't ever thank him enough for what he did in that room. And he won't even take part of the stipend, though I've offered it several times. "Absolutely not," he said when I brought it up. "This is your management position. I'm simply backup support."

At least I've been busy with work and school and spending time with Henri before she leaves, and I've managed to see him so little in the past few days that I've been keeping my nerves at bay. Unfortunately, the Devon Falls Elementary School Fall Carnival put an end to that streak. Traditionally, Henri's always run the medical tent at the carnival on behalf of the festival. When I showed up here this morning, I didn't expect Dr. Evers to be here. But Henri's been CCing him on all our emails about the festival, and for some reason he decided to make an appearance.

And, as per usual, I had no idea what to say to him. Luckily, he just nodded at me and settled into a chair with an e-reader. I'm behind on about fifty pages of reading for chemistry, so I've tried to concentrate on that all morning.

Spoiler alert: after two hours of "reading," I still have no idea exactly what isomers are.

I let those thoughts fall away and try to focus on the person who matters more than all that right now: the crying child in front of me. "What's wrong, Penelope?" I ask her as Dr. Evers and I stand at the same time.

"I fell and bumped my knee!" She bursts back into tears and Mrs. Shoalski sighs, looking slightly harassed as her eyes move out to the baseball field, where the third graders are locked in a heated game of kickball with the fourth graders.

"I don't see any blood or bruising," she says, "but she's clearly upset, and I can't leave my class for too long. Veda Lancaster's serving, and she seems to be out for revenge after her class lost last year."

I glance at the pitching mound, where a four-foot-tall Veda stares at the kicker from the other team with a murderous glint in her eye as she holds a giant rubber ball in her hand.

"We can take care of this," Dr. Evers tells her smoothly. "Please, return to your class, Mrs. Shoalski."

I turn to stare at him, slightly baffled. He remembered the name of a woman he met for all of two seconds earlier today. Then again, I shouldn't be surprised. Dr. Evers seemed to know the names of every single patient of the practice within two weeks of working there. I still get yelled at by Burt Busby for mixing him up with Bill Busby, his brother.

"Now, Penelope." Dr. Evers kneels down slightly to look her in the eye. "May I help you onto this chair next to me? Then Mr. Malachai and I can look at your knee."

I try not to think about the things it does to my stomach when he uses the name that all the little kids who go to Lancer Family Medicine call me. Penelope's eyes widen. "You're the wizard!" she says. "I heard all about you. You use magic to make people better!"

Oh shit. My face goes five shades of scarlet as Dr. Evers cocks an eyebrow and glances over at me. But he quickly smooths his expression back into place.

"You think I'm a wizard?" he asks her as he gently lifts her onto a chair.

Penelope nods seriously. "Yes. George Ryker said that Mr. Malachai said that we shouldn't be scared of you even though you never smile or nothing 'cause you're a wizard and wizards in Devon Falls are so busy doing magic to make us better that they don't have time to smile."

Drat. I am so very definitely caught.

Dr. Evers coughs slightly. "That may be a slight exaggeration," he tells her, sending me another look out of the corner of his eye. "But I do want to make you better, Penelope. Will you let me look at your knee?"

"Okay." She sniffs as she wipes away tears from her face with a dirt-smeared hand, immediately leaving brown streaks over her cheeks. "But can Mr. Malachai stay? He always tells me jokes when I get a shot, and then it doesn't hurt so much."

"I think we can manage that." Dr. Evers begins to gently rotate her leg. "Tell me if this hurts. Mr. Malachai, what jokes do you have for us today?"

Penelope claps her hands together excitedly, and I sort through my brain for one she hasn't heard before. "Did you hear the one about the pony who suddenly couldn't sing anymore? It's because she was a little horse."

Penelope giggles, and Dr. Evers coughs again loudly as he sends something like—is that possibly another smile?—in my direction.

We get the knee taken care of with a Transformers band-aid, and Penelope waves to us as she jogs back toward the field. I turn slightly to find Dr. Evers standing next to the first-aid tent, watching me out of the corner of his eye.

"So. A wizard, huh?"

I clear my throat. "Um, you know how you said you thought some of the kids were afraid of you? I told a few of them that story to calm them down. I think it spread through the school. I swear," I add, "I didn't mean to cause any trouble. I just wanted to make sure they could see what a great doctor you are. Like you said, sometimes you're a little... "

"Terrifying," Dr. Evers says wryly. He crosses his arms over the blue polo shirt he's wearing. It highlights his pecs a little more than I like, and I've been trying not to stare at it all day. "I do prefer not to terrify small humans who haven't even reached puberty yet." He sighs. "Thank you, Malachai. I appreciate you doing that."

"No problem, Dr. Evers. Sir."

He cocks an eyebrow again, and *fuck,* why must that be such an attractive look on him? "Malachai, you're currently living with me and bandaging small children next to me in front of a miniature baseball field. It's certainly acceptable if you'd like to call me Sam."

Sam? He wants me to call him *Sam?* I'm not even sure I can do that. I still struggle sometimes to call Jack by his first name, and *Dr. Evers?* He's... well, whatever he is to me, he's a lot more than Jack is, that's for sure.

"Uh, I'll think about it," I say quickly. "Sir. I mean, sir Sam. I mean, Dr. Evers, sir Sam. I mean—"

"Sam," he corrects softy. "Call me Sam, Malachai. Though I won't deny that I don't mind when you call me sir." There's a tone in his voice that catches at me, tugs at every nerve in my body.

He likes when I call him sir? *Fuck.* That's *definitely* going in the spank bank.

"But I'd very much like for you to be able to call me Sam. I think it's best that you be able to call me by my first name if we're going to continue to be roommates for the foreseeable future."

Foreseeable future.

"Just the next few weeks, of course," he adds suddenly, dowsing my brain with a bucket of cold reality. "Until I leave for New York. Speaking of which, I did talk to my landlord about you staying on at the house until the lease is up. I'll be gone, naturally, but I did pay for the entirety of the year, and you're more than welcome to maintain residence there. That should give you plenty of time to find new lodging in Devon Falls."

"Oh. Yeah, sure, of course." I clear my throat. "Actually, I'm figuring out some things with school right now... so I'm really not sure where I'll be next semester, Dr. Evers. I mean sir. I mean Sam. I mean—"

"Oh." The word cuts through my nervous babbling. "I didn't know you were thinking of leaving," he murmurs.

I shrug. "I'm still not totally sure I am. But I'm nearly done with all the pre reqs I need from the community college to start nursing school. Assuming I can pass chemistry," I half joke, gesturing toward the book on the folding table between us.

He drops back into his seat at the table and picks up the book. "Are you having trouble with the coursework?"

I snort as I fall into the seat next to him. "Honestly? This is the first class I've taken that feels like it might wreck my GPA. I'm worried I'm going to fail my first test next week."

"Definitely not," he huffs. "No employee of my medical practice will fail chemistry. I'm not allowing it. Is that a study guide next to you? Let's look over your answers together." And then, like this level of closeness isn't already making my heart pound its way right out of my chest, he pulls his folding chair closer to mine, pressing it farther into the grass beneath us and leaning hard into my space as he looks at my scrawled handwriting on the page.

He smells like cherry and vanilla, the scents of the shampoo in the bathroom we share. I pull in a deep breath as the sensations of that smell wash through me, imagining what it would be like to stand in that shower with Dr. Evers, imagining what he'd look like, his entire body naked and on display before me.

Chemistry. Think of chemistry, Malachai. Not the way your boss and quasi-landlord smells.

"Problem one," he says brusquely.

We move through the problems really quickly, actually. "You're a good teacher," I blurt out as I scribble out the answer to the final problem. "The way you explain things just makes sense. I kind of wish you'd been my science teacher in high school. Then maybe I'd be closer to the rest of my classmates at the college in courses like these."

"What was your high school like?" he asks.

I wince, because discussing my high school experience is about as fun as discussing mucking out the stalls at Jeb's farm. But I'm good at keeping the most horrific details of my childhood to myself. Hey, I managed to hide how miserable I was from my own mother, didn't I?

"I grew up in Alcott, Vermont," I tell him. "You'll probably never go there. It's just over the mountain pass from Devon Falls, but it's kind of the pits. I guess it used to be a massive logging town, but then the logging industry dried up and it just sort of... died? It's too far from any ski towns to make much money that way, and it doesn't have Devon Falls' tourism or ag industry, and it kind of collapsed." I shrug. "The schools aren't that great. I mean, I didn't know that until I got here and realized that I was behind on a lot of stuff. I have to work my ass off to keep my GPA up."

"Your parents never realized there might have been an issue with your schooling?"

I shake my head. "My mom had to work all the time to keep us going. She did her best, but she usually didn't have a lot of time to pay attention to stuff like that. Or money. I remember my teachers wanted to put me into some after school program for accelerated learners—whatever that means—but Mom couldn't afford it. And during high school I needed my time after school for a job so I could start saving up for my own car and college. I knew saving money would be my best shot at getting out of Alcott. As soon as I graduated I bought a cheap car, enrolled in community college over the mountain pass, and I left."

"That's very admirable, Malachai," Sam murmurs. "I hope you realize just how admirable that is. When I left for college, I had all the support I could need behind me. Help with tuition, housing support, parents who cheered for me at every turn. To take that plunge on your own like that must have been frightening."

I snort. "But I basically sucked at it? I didn't have much money, and the first job I landed at a scrap yard didn't pay well. That's how I ended up living in Darius Fletcher's barn. I'd just saved up enough to get an apartment of my own when I found out he was dealing meth out of the barn. And we all know how *that* turned out." I reach my hand across the table to pick up the paper sitting in front of Dr. Evers—Sam?—but he stops me when he lays his hand over mine.

I swear, every cell in my body comes to a complete pause all at once. "You have nothing to be ashamed of," he says softly. "You've always done the best you could here, and the people who know you best understand that. You're a good person, Malachai. I meant what I said in the town hall the other day. Devon Falls, and this world, are lucky to have you."

My entire body stays stuck in space and time as I try to figure out how to respond to him. "I, um, I, no one..."

There's got to be a way I can express how much those words mean to me. No words can possibly describe the kind of inexplicable faith he seems to have in me. "I, well, I—"

A phone on the table begins vibrating sharply. Sam pulls his hand away from mine, and the sudden absence is like a thousand sharp, quick papercuts over my skin. "It's Jack," he murmurs. "Let me take this and then we can get back to studying." He grabs the phone and walks away from the table, toward the three-legged race.

I close my eyes against the roar of confusion cascading through my body. What the hell is going on? I've got to get over this ridiculous crush of mine. Apparently it's gotten so bad that I'm now hallucinating the idea that Dr. Evers might actually have feelings for me or something.

The idea is so ridiculous I actually laugh out loud, by myself under a budget-priced tent cover.

"Something funny?" says a voice behind me. My entire body stiffens. *Avon Loseff.*

I close my eyes as he steps next to me. "Hi, Avon," I say, keeping my voice as even as possible. "How are you?"

"Perfectly fine." He frowns. "I see you've nosed your way into this town tradition as well?"

"Nosed my way in?" I ask incredulously. "Look, I know I messed up last year, but I promise that I would never do anything to hurt the festival. I care about Henri, and this town, and I want to make the festival the best that it can possibly be."

Avon shakes his head, and his perfectly styled hair whips quietly around his ears. "Oh, I'm not as worried about that now that I know you're being watched all the time. As you should be. Some of the people here are so blind. I see who you really are, Malachai. The town will see too, soon enough. It won't be long before you're back in with the people you've associated with before. Someone with your background is never far from that world. We all know it. Henri's forgotten, clearly, but she'll remember eventually. People like you, from your background, always end up showing the world who they really are."

His words are a jolt through my body, a firm reminder of why he and others in this town have made it clear that I'm not to be trusted. My tongue sticks like sandpaper to the roof of my mouth, and it's like I'm standing next to Ken and Emily all over again as I silently blink back the emotions that threaten to drip from my eyes at any moment.

Never let the assholes see you cry. It's a promise I made to myself years ago after Emily made sure the entire class knew that I was the only one not going on the eighth grade trip to Boston with everyone else because my mother couldn't afford the fees. I still remember watching that large coach bus pull out of the parking lot, imagining what the inside of a coach bus looked like, imagining what a dolphin watch was or what it would be like to stand on a boat waiting to see a dolphin, and then finally racing home on my bike and hiding in the bathroom before I finally let myself break down and sob. *Never let the assholes see you cry.* I've kept that promise to myself for years, and I'm not about to break it now.

"Well," says Avon. "I'm off to see my nephew wreak havoc in the water balloon fight. Toodle-loo."

He steps away while tunnels of anger and sadness and frustration and hopelessness pool their way through my body like rivers of lava flowing down from a volcano.

I have to make sure this festival is a success. I'm so close to earning that stipend money and paying off that deposit. So close to getting the fuck out of this state. So close to proving that Avon Loseff and everyone else in this town who doubts me is *wrong*.

I glance across the tent, to the area just outside of it where Dr. Evers—*Sam, dammit, I can do this*—is deep in conversation with someone, and I have a strange moment of relief. It's a relief to know that whatever happens here in Devon Falls next, he's leaving Vermont before me. I don't want to think about how hard it might be for me to leave him behind when I finally get to leave this place for nursing school.

Because there's no reason leaving Dr. Evers behind should ever be hard; you can't leave something you never had in the first place, after all.

Chapter 8
30 Days to the Devon Falls Leaf Festival

I start sharing confessions of my own. —Sam Evers

"I believe I may have misread the pattern." I twist the hat in front of me, studying the stitches there, while Malachai scribbles away in a notebook on the other side of my home office desk, his tongue tucked between his teeth in concentration.

The way that tongue sticks out ever so slightly, jutting in pink softness between his lips, is deeply limiting *my* concentration. Which is possibly why the top of this hat looks like a cross between a sock and a mitten gone horribly wrong. The recipients of the charity knitting foundation materials deserve better.

Damn it. I'm going to have to rip out stitches again.

Malachai peeks up from his study guide, his hair dangling in his face. It's the first time I've been able to closely study him since the day we spent together at the school, and memories from that day that have been lingering in my mind ever since.

Malachai's soft smile. Malachai's high laugh when the three-legged race turned into a puppy pile on the school lawn. Malachai's hair, dancing innocently in front of his forehead.

The event was only two days ago, but his typically busy schedule has limited our interactions since then largely to the Lancer Family Medicine office. Today, though, we both found ourselves leaving the office at the same time, and I was surprised when Malachai told me he was planning a quiet evening of studying and working on the festival books. It is a Friday night, after all.

Benson and Jack had invited me for dinner, but I found myself turning them down and in lieu of making Malachai my mom's spaghetti recipe and sharing some study space with him in my office.

It's been the perfect evening in so many ways. We made small talk and joked about misbehaving pilot lights while I cooked. His burn continues to heal nicely, thank goodness, which is the only reason I can joke about the stove I deeply considered taking a baseball bat to after it harmed Malachai. Once he began studying, I picked up my knitting and for the last hour or so we've enjoyed the quiet of my den, a room of this house I've loved since I first moved in. It's a space filled with built-in-bookshelves, all of them a dark and deep mahogany, along with a very comfortable leather couch that sits along one wall. Malachai's working at the large two-sided desk that takes up much of the room.

I'm trying very hard not to think about the fact that Christian and I never, ever shared working spaces like this. I enjoyed quiet evenings; Christian did not. He found inactivity deeply boring, my husband. His career as a sports agent lent itself well to nights out and parties; my career as a doctor lent itself much better to naps. Our social habits were one of many things we did not have in common.

Still, I have no regrets about asking Malachai to join me in my office this evening.

In fact, this evening is proving that asking Malachai to move in and offering to help him with the festival were not mistakes I should deeply regret. I can have him as a roommate, and even my friend, and still hold myself to the debts I owe Christian. Perhaps my willpower has not completely left me after all.

If only my knitting were hitting such heights of success. I can't stop the curse that escapes my lips as I notice my latest error in this poor hat.

"Did you say something?" Malachai looks up from his work.

"No. Nothing. I was just bemoaning a difficulty I'm having with this pattern."

Malachai shakes his head. "I still can't believe you're in a knitting group."

"Why wouldn't I be in a knitting group?" I ask him innocently.

"Because you're—" Malachai's eyes widen as I carefully leave my expression stoic. I enjoy telling people I've recently taken up knitting. Reveals all kinds of gender-based biases they usually didn't realize they had. The conversations that follow are always interesting, and usually highly amusing.

"I just don't think of, um, people like you as knitters," Malachai goes on.

"People like me?" I ask, and now I'm working desperately hard to keep the smile off my face.

"Yeah! Um, you know, doctors. Because..."

"Why wouldn't doctors knit?" I ask. My voice stays even as his goes up with fluster, and now I'm beginning to feel guilty about this little game I'm playing with him.

"It's just that you're all so busy," he goes on. "And also, you're, ummmm..."

"Male? More likely to be seen in a gym than a knitting circle, as per my physique?" I decide to let the poor guy off the hook, even if he is awfully adorable when he's flustered like this. "It's fine, Malachai," I tell him soothingly, and his entire body relaxes when I flash him a quick smile.

It's probably wrong how much I enjoy having that effect on him.

"I know I don't exactly fit the stereotype for a member of a knitting circle," I say. "The truth is that I only took up knitting after Christian died. My therapist recommended it, and I find it soothing." I shrug. "Somehow your nosey mayor found out about my hobby and talked me into joining her knitting circle, where I currently spend an hour a week being reminded that my charity knitting is very much subpar to her charity knitting. And everyone else's charity knitting."

"Oh. I didn't—I mean—I should have known—"

I sigh and set my project down. Making Malachai uncomfortable by bringing up his unconscious gender biases may have been purposeful, but I did *not* intend to make him uncomfortable by bringing up my dead husband. "You don't need to apologize," I tell him. "I brought up Christian because I wanted to, and if I hadn't wanted him to come up in conversation, I would have said so." Malachai looks stunned by my words, his beautiful brown eyes rising below tented eyebrows, and I resist the urge to brush the unruly locks from his forehead. "You don't need to walk on eggshells around me, Malachai. I know Jack and Marie have half the office convinced that I'm either a fragile vase or a powder keg that must be stepped carefully around, but I assure you, I'm neither."

"I don't think you're a powder keg, sir."

My dick twitches in response to the phrase, and I wonder, not for the first time, when I became someone so easily turned on by this formal business term. Christian and I never had the sort of dynamic where he called me sir, and I've had plenty of employees and patients call me that in the past without the word eliciting any sort of reaction from my dick.

I should probably talk to someone about this. If only my current physician wasn't also my infamously nosey best friend.

"I suppose that's nice, at least," I murmur. "It's good to have one person in my life who isn't waiting for me to fall apart at any moment."

Malachai frowns, his brow knitting together in thoughtfulness. "Sometimes," he says, almost wistfully, "I think the world is asking an awful lot of us by wanting us to keep our shit together all the time. I mean, life can be kind of terrible. Wouldn't things be a whole lot easier if we could just be hot messes in front of each other without having to worry about everyone else noticing?"

I don't bother holding in my bark of laughter. "You have no idea how many times I've thought exactly that same thing," I tell him.

Malachai's ears turn a bright shade of pink as he nods, a hint of a smile forming at the corners of his mouth. He smiles far too little, I've decided. I know Jack and Marie agree with me. They cornered me at the office yesterday, demanding to know if Malachai was safe and how we could all help him find a new place, particularly since I still refuse to sign that paperwork of Benson's.

I assured them again, of course, that they have nothing to worry about. Whatever feelings I may have for Malachai, I have fully forbidden myself from acting on them. I assured them both that Malachai has extended use of this house after I leave, and until then it remains a safe place he can reside for as long as he needs it.

Marie mentioned that Malachai brought up the possibility of leaving the practice at the end of the semester, and ever since I've felt even more curious about his future. "Marie and Jack and I were discussing the office operations yesterday," I tell him casually, which isn't a complete lie. "Do you know yet if you're going to stay on with them in the spring?" I know Jack and Marie worry about Malachai's future almost as much as I do. They certainly don't want to hold him back from his schooling, and they also don't want to lose him from the office. He's very competent at what he does for everyone on staff at Lancer Family Medicine. Henri trained him well.

"Oh. Um." Malachai frowns. "I'm not sure yet. I know you'd probably like me to move out, and I can look harder, sir, I promise. I know it's a bother having me here, and I—"

"Malachai," I interrupt quickly. "I told you already that you staying here is no bother whatsoever. You're welcome here until the lease is up in January. I was only asking out of my own curiosity." He frowns. "I'm not sure where I'm going next," he finally says softly. "I just know I need to get the hell out of here."

That's a vague and rather disturbing statement. "Has someone been bothering you around town?" I ask. "Avon again?"

He shrugs. "Not really. Not more than usual. I just... I guess I just get tired, sometimes. Of feeling like I'm never going to belong anywhere." His eyes dip with a hopelessness I recognize, and I fight the urge to rush around the desk and take him in my arms.

Instead, I do something else that is probably equally stupid.

I start sharing confessions of my own.

"I know exactly what you mean," I tell him. He looks up at me, clearly shocked.

"But you're... you," he says. "You always belong anywhere you are. I've seen it. You just walk into a room, and everyone there looks at you like you own the place."

I chuckle at the vision he seems to have of me. If only he knew how inaccurate—or incomplete, at least—that vision really is. "I wish that were true," I tell him. I sigh. "I don't know if you've ever heard how my husband died. Do you mind if I tell you?"

He shakes his head, clearly confused. And curious. I don't blame him; he has every right to be curious. He's living in a house dotted with pictures of my dead spouse.

"Christian and I were childhood friends. Our families were very close. In fact, my brother, who's only a year younger than me, is best friends with Christian's brother. We were together all the time. I can hardly remember a time in my life when Christian wasn't beside me." I set down my knitting and swallow the bile rising in my throat. "Our marriage seemed like an obvious choice: we had dated on and off through most of our teenage and college years; neither of us ever seriously dated anyone else. That we would spend the rest of our lives together seemed like a foregone conclusion. But Christian and I were very different." I rub at my temples, determined to say the next words I must say without stuttering or mumbling through them. "Christian loved people, and he loved being the center of attention. I preferred nights alone at home. Our apartment had a rooftop pool, and Christian greatly enjoyed throwing parties up there. I almost never agreed to go to any of his soirees. One day he had a party and I declined to go."

Malachai visibly gulps. I don't blame him; it isn't hard to fore-shadow how this story ends.

"There was a lot of drinking, and Christian slipped. He drowned. I have every certainty he would not have died if I'd been there. And ever since that day, the people in my life have looked at me differently. Like I'm broken and need to be fixed." I lean across the desk. "You never look at me that way."

Malachai purses his lips and shakes his head. "I could never think of you as broken," he finally says after a long moment of silence. "Ever."

And then, almost before I realize what's happening, I've moved around the desk to sit on the bench window seat next to his chair. Then Malachai's arms are around me, his cherry-vanilla scent, one I know all too well, enveloping me in soft sweetness. His body fits so perfectly against mine, his head nestled into my chest, that it never occurs to me to push him away or remind myself how highly inappropriate it should be for a boss and employee to hug like this. Instead, I lean farther into the embrace, allowing my own cheek to brush against his, allowing myself to feel the scrape of our skin together, the tingle of sensation as his hands move further around my back.

For a moment, I even let myself wonder: what would it be like to give into my fantasies and kiss him? To press my lips against Malachai's and feel—

"What's going on here?"

Malachai and I jerk away from each quickly as I register the sound of a voice I know all too well. We both turn in our seats, and Malachai's eyes widen even further as he sees who's standing there.

"But that's... is... is that *Christian?*"

Chapter 9
30 Days to the Devon Falls Leaf Festival

I swear, the statue's poop-emoji eyes narrow slightly. —Malachai Flynn

How's a dead man standing in front of me right now? More importantly, how is the dead husband of the guy I'm not supposed to be crushing on standing in front of me right now? I glance back and forth between the picture of Christian that sits on Sam's desk and the man in the doorway of the room, but aside from outfit choices—the Christian in the picture is wearing a dark blue tuxedo; the Christian in front of me is wearing a muted red sweater—and a few extra arm muscles, the two men are identical.

"Honey, I'm home!" A loud, bright voice shouts from the hallway just before another head pops into the room, and now I'm definitely certain someone's fucking with me. Has Jack's dad been putting his "green mayo" into the sandwiches Benson and Marie leave on my desk periodically?

Because now there's a movie star standing in the doorway. A tall, blond, green-eyed movie star, who I am only now just realizing looks vaguely like Dr. Evers.

"Oh no, we've stroked someone else out." The movie star puts his hand on his jeaned hip. "Sammy, I keep telling you to warn people who've never met us about this before we come visit."

"In my defense, I didn't know you were coming to visit," Dr. Evers says mildly. "Telephones do exist, Tom."

"Yes, and they ruin surprises." The Double walks across the room and stretches a hand out to me, smiling brightly. "I'm Tom Evers. Sam and I are brothers. The way you're staring at me suggests you've possibly seen me on a screen somewhere, so thanks for watching. Yes, I go by Tom Michaels in the media; it's an old family name. And that hunk of handsomeness behind me who you can't stop staring at is Christian's twin, Colin. I'm guessing that's why you're staring at him."

I open my mouth.

I close it again.

I open it one more time.

Nothing. No words come out.

Tom pats my shoulder sympathetically. "Wouldn't be the first time we saw the doppelganger effect in action. Give yourself a minute; you'll catch up."

Dr. Ever sighs. "I would have warned you if I'd known they were coming," he says softly to me. "Colin." He stands up and walks across the room to wrap the Christian-lookalike in a long embrace. "It's so good to see you."

Colin hugs him back while Tom huffs. "What, no hug for your own brother?"

"No hug for the brother who can't be bothered to call me and tell me he's about to show up on my doorstep," Sam says as he releases Colin. "I thought you were on set this week."

"There were some delays, so I ended up back in New York, and Colin was..." Tom trails off, apparently without words for the first time since he's walked through the door.

"Colin was lonely," Christian's twin interjects with a sigh. "You can say it, Tommy. I'm not ashamed of it." He glances back and forth between me and Sam. "Sammy, you're looking... well."

"Not so lonely?" Tom arches an eyebrow in the air. "Looks like Sam's skipped introductions, as always. Mom would be appalled by his manners."

Dr. Evers sighs and rolls his eyes.

"What's your name?" Tom asks me. "And hey, man, I am seriously sorry about freaking you out like this. Colin and I were just trying to surprise Sammy. We didn't realize anyone else would be here."

"Didn't occur to us," Colin says softly, his expression neutral, and my cheeks burn.

"Malachai," I manage to get out. "Uh, my name's Malachai Flynn."

"Malachai works for me at the practice, as our office manager, and he's staying with me while he's in between apartments," Dr. Evers adds brusquely. "That's all we are to each other. Nothing more."

The words sting against my eardrums more than they should. I know exactly what Dr. Evers and I are to each other. So what if I thought we had a moment just before Christian—Colin—walked into the room? People hug each other all the time. Of course that's all it was.

Just a hug. Just a regular, ordinary hug.

"You work for Sammy, huh?" Tom tilts his head at me. "You know, if you're tired of his poor attitude, I'm in the market for a personal assistant, and—"

"Absolutely not," Dr. Evers barks.

"I'm a very good boss!" Tom says indignantly.

"You're a horrible boss. That's why you're always in the market for a new personal assistant."

"Said the man who was fully embracing his employee when I walked in just now. Listen, Colin and I had a long drive. We'll debate who the better employer is tomorrow. Can we grab some dinner? I'm starving, and I bet Luis would whip up some of his famous empanadas or meatloaf if I asked nicely."

The room feels like it might very possibly be spinning around me. "Bed!" I announce, jumping up from my chair.

"I'm sorry?" Colin turns to stare at me, clearly startled.

"Um, I mean, I need to go to bed. I have an early Saturday morning class tomorrow." I rush to tell them. And for the first time all semester, I'm glad my math class is at ass o'clock on a Saturday morning.

"Of course you do." Dr. Evers sends me a tight smile. "Get some rest. Good luck with your class tomorrow. I'll have Tom and Colin stay in the rooms on the first floor so we won't bother you when we come in."

Oh, fuck. That's right. I'm about to be living with my crush's dead husband's identical twin.

I gulp back the rising panic in my throat, squeak out a goodbye, and rush upstairs to my bedroom to slam the door behind me.

"So, anyway, things are kind of a mess, as usual." I scrub my hands over my face. "I'm finally on track to get the money I need for my tuition payment, but I have to make sure the festival's a success. Otherwise I might not get the stipend money. Not to mention that I'd be letting this whole town down yet *again*."

My conversation partner doesn't answer me.

"Not to mention that I'm still obsessed with a guy who's mourning his dead husband. Oh, and did I mention that he's my boss and

I'm living with him *and* he's leaving town in just a few weeks? So yeah, kind of a total mess."

The poop emoji statue doesn't respond.

I take another bite of my sandwich and lean toward the statue. The Devon Falls town square has become one of my favorite places in the world, and I eat lunch here every Saturday after my math class gets out. The square stretches between the town hall, main street, and both of the Devon Falls churches, and it's home to the most recognizable thing in Devon Falls: the poop emoji statue.

It's not *actually* a poop emoji statue, of course. It's supposed to be a statue of some children dancing in a pile of falling tree leaves. Apparently it's a nod to the famous Devon Falls Leaf Festival, the one I'm now in charge of. But whoever made the wire statue clearly didn't get many opinions from other people before they locked it into cement or they really surrounded themselves with liars because *wow*, does that thing look exactly like a poop emoji. People come from all over the state to take pictures with it. It's gone viral more than once.

And this isn't the first time I've started talking to it out loud. I don't happen to have a whole lot of people to talk to, and sometimes you just need to get things off your chest, you know? At least there's not a lot of danger of a metal statue spilling all my secrets.

I rip a section of the sandwich off with my teeth and chew like I'm on a mission to destroy it. "The wild thing is," I tell the statue, "I thought for a minute he might actually have wanted to kiss me last night." I glance around, suddenly nervous that someone might have overheard me, but the park's unusually empty for a Saturday. More than a few of the Vermont leaves are beginning to turn now, a nod to how close the festival's getting, and a few reds and yellows dance across the darkening grass. The youngest Ryker kid and two of his friends are rushing around, throwing those early autumn leaves in the air like extras in a cable TV movie. But other than some falling leaves and five-year-olds, I have the space to myself.

"I mean, isn't that wild? As if someone like Dr. Evers would ever want to kiss *me*. He's Dr. Evers, for crying out loud! And my boss! And I'm..."

I don't finish the sentence, but I'm sure the statue knows what I haven't said. *I'm the town disaster. His employee who can't even afford khakis without holes in them. The kid who lives in his house and is like a million years younger than him.*

"There's no way I can hold a candle to his dead husband," I whisper to the statue as I wipe some peanut butter from my cheek with a napkin. "Christian was an amazing guy, I'm sure. He must have been if he was married to someone like Dr. Evers." I sigh. "I wonder if it's weird for him, having to see the exact mirror image of Christian all the time. I mean, Colin looks exactly like Christian. Like, exactly." I sigh. "Anyway, when Colin and Tom showed up, Dr. Evers made it pretty damn clear to them that he wasn't ever thinking of kissing me at all. That was totally in my head. So yeah. That's fun."

My phone pings and I sigh as I pull it from my pocket. *Please don't be Mom*, I beg the universe. After that impromptu episode of *The Parent Trap* in Dr. Evers' living room last night and three hours of equations this morning, I have zero energy for putting on the fake-happy front our conversations require.

It's Benson. Right now I can't decide if texting with him is better or worse than texting with my mom.

Benson: Hey, Marie's having a get-together at her place since Sam's family is in town. Can you come over?

I groan out loud again.

Benson: Marie says if you don't show she's going to track you down using the town message boards. Is she joking? IDK. May not want to risk it.

"Well, fuck." I chuck the phone down on the bench next to me. "Don't get me wrong," I tell the statue. "It's really nice that Marie and Alan always invite me to these things. Really, really nice." The Lancers have been so warm and welcoming from the moment I showed up to interview for the position at their office. I really do appreciate how much they try to include me in Devon Falls events.

"But," I add, "they don't get that their parties always have at least three people giving me weird side-eye. And now this one's going to have a living, walking reminder of the guy Dr. Evers is still probably in love with. And going means I'll have to spend even more time making conversation with that guy. Did I mention that he looked pretty weirded out when he saw me and Dr. Evers together in the den last night?"

Not that I blame him. *I* was pretty weirded out by whatever happened between the two of us in that den last night.

"But I have to go to the party." I crumple up the wax paper my sandwich was wrapped in and stand. "If I don't, Marie will be upset. Plus, I need people to trust me now that I'm running the festival. Skipping out on town events isn't going to help me build that trust."

I swear, the statue's poop-emoji eyes narrow slightly.

"I know, I know," I tell the statue. "It seems like I'm just going because I want to be with Sam—ah, Dr. Evers. And okay, maybe I do, just a little. But look, I'm not an idiot. I know nothing's ever going to happen between us. Really. I get that. Even if it weren't for all the weird baggage and the whole 'he's my boss' thing, someone like Dr. Evers is always going to be off-limits to someone like me. It's like we're not even from the same world. But I'll go. Just to show people like Avon that I really do care about the town."

Statues can't raise their eyebrows, right? Because I could swear this one just raised an eyebrow.

"Oh, whatever. I'm leaving now." I collect my trash and turn around. I guess it's time to get ready for this party.

Time to remind myself of all the things I want that I can never, ever have. Time to remind myself, I guess, exactly why I need to get the hell out of Vermont and far away from Dr. Sam Evers.

Chapter 10

29 Days to the Devon Falls Leaf Festival

Sadly, this particular goat brings me no sense of calm. —Sam Evers

Usually I avoid Marie's picnics and parties. She's been like a second mother to me since I first met Jack, but I'm all too aware why I'm invited to the many gatherings she and Alan, Jack's father, like to hold.

I'm supposed to make friends. Connect with the town. Possibly find a brand-new boyfriend to fall in love with, one who will magically make me forget about all the problems in my life and want to move to Devon Falls permanently so that I may stay here forever and be fully Happily Ever After.

Not that Marie wants me to entirely forget New York. If that was the case, I know she wouldn't have rushed to create a party today so that she could invite Colin and Tom over. It's more like she wants me to forget the pain of New York. And I appreciate that.

But forgetting is simply not possible, for so many reasons. And that's why I rarely make appearances at these events.

I have no choice today, of course. Tom loves a party, loves Marie and Jack, and I'm all too aware that he's brought Colin here because Colin's clearly not doing well in New York. Colin and Christian were always exceptionally close, as are Tom and I. The four of us, as I told Malachai last night before they arrived, have been bonded together since childhood.

Tom and Colin's bond only strengthened with celebrity. Tom's a long-time actor who's recently had some big breakthroughs in his career, and Colin only recently retired from a career as a Formula 1 driver. They've always run in the same celebrity circles. Christian and I used to wonder if the two of them were possibly on the path to being more than friends, but as far as I know, Colin is straight. If there is anything more than friendship between Tom and Colin, they've never shared that with me.

One of the things that worried me most about moving out of New York was leaving Colin behind. Colin retired from racing shortly after Christian died, a choice that concerned both Tom and me deeply. I know he keeps busy with his various commitments to the racing community, but I still worry he has too much time on his hands these days. Tom promised me he could take care of Colin after I left, but then Tom's career began to send him across the world on a regular basis. I know he hasn't been in New York much lately, and that means Colin's likely been on his own a great deal.

So we will attend the party. And if it makes Colin smile, I'll declare the experience to have been worth the trouble.

Marie's backyard is just a large expanse of land that backs up against a field, with a patio on one side that's covered in folding tables and camping chairs. Alan is serving hot dogs and veggie burgers onto the end of a table covered in salads that have far more mayonnaise than vegetables in them, and a small crowd of people that I know fairly well are milling around talking when I walk in, flanked by Tom and Colin.

"I just love this place," Tom gushes. "It's so quaint. Look! Marie and Alan have goats now! And Benson's going to show me his tomato garden today. Someday I'm going to move to Devon Falls too. Then you'll never be rid of me, Sammy."

Colin and I share an amused glance. Tom says this all the time, but we both know he'll never move to Vermont. His personality wouldn't even fit inside the borders of Devon Falls.

"Of course," Tom goes on. "I'll get my own place. Wouldn't want to interrupt whatever you and that employee of yours have going on right now."

Colin's eyebrows go up. I wince.

"There's nothing going on between me and Malachai," I say, and I don't bother to hide any of the growl in my voice. "And there never will be. I believe I've made that quite clear."

Tom groans and rolls his eyes. "When Jack told me that you'd been speaking fully in your prep school voice since you got here, I was hoping that he was exaggerating. Guess not. What about a place with more cows than humans has brought out the prim and proper version of Sammy Evers, huh?"

I don't bother to answer him. Any answer I could give would only raise more questions and potentially some conversations that I am *not* willing to have in front of Colin.

As far as I know, Colin has absolutely no idea that Christian and I were ever anything but deeply and madly in love. After all, my own marital problems weren't even fully on my radar until after Christian passed. Colin is one of the many reasons that I am so determined to make sure no one ever finds out about these inappropriately obsessive feelings I have for Malachai.

Therefore, telling Tom that I've adopted a more formal approach to my interactions in Devon Falls because it helps me keep my employee at more of an arm's length seems like a poor choice. So I hedge.

"Like you don't bring that voice out when it suits you," I remind him. "I'm just keeping a professional distance here. I'll be returning to New York in just a few short weeks, after all."

"Yes, Jack's mentioned your plans to leave a time or thirty." Tom crosses his arms. "Speaking of people who never stop talking to me about you, Mom and Mother want to know if you ever plan to call them back?"

I swallow down the taste of discomfort. I love both of my parents, and Tom and I have always been very close to them—but our mothers are deeply, passionately in love. Since Christian died, watching the two of them together has become yet another reminder of everything our relationship lacked. Everything that was missing from our marriage which eventually led to Christian's death.

In my defense, last year they bought one of those houses in Sicily that costs a Euro, and since then they've all but moved to Italy to spend a small fortune fixing it up. It's not as if I'm ignoring constant invitations to visit their apartment down the street.

"Time differences," I tell Tom in a strangled voice. "I'll call them this week."

Tom arches an eyebrow at me. Colin stays silent.

The problem with marrying a twin is that if you happen to lose your husband, you can spend the rest of your life staring at a copy of his face: the eyes are identical. The expressions are eerily accurate. Even the cheekbones match.

But something about the full picture is never right. For two months after Christian died, I couldn't look at Colin without flinching. Right now, though, I'm looking at the exact same expression Christian used to wear whenever we were having a difficult conversation and he was trying to decide if he should push me with more questions and poking or leave me be.

"You're Tom Michaels!" A young man with golden brown hair and eyes as wide as planets rushes up to us. "Oh wow, I can't believe this! You're actually *him*. I've seen all your movies, and I can't wait for *The Good Sword* to come out! Sorry, I know I should probably try to be cool around you, but I'm not very cool? So, yeah,

I just want to tell you you're amazing." He beams at my brother, face wide with adoration.

"Please don't apologize! It's always a joy to meet a fan! Would you like a selfie?" Tom smiles as his new admirer pulls out a cell phone.

"That would be great! I'm Gabe Gomez, by the way. Hey, do you think someone could take the picture for us?"

Colin and I look equally horrified by the idea of playing photographer, and it must show on our faces. Gabe blinks at us and starts looking around the crowds of people standing behind us.

"Oh, there! Hey, Malachai, do you remember me? Gabe, from the farm! Will you take a picture for me?"

Malachai appears behind him, blushing. "Sure, of course. Um, hello Dr. Evers. I mean Sam."

He keeps his eyes away from me as he speaks; his head tilted toward the ground. I fight the urge to reach for his chin and demand that he lift his face up. He should be able to look me in the eye. He should be able to look anyone in the eye. He's worthy of so much more than a life of looking at the ground.

I swear softly to myself. I let things go too far in my home office last night, and now I'm certain I've pushed him further into the shell he hides behind.

"Malachai, it's delightful to see you again." Tom strikes a pose with Gabe and Malachai snaps several shots of the two of them together. "Malachai, I know you've met Colin. Have you, Gabe? If you'd like to walk to the hot dogs with us, I can tell you all about what to expect from *The Good Sword*."

Gabe's jaw drops. "I—you mean—but you're Colin Templegate! You won the F1 championship a few years ago! Really? I mean, we could really get hot dogs? Yes! Yes, of course! I could help you with your toppings, if you want? And get you a drink!" He rushes toward the food table with Tom sauntering just behind him, and Colin and I share simultaneous amused eye rolls.

"He never changes," I say dryly.

"You wouldn't want him to," Colin says. "Hello, Malachai," he adds. Malachai manages to make eye contact with Colin and briefly nod at him. "Hello."

Colin's eyes move back and forth between the two of us. "Well. I should probably go help those two with the food." He casts me another glance I can't fully read out of the corner of his eye and then starts making his way toward the table where Gabe and Tom are eagerly chattering at one another.

"Malachai, can I speak to you for a moment? Privately?" I ask. Malachai's eyes widen with surprise, and I quickly lead the way across the yard to the goat pen before I can find a reason to run away from a conversation I'm now certain we need to have.

We stop in front of a goat with brown circles around her eyes offsetting an otherwise white face. Marie keeps insisting I get goats; she says they bring up her mood. The tree farm Malachai's been moonlighting with is known for putting Santa hats on their mascot goat around Christmas time. Sadly, this particular goat brings me no sense of calm as I try to put together the words I now know for certain that I need to say to Malachai.

I decide it's best not to beat around the bush. "What happened between us last night should not have happened," I tell him roughly.

Malachai purses his lips together and doesn't say anything.

"I'm your boss. And your landlord. It was highly inappropriate of me to ever behave as though we might be more than that." I shake my head. "You're my colleague and my short-term tenant. Having Colin and Tom here to visit has reminded me of how far past those boundaries I've pushed. From now I can promise you that I'll stay firmly behind them."

Malachai swallows. "I'm sorry too," he finally says. "For forgetting my place."

"Your place?" I'm not sure exactly what he means by that.

He shrugs. "Like you said. I just work for you. I'm your office manager; that's it. And you've been very nice to let me stay with you, but we both know you never had to do that. I mean, I get it. It's not like I belong here anyway." He sighs.

What the hell is he saying? Is he comparing the way he feels with me to the way he feels about how all of Devon Falls treats him? I'm starting to feel as though I may have lost control of this conversation. "Malachai, I didn't mean to imply that—"

"No, you were right to say it," he interrupts. And now I'm certain that something is wrong here, because Malachai has never interrupted me before. I've never seen him interrupt anyone before. It's simply not a thing that he does. "It's true. I know my place here in Devon Falls. I know yours. I should have remembered what those places are. I will from now on."

I'm not sure what to say next. This was the end goal I had for this conversation when I asked to speak with him: I wanted to make sure he knew that we'd gone too far last night and that I wouldn't be crossing such lines with him again in the future. Boundaries like that, I know, is the only option moving forward. I've had an entire day of staring at another version of Christian's face to remind me that I cannot ever give into my feelings for Malachai.

I owe too much to the memory of Christian. I owe too much to everyone who loved Christian. Especially Colin.

I simply have to put a stop to whatever might have begun to happen last night. Speaking to him about it, I'm sure, was the right thing to do.

But Malachai's words, for some reason, are crawling across my skin in the most uncomfortable of ways. They ring like discordant tones in my ears. He's taken something incorrectly from what I've just said; I'm sure of it.

I just can't quite figure out what.

"I think I'm going to get some food too." Malachai sends me a weak smile. "But don't worry, I'll try and stay out of your hair."

"No." The word falls out of my mouth like it's been strangled somehow, and Malachai stops to look at me curiously.

"No?" he asks.

"Don't avoid interactions between us," I add in a rush. "Just because we need to hold to certain boundaries doesn't mean I don't enjoy your company."

Malachai frowns. Nods. "Thank you," he says softly.

And then he leaves me standing alone by the goats, wondering how a conversation with someone can be such a success and such a failure all at the same time.

Chapter 11
28 Days to the Devon Falls Leaf Festival

I'm grasping for any inch of air I can find. —*Malachai Flynn*

"Okay, I can do this. I can do this. I can absolutely, positively do this." I draw in a deep, long breath and then let it out, just like my high school counselor always said to do when my anxiety started to choke up deep inside of my chest and lungs. "It's just a quick thank you. Two minutes. No one will even remember I talked at this stupid thing."

I lean back awkwardly against my car, which is lined up in an old cow pasture and looking much like the oldest vehicle in the pack, while I study the sign at the bottom of the driveway in front of me.

NORTHERN STARS WINERY.

"Really wish you'd given me more of a heads-up about this, Henri," I mutter as I pull my phone out of my pocket and review the text she sent me this morning for the eight hundredth or so time.

Henri: Hey sweetie! Listen, I know this is last minute, but I forgot to mention one other festival lead-up event before I left. That new winery that's opening up outside of town, the one on the

Canadian border that's claiming to be the most northern winery in the whole country? They're a major sponsor for the festival this year, and I said I'd go to their soft launch this afternoon to say a few words about how much the festival appreciates them. Totally understand if you're too busy to go last-minute, but if you can make it I know they'd appreciate it!

"I can do this," I mutter again. I close my eyes and will my legs to move forward, up the driveway to the large renovated barn sitting on the top of the hill.

The barn that is currently surrounded by a very large crowd of laughing, excited people who are all clearly very happy to be here. The barn that sits next to a large stage, which I am apparently expected to stand on in approximately ten minutes' time.

"What did I do in a former life," I murmur to the cars around me, "to deserve making appearances at social events two days in a row? And now I have to speak *on a stage* at one of them?"

I *hate* speaking in public. I've hated it ever since I was ten years old and Ken Davidson and his cronies "spilled" a bottle of orange soda all over me just before I had to go out into the Alcott Elementary Auditorium to be a fairy in our school play. I was already nervous, and the tittering laughter of the audience when they saw me covered in Sunkist only solidified my desire to never, ever be the center of attention again.

I could have texted Henri back that I couldn't make it today—that I was too busy studying, that I was working on other things for the festival, that I was too tired. But I just couldn't bring myself to send that message. I know exactly how much faith Henri placed in me when she rested Devon Falls' beloved festival on my shoulders. There's still about a month left until the festival, and I know I'm going to have to make it through a lot more moments like this if I want to successfully pull the festival off, make Henri proud, and earn that stipend check I need so badly.

I make my way through the field of cars and up the driveway toward the large, wooden barn that screams of high-level craftsmanship. A row of flower beds surround the makeshift stage under a tent where I recognize Jack's nephew setting up sound equipment with his friend Pat and the rest of their band. People are setting up camp chairs all around the perimeter of the property, and there are corn hole boards set up at random intervals, just waiting to be used. On a porch nearby someone has placed a row of wine bottles out and ready for tastings. Henri mentioned in another text this winery is the dream of one of the Shoalski grandchildren, and their entire family has provided the financial backing for it.

I wonder what it would be like to have a family that could provide for your dream like that. I wonder what it would be like to have a family that believed in your dream strongly enough to put their life savings behind it.

I manage to put one foot in front of the other long enough to make it to the side of the stage. A few people wave at me as I pass, and no one glares or steps obviously out of my way, so I take that as a good sign. I'm looking around for the winery owner, trying to figure out exactly what I'm supposed to do and when. I'm about to ask Elijah, Jack's nephew, if he knows what's going on when a face that's becoming more and more familiar appears in front of me.

"Malachai?"

"Gabe?" I'm starting to wonder how I managed to go an entire year in Devon Falls without ever seeing this guy; this is the third time he's shown up in my life in just the past week. "Um, what are you doing here?"

"Oh, I'm working at the winery too! Not full-time or anything. Basically just for events like this, and once they get their new inn up and running they said they might be able to hire me for the front desk. And next year I might actually get to finally learn how to make wine!" He finally stops and takes a breath. "What are you doing here?"

I glance past him, to the stage where Elijah's frowning as he plugs in a guitar, to the lines of people that suddenly seem to be streaming up from the makeshift parking lot, over to the people starting to line up next to the wine tasting porch.

And I spot Avon Loseff. He looks up just as my eyes find him, and our gazes lock. His eyes narrow, his face contorting into a quick expression of disgust, and just like that, I can't breathe. A sudden pain, aching and mildly sharp, runs through my chest and my heart starts racing at double its normal pace. I gasp for air, desperate to calm my entire nervous system down, but I know that won't be easy. This isn't my first panic attack, unfortunately. I haven't had one for months, but the symptoms are horribly familiar. I gasp again for breath, because I know all too well that a whole lot of breathing is the only way I can ever get these under control, but there are so many people nearby and the air feels so thick all of the sudden and that stage is locked in my peripheral vision and—

"Malachai? Malachai? Hey, I think we need a doctor!"

I'm grasping for any inch of air I can find, and trying *not* to focus on how hard and fast my heart is pounding in my chest, when I hear a low voice next to my ear.

"Darling, you're okay. I've got you, Malachai. Let's go behind the barn."

That voice, so familiar and strong, is like a shot of Vicodin to my entire nervous system. Dr. Evers puts his arms around my shoulders and gently guides me behind a building near us. The world is fuzzy around the edges, hazy, but it's hard not to notice when he settles down onto the grass next to the building and gently tugs me down to sit between his knees.

He pushes my head toward my legs and holds onto both of my shoulders. "Just listen to my breathing," he murmurs against my ear. "Breathe with me, darling. You're okay. Nothing's going to happen to you. I'm not going to let anything happen to you. I promise you that."

Something in my brain takes those words as instant gospel, and suddenly I can focus on the sound of his breath, soft and smooth in the air next to my face. I can breathe alongside him, in time with him, enjoying the way the sounds start to mingle together in time with one another.

"That's it, darling," he says. "You're okay. You're going to be just fine. Let me take care of you."

The strangest thing about panic attacks, I've always thought, is how quickly they appear and disappear. One moment I'm absolutely convinced I'm going to die, and the next minute it's as though nothing ever happened. As though the world was just set back upright on its axis again and everyone's just going about their business.

I glance up at Dr. Evers as I take in exactly how closely we're sitting together. Holy fuck. Just yesterday he was telling me that we need to hold to stricter boundaries when we're together, and now I'm basically sitting in his lap. I scramble to stand.

"Hey there, calm down." He moves slightly to the side of me so that his arm is still around me but we're not quite so physically connected. "How are you feeling? Do you often have panic attacks?"

Breathe in and count, hold and count, let it out and count. I follow the sequence my old high school counselor taught me twice before I know I'm ready to answer him. "I used to. But it's been a few months now. I thought maybe they were gone."

"Any idea what brought this one on?" His tone is so mild, gentle, and that tone makes it much easier to tell the truth.

"I have to stand on that stage and thank the winery for supporting the festival. I'm not exactly the best at public speaking."

"Ah, I see." Dr. Evers nods. I notice he's picked up a piece of grass and is chewing it thoughtfully now, holding it in between his teeth as he looks off over the rolling hills in front of us, the green grassy lanes there intermixed with fallen yellows and reds and oranges. Every newly fallen leaf brings us closer to the festival. "That makes sense."

I snort. "Yeah, sure. Because everyone has a panic attack right before they have to talk to people."

He shrugs. "Many people do," he says softly. "You won't be the first or the last."

We sit in silence for a moment. He chews his grass, and I breathe.

"I admire so many things about you," he finally says.

I jerk my head up so fast my neck hurts. "What would you ever admire about me?" I ask incredulously.

"As I said, many things. Your kindness. Your desire to be good at everything you do. Your fortitude." He glances behind the barn, toward the stage that's so quickly become my nemesis today. "You never give up, Malachai," he murmurs. "Some of us, we give up on things so quickly. We settle. I can never imagine you settling for anything less than what you deserve."

I gulp back the shock that quickly courses through my system; I doubt anyone else in the world sees me that way. I certainly don't.

Dr. Evers stands and holds out his hand to pull me up. I take it without thinking.

"If you don't want to speak, I imagine you don't have to," he says. "But know that I have every faith you can do it. I have every faith you can do anything you set your mind to, Malachai."

It takes a few more minutes of counting my breaths before I'm ready. But then I nod, turn, and start walking toward the stage.

I let the memories of everything he's just said to me carry me through each step I take to the stagefront, through my short remarks thanking the winery for their support, through the applause and cheering of the crowd as I step back down the steps and away from the stage. My sneakers touch the grass with a *thump* as I glance around me and find Dr. Evers standing next to the barn, still chewing on a blade of grass while he sends me a thumbs up.

Breathe in. Breathe out.

Don't think about him leaving Vermont without you.

Don't think about you leaving Vermont without him.

Just. Breathe.

Chapter 12
28 Days to the Devon Falls Leaf Festival

It looks as though this afternoon will certainly require the support of wine. I suspect we'll need more than two bottles. —Sam Evers

"Devon Falls continues to surprise me," I tell Tom mildly as we stretch out next to each other across blankets on the side of the winery's lawn and listen to Elijah and Pat's band play some song I only half-recognize. Colin sets up a camping chair next to us, watching carefully for cow pies. The three of us may be city boys, but we've all quickly learned that almost any outdoor activity in Vermont requires carefully scouting the area you sit in before you make bodily contact with the grass. "How did you two even hear about this place before me? Devon Falls doesn't exactly keep secrets."

"We just listen better," Tom answers cheerfully. "And today is the winery's soft open, so they're not really spreading the word about themselves loudly yet. Their plan is to open the weekend of the festival."

That explains why they're sponsoring the festival and why Malachai was asked to speak today. I haven't seen him since that speech, and I look forward to congratulating him when I do. He was poised, calm, and clear, easily thanking the winery owners for their support and reminding everyone to make sure they attend the festival that's coming up in less than a month now.

Anyone who hadn't seen him twenty minutes earlier would have never guessed that speech gave him a panic attack.

He's so strong, Malachai. I wish he saw that strength in himself.

"So hardly anyone knows about this place yet, and here you managed to collect an invite to the soft open within twenty-four hours of arriving in town," I say to Tom wryly.

"Like I said, I'm a good listener."

"More like the owners of the place saw him at Marie's party and immediately begged him to come," Colin adds, clearly bemused. "I wouldn't say this is so much a matter of you not listening, Sam, as a matter of you not being in a big-budget franchise film."

"Yes, shame about me not landing that role in Tom Hanks' new flick," I say, and Colin grins.

That's the first time I've seen him truly smile since we got here. I raise my plastic glass of red wine to him, and we soundlessly clink our cups together.

"Tom! Colin! Sam!" Gabe Gomez is standing next to a flower bed down the hill from the stage, waving enthusiastically. Next to him, Malachai is standing awkwardly, hands wrapped slightly around his waist.

"Well, will you look at that?" Tom beams at Gabe and waves brightly. "Looks like your housemate and my new fan are trying to get our attention, Sam. Isn't that convenient?" He and Colin exchange a look I don't have time to parse before Tom begins to jog across the lawn toward Gabe and Malachai.

"Very convenient," Colin agrees mildly. I don't have time to parse that phrasing either before Tom's returning to our blanket with Gabe and Malachai in tow. Gabe's carrying two bottles of wine.

"I'm done working for the day!" he says excitedly. "I told Malachai he should stay and hang out with me, even though he really wanted to go home. And I got free wine!" he lifts the bottles in celebration.

My eyes dart back to Malachai, who seems to be making a very concerted effort to look anywhere but at me. I wonder how I can begin to convince him that if he's ashamed about what happened earlier, there's nothing at all to feel shame about.

Colin's watching me, I realize, out of the corner of his eye. I quickly jerk my gaze back away from Malachai.

It looks as though this afternoon will certainly require the support of wine. I suspect we'll need more than two bottles.

Two hours later, the band is finishing a rollicking set and people dance across the lawn around us, sharing cheese and cookies and games of cornhole while they sing along to Pat and Elijah's playing in what's becoming an all-out karaoke fest. Our group has already finished off four bottles of wine and Tom's just opened something called ice wine—I'm given to understand it's made from frozen grapes and is a bit of a specialty in this area of the world—but it's clear who the lightweights on our particular blanket are.

"I love wine!" Gabe squeals as he reaches for a nearly empty bottle of something rose-colored. Colin captures his hand, an amused expression lighting his face, and tugs Gabe gently away from the bottle and into a sitting position that's nearly in his own lap.

"Maybe time for a rinse cycle?" he says kindly. "You've had an awful lot, little one."

"I'm not little!" Gabe's voice nearly squeaks with his outrage, which of course makes Tom laugh out loud. "And Malachai and I need more wine!" He yells out the last word with emphasis and begins banging on the ground next to him, making Malachai laugh. Malachai's had plenty of wine in the last few hours himself, but he's clearly a very different kind of drunk than Gabe. Gabe is loud, excited, and easily prone to touching and feeling everything and everyone around him, while Malachai seems to sink more into himself with every sip of alcohol. He sits across from me on the blanket, staring around him as though the world is a mystery being unraveled by the fermented grape juice coursing through his system. I've watched him carefully as he takes small sips and studies the scene around us, then closes his eyes in happiness when Pat and Elijah begin playing a particular song. I've watched his expression go glassy, watched the tension from his body seemingly dip away, and I will not lie: I've encouraged him to drink more, not less.

Malachai is always so tense. I'm enjoying watching his shoulders fall away from his ears. I'm enjoying watching the corners of his mouth stay upward in something approximating a long-term smile.

Onstage, Elijah lets out a loud excited yell. "We're so excited to be here today!" he announces to the crowd. "We're definitely honored to be playing the opening of the first winery in the county!" The people around us cheer in excited agreement.

"Now," Pat goes on, "we figured all you old folks in the crowd might want to hear a little 80s music."

Their statement draws the expected boos from the crowd, and Elijah and Pat both laugh on stage. "I'm telling your uncle about this," Tom yells to Elijah. My brother's local fans, who already got their share of autographs and pictures when Tom opened a bottle of Cab Franc with the vintner earlier, applaud him excitedly.

"Oh, we're counting on that," Elijah answers Tom cheerfully. "But you all know you want some 80s music, right?"

The crowd, with exceptions like Gabe and Malachai, is largely in their thirties, forties, and fifties. Everyone cheers excitedly.

"Great!" says Elijah. "Then here's your first song."

He strums his guitar excitedly, and soon the first chords of Madonna's song "Like a Virgin" are echoing through the air.

"Yay!" Gabe calls excitedly. He throws his hands into the air, nearly spilling what's left of the wine in his cup everywhere. Tom rescues the cup from him quickly as he clearly tries not to laugh. "Virgins!" Gabe whoops. "Just like me! I'm a virgin!"

Tom lets out a loud cough.

"I bet Sam and Tom and Colin aren't virgins," he says loudly as he sways on the blanket. "But Malachai, I bet you are!"

Malachi's face immediately goes bright pink. All the tension in his body that I've watched dissipate over the last hour is back now. I watch, nearly horrified, as his shoulders rise up toward his ears as embarrassment seems to flood his body. I push myself slightly closer to him on the blanket, determined to end this discomfort Gabe's created in him.

"Well," I say mildly. "There's absolutely nothing wrong with being a virgin. Nothing at all."

"Virgins are the best! It's great to be a virgin!" Gabe collapses in giggles while a bottle of rosé gently overturns itself and sloshes onto his shorts.

"Okay, that might be enough for you." Colin tugs Gabe upright as Tom rights the bottle, but Gabe tips a little too far to the left, and Colin ends up grabbing him up into his arms and onto his own lap just before he hits the ground sideways.

"Oh!" Gabe's eyes widen as he looks up into Colin's face. Tom bursts out laughing and rubs at his hair fondly. Colin just shakes his head, the right corner of his mouth turned up slightly.

"You're quite the troublemaker, aren't you?" he says softly.

Gabe shakes his head back and forth so quickly it's almost comical. "No, uh uh! I'm good! I promise, I'm a good person! Everyone likes me. Well, Malachai doesn't know me very well yet, but eventually he's going to like me!"

We all turn to look at Malachai, and I'm immediately appalled to find his seat empty. A quick glimpse upward alerts me to Malachai darting across the pasture toward an outbuilding next to the porch where wine is still being poured in large quantities.

"Oops." Gabe winces. "Maybe I shouldn't have said all that stuff about virgins," he slurs. "I'll go talk to him."

"I think you should stay put," Tom says. I don't pause to listen to Gabe's response. I stand and begin charting my own quick path across the yard to find my young tenant.

I catch up to him on the other side of a small, darkly wooded shed, where he's bent over and using the barn to hold himself upright. "Don't worry," he calls out when he sees me. "I'm not having another panic attack, I swear. Just... felt a little sick."

"That's understandable," I tell him mildly. "It's been a busy day, hasn't it?"

"That's for sure." Malachai groans as he stands upright and falls back against the barn, dropping his hands to his sides. "How do I always end up looking like such a *loser* around you?" The words start out as a whisper and end in a slur. Strains of Elijah's guitar wind their way into my ears; he and Pat have finished their time with Madonna and now pieces of Peter Gabriel's "In Your Eyes" take up the space in the air around us. It feels like a fitting song for Malachai's expression, which is hollow and almost bereft but still alive with the same light I've grown so used to seeing there.

"Malachai." I place my hand under his chin and lift it up gently toward me. "You never have, and never will, be a loser. Gabe owes you a very large apology when he's sober enough to give one, that's certain. But if you are a virgin, that's nothing at all to be ashamed or embarrassed about."

Malachai purses his lips together and sucks in a large breath before he groans. "Easy for you to say," he slurs. "Do you know what it's like being a twenty-one year old who's hardly even kissed anybody? I'm beyond virgin. I'm like virgin-plus. It's embarrassing." He groans again.

"Are you feeling unwell?" I ask him. "Do you need to be sick? How can I help? Let's find you some water."

Malachai shakes his head as he sways slightly on his feet. "You always want to take care of me," he whispers. There's a tear sitting stagnantly at the corner of his left eye, and I fight the urge to tug it away from his body with my thumb. Someone as wonderful as Malachai should never have to cry. "And you're always so *nice* to me. No one's ever been like that with me before. Not like you." He shakes his head.

I grab hold of him before he can tip over and ease him down to the grassy ground beneath us, just like I did earlier in the day, holding onto him as we land together. "You deserve nothing but the best of care from the people around you," I tell him as I tilt his head up again to examine him further. His eyes are shadowed, almost sunken. Is he not sleeping well? Perhaps I should change the comforter in his room? Purchase new sheets? I wonder if—

And then, just as I'm pondering the true merits of Egyptian cotton, Malachai leans over and presses his lips firmly against mine.

The kiss is soft and almost innocent in its lack of innocence. His arms wrap into mine as he moves his bottom lip closer to my top one, as though he's taking on an exploration to discover every part of my mouth. For a moment my brain blinks in a sea of white noise. I haven't been kissed in a very long time, and it takes a second for muscle memory to intervene in this experience.

And then? Intervene it does.

Before I can think logically through the static that's intercepted my brain, my own lips begin moving against Malachai's, my tongue brushing into his mouth in what feels like some kind of primeval urge to claim him as my own. I tug him against my body, cherishing the feel of his skin where it brushes against mine, savoring the feeling of the energy coursing through my body. For a long moment all I can concentrate on is that energy, the heat moving between us, the thrill of connection and excitement and *rightness* that courses, through my body, and then—

And then my brain catches up with my body.

And I pull away. Immediately.

"I'm so sorry," Malachai whispers. "Fuck. I know I shouldn't have done that, Sam."

He takes off again across the lawn, disappearing in front of my eyes yet again today. I sink down onto the grass, desperately trying to sort through the tornado of thoughts in my brain.

I gave in to him. I gave in to every feeling I've had for Malachai. I let myself kiss him.

Everything I felt in that kiss—it was like nothing I've ever felt before.

A jolt of guilt, ink-black and slippery, moves through me. But it's quickly interrupted with another thought.

He finally called me Sam.

Chapter 13

25 Days to the Devon Falls Leaf Festival

Sure, of course. Happy to talk with you about prostate checks, Doc.
Please just don't ask me not to smash my lips into yours again.
—Malachai Flynn

Unknown number: Hi, it's Gabe Gomez. I got your number from Shandra LaPiece who got it from Burt Busby who got it from the mayor who got it from one of your bosses.

Unknown number: I just wanted to say I'm really sorry about how I acted at the winery launch. I've never had wine before? I think maybe I'm allergic to it.

Unknown number: Which might be a problem if I'm about to start working at a winery part-time.

Unknown number: Anyway, I wouldn't blame you if you never want to speak to me again. But if you feel like texting me back, maybe we can hang out or something. Do you like pie? Luis' place has great pie. I like pie.

"You know your phone's blowing up right?" Benson eyes me from across the office in Lancer Family Medicine. He would have to be waiting for Jack just as Gabe Gomez decided to start this apology texting tour.

I frown at my phone. "What are you supposed to do when someone apologizes for being, well, kind of a jerk to you?"

Benson blinks and looks up from his phone. "Malachai, I think we both know I'm usually the jerk in any given scenario where someone is behaving like a jerk. But in my experience, if someone apologizes for being an ass, it's usually a good thing." He shrugs. "Now you just have to decide whether or not you forgive them."

I frown as I look down at my phone again. Huh. I'm not used to getting a whole lot of apologies when someone hurts me. Eighteen years in Alcott, and not one person there ever apologized for how they treated me. I'm sure that if I went home tomorrow, Ken Davidson would slap me on the shoulder and go right back to making fun of me.

"You forgave me," I said slowly. "After what happened last year." People like Avon may still not have let go of what happened back then, but Benson and the Lancers certainly forgave me right away. And it was Benson who dealt with the worst of consequences of the secrets I kept.

Benson looks up again, his eyes narrowed slightly. "What happened last year wasn't your fault, Malachai," he says softly. "You had nothing to apologize for."

If only people like Avon Loseff agreed with him. Still. I wonder if apologies are the kind of thing you should pay forward. I let my fingers drift back and forth over the keyboard on the screen. Maybe I should text Gabe back. I'm not exactly swimming in people who want to hang out with me. And I do like Luis' chocolate pie a whole lot.

"How are things going with the festival?" Benson asks as he puts down his phone and flips over a piece of paper in the file folder on his lap in front of him. I've never quite understood exactly what lawyers do all day. Benson seems to spend a lot of his time making sure that his practicing-nudist boss, Ellie, is fully clothed before she goes into a meeting, and the rest of the time he usually seems to be reading something. I always thought lawyers did glamorous things like go to court all the time. "Any updates to my wedding I should know about? I've got a resort in Belize on speed dial, just so you know."

I laugh and shake my head. "No new developments, I promise. Henri wanted me to remind you, though, that you and Jack should be working on your vows."

Benson sighs. "Yeah, I know. I'm on it. Writing poetic words of love isn't exactly my strong suit. I wonder if anyone's ever written their wedding vows in legalese. You know: *hereafter we will refer to Groom One as...*"

"My guess is no," I tell him. "Anyway, things are on track right now." I stifle a quick yawn. Things arc on track, but that doesn't mean they're not taking up a lot of time. I have two tests this week and I had to do billing for the office, and then there was all the time I lost being massively hungover and panicky after the winery event three days ago.

A spike of nervous energy moves through me as I think back to that day, and my dick rises to a quick salute at the memory of me kissing Sam Evers. I still can't fucking believe I did that. We haven't seen each other much since he drove me home from the winery on Sunday, and I'm exceptionally grateful that he hasn't brought up The Kiss once during the past few days. The last thing I need is him reminding me all the reasons that my kissing him that day was a mistake.

Especially when nothing about that kiss *felt like* a mistake. Granted, it was my first kiss ever, if you don't count a really bad game of spin the bottle in fifth grade and some awkward and definitely failed experiments in high school. But still...

The way every nerve in my body lit up as our mouths touched. The way his skin felt hot and right and certain against mine. Is that the way every kiss is supposed to feel? If it is, I'm kind of sad

I've let myself stay a virgin—in almost every single sense of the word—until now.

At least Colin and Tom left for New York City the day after the winery event. I'm awkward enough around Sam right now without his brother and his deceased husband's twin watching my every move.

"Benson!" Jack beams as he steps into the front office, and the two of them rush toward each other like they didn't just see each other eight hours ago before work this morning. Maybe kisses *are* always supposed to feel that otherworldly, then. Jack and Benson sure act like theirs are.

Sam steps into the front office behind Jack, and my entire body immediately goes on high alert—I'm surprised my hair doesn't stand upright.

"Ready for dinner?" Jack asks Benson. "Sam, Malachai, want to join us? We're going to Thai for Two. Elmer's doing his comedy routine tonight."

Sam shakes his head. "I have some more files I need to update. Malachai, will you be here for another few moments? I have a question about the Rothski appointments next week."

Sure, of course. Happy to talk with you about prostate checks, Doc. Please just don't ask me not to smash my lips into yours ever again.

"No problem," I answer, and I *really* hope no one in the room can hear the strain in my voice.

Sam nods, and Jack and Benson sink into their own world, talking and laughing together as they find their jackets and head out the front door, locking it behind them.

I follow Sam back down the hall to his office, which is smaller than the one Jack and Marie share but still fairly good-sized. The large, polished dark wood desk in the center reminds me a lot of the one in his office at home—well, at his home.

Damn. I've really got to stop thinking of Dr. Evers' house as a place where I live. Belong.

"So, Mr. Rothski has a 4:30 appointment on Thursday," Sam says as he leans over his computer, flexing butt and thigh muscles that might as well be teasing me personally from his perfectly tailored pants. "But I noticed he also has an appointment for Friday, so I wanted to check that."

"I'm sorry about kissing you on Sunday," I blurt out.

He stands up straight, right eyebrow raised. He says nothing.

I squirm in front of him. "I mean, I understand why it was a mistake. We've talked about boundaries. You're my boss, and I put you in a really crappy position when I did that. Especially with Colin and Tom there. Plus, I know you're not interested in me like that, and you're still getting over the loss of your husband, and I—"

"Malachai." He interrupts me, his voice steady and even. He shakes his head. "You have nothing to be sorry for."

"But I do!" I practically shout the words through the room. "I didn't have your permission, and like you said, it was a mistake!"

Sam crosses his arms and frowns. "It was a mistake," he says softly. "But that doesn't mean I didn't want you to do it."

I swear, my heart stops beating. Just for a split second, but it definitely stops.

Did he just say what I think he said?

Sam shakes his head. "There are a lot of reasons you and I shouldn't have done what we did that day. Some of those reasons are more personal to me. Others are obvious to both of us, I know. There's a great deal of power imbalance in this relationship, Malachai. I am your boss. You live with me." He shakes his head. "And whatever feelings might exist between us... I have to be careful. I've made mistakes in the past that I can never atone for."

I assume he's talking about Christian's death, though I still don't understand exactly why he holds himself so responsible for that. He couldn't have ever known what would happen when he decided not to go to that pool party that day.

Still, I think I get where he's coming from. I understand what it feels like to carry all your regrets and mistakes on your shoulders.

I nod. "I understand that. Really. And from now on I'll be more respectful of your space, I promise. I shouldn't have had all that wine. And then you were being so..."

Sam tilts his head slightly as he studies me. "So what?"

"So nice," I whisper, more to the ground than to him. "Like I said. So kind. So caring. I mean, you're always kind and caring, Sam. And maybe that's why—"

He steps out from behind the desk suddenly, his arms crossed. "You've finally started calling me Sam," he interrupts.

It takes me a moment to connect the dots of what he's saying, and then I realize he's right. I have started calling him Sam, and not only out loud; I call him that in my head more often than not now. Maybe that kiss shifted something in my brain, because calling him Sam instead of Dr. Evers hasn't felt unnatural or strange at all—and it took me a lot less time to make that shift than it did for me to start calling Marie and Jack by their first names. "Is that okay? If I call you that?" I ask him hesitantly.

"It's more than okay," he says softly. "It's what I've wanted for some time now." He takes a step toward me, capturing my chin in his right hand. He seems to take my chin in his hand an awful lot, and I can't say that the movement doesn't make every cell in my body immediately respond. "Malachai, you and I can never... be. That's why the kiss was a mistake. But just to be clear: that unfortunate fact doesn't mean I didn't want you to kiss me that day."

I'd probably jolt back from him in shock if he wasn't still holding my chin in his hand. Sam Evers seriously wanted me to kiss him? On what kind of planet do doctor-gods like Sam Evers want minions like me to kiss them?

"What?" My voice comes out like a squeak. "How? Why? You've got way better options than me."

Sam snorts. "Better options." He shakes his head. "You really don't understand, do you Malachai? How you affect me. What you do to me."

"Me?" The word squeaks again from my mouth. "I'm not anything. I'm nobody. I'm from Alcott, Vermont, and I don't even fit in there! Do you know how hard it is not to fit in when you live in Alcott? My elementary school's mascot was a log!"

Sam bursts out laughing. "Malachai, this is exactly what I mean. You don't see all the power and light you bring to this world. You *can't* see it. No one's ever reflected that light back to you." He sighs. "All I wanted to do on Sunday was to keep kissing you. But like I said, I've made mistakes I can never atone for. I owe debts to the world. Even outside of the other boundaries between us, those debts mean that you and I can never be anything more than what we are to each other now." He shakes his head as he drops his hand from me and steps back.

"I want to lose my virginity to you!" I blurt the words out, an unexpected revelation from my mouth before my head can catch up to them, and then I just stand there, clearly as stunned by their presence as he is. "Shoot, I shouldn't have said that," I add. "But, I mean, what if we didn't have to be together? What if you just, like... helped me out? Because honestly, that kiss the other day was *really excellent.* And when I say I'm a virgin, well, I mean I don't have any experience with anyone. Like at all. And like I was telling you on Sunday, that's kind of embarrassing. It's just one more thing that makes me, you know, different from a lot of other people." I bite my lip and then force the next words out of my mouth before I can lose my nerve to say them. "I'd never even really kissed someone until last Sunday when I kissed you. And when I am with someone, well, more physically or whatever, I want it to feel like that kiss did."

"Malachai." Sam's voice is a growl now, echoing through the space. "You can't stand there and say things like that to me. I'm only human, after all."

And just like that, I know what I'm going to do next. I know what I want to do. I know what I want to convince *him* to do.

I perch myself up against the desk and slide my body ever so slightly closer to his. I gently roll one finger over the edge of his hand, and I know I've got him when he shivers slightly as my skin crosses his. "Of course, sir," I say softly. "Whatever you say, *sir.*" I add as much emphasis to that final syllable as I possibly can. "I promise to leave this office right away, if that's really what you want. Sir." I clear my throat as his eyes grow darker and brighter, somehow at the same time, with each of my words.

It's working. It's fucking working.

Huh. Maybe I'm really onto something here.

"But, sir," I add, "if you *did* want to help me, I hope you know that whatever we do wouldn't have to mean anything. It could stay just between the two of us. And I would be very, very grateful."

"Careful what you say, Malachai," he whispers. "Be very, very careful."

I shake my head. "I'm not worried, sir. You're leaving Devon Falls in just a few weeks. Debts and power imbalances and all that stuff don't have to matter. This can just be for us. Nobody else." I gulp in a large breath of the air and pause to wonder where I managed to get all of this confidence from. I hope I can pull some more of this out of thin air again for my next lab presentation.

"Please," I add. "I want this. And like I said before, I know you'll take care of me." I tug in one more gulp of air and add the words that I somehow know, in my innermost soul, will push him across the edge I want him to fall over. "You could tell me what to do," I say. "You are my boss, after all."

I whisper the words as if they're the key to unlocking a door I've been staring at for months. And then, just as I'm wondering if I've actually unlocked Pandora's box, Sam moves.

He pushes me up against the desk, almost roughly, but with a soft smoothness that lets me know he's thinking of my comfort even as he's taking control of my body. "Are you saying," he whispers in my ear, "that if I ordered you to get on your knees right now, you'd do that for me? For your boss, Malachai?"

I gulp and pant back a whimper. "Yes," I whisper. "Anything you want, sir. Anything at all." I'm so hard in my boxer shorts that my dick feels like it might be about to poke its way straight through my worn khakis.

He nods, mouth straight and eyes sparkling with a kind of excitement I've never seen in them before. "Or perhaps," he adds, "I'll order you to let me show you how good it can feel to have someone put their mouth on you, and then explore your body—"

"Sir!" I gasp the word out, loudly enough that I'm immediately grateful we're the only two people in the office. And if I unlocked a door with my words to him before, now it's as if I've pressed the trigger on the starting gun at a race. "Yes, yes! I want that! All of it!"

He pulls back from me, face bright and focused fully on me. "Take off your pants, Malachai," he whispers loudly into the room.

I gulp. "Yes, sir." I pull at my belt, desperate to get my pants off before Sam remembers all his worries about power imbalances and his past and everything else he kept talking about earlier. I don't want to risk doing anything that might take him out of this moment we're having together. I successfully get my belt undone and drop my pants to the floor. Sam studies me for a moment, eyes narrowed with a kind of hunger I've definitely never seen directed at me before. I push my boxers down more slowly as he studies me, and despite all the energy in the room, I find myself waiting for the moment when he realizes exactly how ridiculous it is that he ever thought he might want to be with me like this. Maybe it will be when he sees my ramrod-thin thighs, or my slightly-too-small cock, or my just-a-little-too-hairy balls, or—

And while I'm waiting for Sam to discover what a truly terrible mistake he's making, he does the impossible.

He drops to his knees and takes me in his mouth.

Chapter 14
25 Days to the Devon Falls Leaf Festival

It is a truth universally acknowledged that when someone your heart craves steps in front of you, and tells you unequivocally that their heart craves you back, that they will be impossible to resist.
—Sam Evers

After Christian died, and I began to come to terms with all that was lacking and wrong with our marriage, I went through a period of time where I obsessively read every romance novel I could get my hands on. I was studying, I suppose. Trying to determine what love and romance were supposed to look like objectively. I read every happy-ever-after I could find, starting with the most historical of romances, and I read my way all the way through the contemporary tomes of authors like Alyssa Samuel.

It wasn't until I moved to Devon Falls and was hit with the force of my problematic feelings for Malachai that the lessons from those books began to make sense. Since then, Jane Austen's first words in her romance novel *Pride and Prejudice* have continually reappeared over and over again in my mind.

It is a truth universally acknowledged...

I wasn't sure, even after I began spending time with Malachai, if I thought that any truth about love could ever be universally acknowledged. But now, kneeling in front of the first person who's made me feel alive, possible, *real,* in years, I finally see a truth universally acknowledged.

It is a truth universally acknowledged that when someone your heart craves steps in front of you, and tells you unequivocally that their heart craves you back, that they will be impossible to resist.

And I'm quite certain that is why, against my better judgment, I find myself with my mouth positioned fully in front of the hard cock of a young man that I have no business being alone with in my own professional office space. The power imbalance between the two of us still rings loudly in my ears. The wrongs I did to Christian weigh heavily in the back of my mind.

And yet, all I know at this moment is that Malachai has asked me for something. And once again, as the day I found him alone in his car, I know I cannot resist giving him anything he needs or wants.

His body is perfect. His thighs are a sweet, soft milky color, a stark contrast to the dark wood of the desk he leans against. His boxer shorts are holey and worn where they've fallen around his ankles, and I take a moment to wonder if perhaps Malachai would allow me to take him shopping. But until such time as that, it does seem rather convenient that I could rip through this soft cotton cloth of his boxer shorts at any time I like.

But there's no time to think of clothing or new wardrobes right now. All I can think of at this moment is the opportunity in front of me: an opportunity that goes against all odds and logical thinking. An opportunity I am quite certain I cannot pass up. I take in a deep, dark breath, full of pure *want* that I haven't felt in so very long, and I take Malachai deep in my mouth.

He lets out a soft, sweet gasp. It's the kind of noise that could make me come in my own pants if I wasn't a man of very strong endurance and great patience. Still, it's difficult, hearing his noises of soft desperation as I gently circle my tongue around him. I shift and move, first slowly and then quickly, back and forth and over and across his cock. I pull all of him in and then release him, over and over, feeling the warmth and hard excitement of his body. It feels nearly impossible in this moment not to lose myself to the sort of pleasure and excitement I haven't felt in so, so very long.

"Sir." He whimpers the word. And how *does* he know? How does he know that one word is enough to nearly push me over the edge? How does he know exactly when to utter that word in exactly the right tone, and how has that word become something that has so much power over me? "I want... more. Need more."

"Don't come." I growl the words out of the corner of my mouth, knowing that they will echo around his cock and their vibrations will only add further excitement to this moment. "Not yet."

Great fuck—are these words as exciting in his ears as they are on my tongue?

"Yes, yes, sir. I've never... I've never done this before. Anything like this. It feels..." I hear his unfinished response fall from his mouth, and I know without a doubt that he is ready. I gently push one finger up inside my own mouth, just one finger, until it intersects between my cheek and his cock, and I begin covering it with the warmth of the two of us together, gathered and connected in one space.

"Oh. Oh. Sir!" More of Malachai's words echo across the quiet space of the room. They're the kind of words that are so often mocked and joked about, words associated with pornography and societal shame, but here in this room those words feel like magic. Like a kind of emotion that I didn't even know was possible to feel again, an emotion that was once dead to me.

And all I want to do is hear more of those sounds come from Malachai's mouth. I pull off of him gently with a soft pop, and he grips the desk behind him as if it's holding him up. Perhaps it is, but I cannot risk him falling. I cannot risk anything happening to his small, soft, perfect body.

Quickly, I sweep aside a section of small, unimportant items on my desk. It's a desk that houses very little, and yet I still somehow manage to feel like one of those people in the movies who's just flipped everything off their desk willy-nilly in the name of a romantic encounter. How have I become that man? How have I managed to meet every possible touchstone of every one of those romance novels I read all in one day?

If anyone could cause such a rush of emotion, it would appear to be Malachai. Some cliches, I suppose, are beloved for a reason.

"Don't come," I whisper again to Malachai. I pull his pants fully off his body and lift him up on top of my desk. He's splayed out before me now, his legs parted wide, his mouth and eyes open wide in wonder. He's giving himself completely to me in this mo-ment, and we both know how much vulnerability and how much importance there is in that. I won't ever take his vulnerability for granted. I hope beyond all hopes that he knows this.

"Tell me." I say the words sharply into his ear and then immedi-ately curse the tone of voice Jack keeps telling me to watch for. I soften it again before I continue. "Tell me if you want me to stop. Say the word, Malachai. That's all you need to say."

He shakes his head quickly. Firmly. "I don't want you to stop, sir."

I nod, and then I quickly suck the first finger of my right hand into my mouth again. I suck as hard and as fast as I can—there's no lube in this office, and I will not risk harming him. And then, when I'm fairly certain that I have reached a level at which I am ready to enter him, I take two actions at once that I can only hope will be his undoing.

I lean over his body, taking him back into my mouth once more at the same time that I slowly tease his entrance with that one wet finger.

"Sam." It's the first time he's spoken my name since we first began engaging in these acts together, and once again, I nearly lose myself in the moment. It takes every ounce of fortitude and composure I have to hold myself together as I continue to push gently inside of him, testing the boundaries, feeling the pull of his body against my skin, feeling his passion, his fear—his readiness as he moves and jerks in my mouth, gently at first and more harshly. I can hear him gritting and grinding his teeth, but he's not telling me to stop.

I push a little more firmly into him. Just slightly. "Push back against me," I tell him. For someone who claims to have absolutely no experience sexually, he's responding instinctually to every single move I make, and he pushes back down against me like a determined rock pulling away from a slide. The rest of my finger is sucked into his body as he drives his cock farther into my mouth, a sure sign that he is ready.

A sure sign that he's feeling everything I had hoped he would feel right now.

"I... I..." Words are drifting off his tongue. They are desperate, but they are the exact right amount of desperation I hope to hear from him right now. "I'm going to come, sir," he finally adds in a quick and breathless voice.

"Come for me," I order him as I twist my finger ever so slightly inside of him and tease that I might add another. He gasps against my body, and I know.

What's coming next is solely for him, and yet my own body is responding to his need. Every muscle and bone inside of me feels the excitement of this moment, and I cannot stave off what's coming much longer.

"Sam! Doctor! Sir!" He calls me every name he possibly can just as I feel him explode up and into my mouth. His warmth circles my tongue. I stay exactly where I am, sitting in the feeling of holding him in a space inside of me.

This is, of course, not something I would normally do. Blow jobs without condoms are certainly not something recommended by any medical association, but then again, nothing about this moment would likely be condoned by any professional governing body. Malachai and I are off the beaten path, doing something that surely almost nobody outside of ourselves would approve of. Something *I* don't even fully approve of. And yet everything about this moment feels entirely right—even more so when Malachai gasps once more and juts up against me.

And that's all it seems my own body can stand.

Everything within me explodes in that one moment. I come without ever even touching my own cock, wetting the inside of my pants as I feel a kind of release I never thought I could feel again. This is the kind of release I certainly haven't felt alone in my bed, silent and determined to find some solace in dark, sleepless hours. No. This is an explosion of release I was almost certain my body was no longer capable of. I collapse into it, into the moment, as the moment itself softly collapses around us.

A sea of gray and white light from my office lamp covers us as I fall slightly over Malachai's body while I stroke his cheek with my less disheveled hand. "How do you feel?" I ask him.

Must make sure he's okay. Must make sure he's alright.

The words echo through me. What if what I've done here has caused harm? What if all my initial trepidations were right? Or what if I've gone too far, too fast with him?

But then Malachai hitches himself up in his elbows, grabs at my mouth with his own, and kisses me again the same way he kissed me that day at the winery. And then I know something for certain: there is nothing I will be able to regret about this moment. However forbidden it may be, whatever lasting consequences lie beyond these office doors, I won't be able to apologize to myself or the world for this choice. Because nothing of that world matters now, as Malachai rolls his tongue around mine, tasting himself in me and deepening whatever strange and taut connection is constantly pulling between us.

"I'm more than fine," he tells me after he finally pulls away from me. "I'm better than I've ever been. Sir."

The word sings through the air as we cling to each other. Even if only for just this one moment.

Chapter 15

23 Days to the Devon Falls Leaf Festival

This protective vibe is turning me on a whole lot more than it should. —Malachai Flynn

"Um, hi? Malachai?"

I jerk my head up from my desk, where I was very definitely *not* falling asleep on the math book I was very definitely *not* studying while I'm supposed to be doing billing for Lancer Family Medicine.

Hey, calculus and billing both involve numbers. And I'm a good multitasker.

"Gabe?" I squint at him, not entirely sure this is the same Gabe Gomez who's been texting me obsessively since our unfortunate afternoon together at the winery last weekend. He looks different, somehow. His usual beaming smile is nowhere in sight. He's wringing his hands together in front of his flannel shirt, and the baseball cap he's wearing hangs low on his head.

"Yup, it's me. How are you?" He sends me a shy smile.

"Tired." I blurt out the word before I can come up with the kind of half-lie I usually give in response to that question. I'm fucking exhausted, honestly. Yesterday, I got a text from the festival's tent vendors that they needed to have an emergency meeting right after I was done with work, and that meeting ended up lasting for over three hours. And of course I also had a massive lab assignment due for chemistry class this morning. I slept for about two hours last night.

"Oh." Gabe blinks at me. "Geez, I'm sorry. I can come back, if you want. I just needed to apologize in person."

Wow. Apologies like the ones Gabe has been texting me were already new territory—now I'm getting an in-person version? I don't even know what to *do* with that. Despite Benson's advice, apologies remain confusing territory for me.

"I'm sorry I didn't answer you right away," I tell him. "I just needed some time." The truth is that I wasn't sure I was ever going to be able to answer Gabe's texts after what happened at the winery. Not because I didn't want to, exactly. I knew Gabe was drunk and he never meant to humiliate me by saying what he said. But that humiliation, the way I felt stripped down that day, was just too damn close to all the ways I often felt unworthy or lesser when Ken Davidson would follow me to the bus stop at the Alcott Trailer Park so he could make fun of my thrift store jeans or budget haircut. Way too close to the feeling I still get in the pit of my stomach whenever Avon Loseff turns his super judgy gaze on me.

I wasn't sure I could let those feelings of humiliation go. But then Sam and I had that afternoon together in his office, and, well...

What can I say? It's hard to stay mad at someone when you're riding the throes of post-orgasm bliss.

Not to mention that Sam has been even more perfect since that afternoon. We haven't really talked about what happened, not exactly. But he packed a lunch for me to take to work today—and that's definitely the only time anyone's packed me a lunch since I was in the second grade—and last night he had dinner waiting for me in the fridge after I missed eating with him because of my meeting.

Pork chops. He even waited with me while he warmed them up.

We talked a lot while we waited for dinner to heat through. Not about what had happened in his office or about anything that matters, necessarily. We chatted about how I always wanted to play soccer growing up but never got to (because I didn't have anyone to drive me back and forth to practice—I left that part out), and why he likes knitting except when he hates it. We talked about how I used to borrow paddleboards to use on the lake in Alcott and how I really wish I could buy one of my own someday. We talked about the athletic club he belonged to in New York and the strangely competitive racquetball group there that once sabotaged a bunch of matches by strategically removing their opponents' favorite paddles from their lockers and dumping them into the swimming pool.

We laughed together too. A lot. So maybe those things we talked about *did* matter after all. Before she died, my grandmother used to say that the little moments sitting around you are what make up your whole life, even as you forget to notice them.

I still want more moments with Sam like the one we had in his office, but I'm not going to push him. And I'm going to keep making it clear to him that whatever else happens between us needs to stay strings-free. I doubt I could ever understand what he still feels for Christian and exactly why those feelings keep any relationships so off-limits for him, but none of that is really my business anyway.

He's going back to New York in a few weeks. If everything goes according to plan, I'll be leaving for Boston not long after that. Our time together has an expiration date, and I've always known that. But that's all fine with me. What matters right now is that for the first time in my life, I'm starting to ask for things I really want. Things that really matter to me. And asking Sam for what I wanted that afternoon more than paid off; as sexual experiences go, that was the most magical first time I could ever ask for.

I want a second. And a third. Hopefully a fourth. And I'm more than okay with the limitations that come with asking for more afternoons with Dr. Sam Evers.

Gabe gulps. "I understand why you didn't answer me," he says softly. "What I did that day was way, way out of line. I know that. I totally understand if you can never forgive me. I just wanted you to know how sorry I am." He says the last words softly, then turns around to leave.

"Gabe? Wait."

He turns around on his heels, twirling like a ballet dancer. "Yes?" he says eagerly.

"When you and I first met at the Stock Tree Farm, you said something about me being *that* Malachai Flynn. What did you mean, exactly?"

He bites his lip and doesn't answer me at first. "I'm sorry about that too," he finally says. "I was surprised. When people talk about you, well, I guess I just expected someone a little different. You're not like what I imagined at all! You're nice and funny and you seem really smart, and you don't seem like the kind of guy who deals drugs!"

I can't help the snort of laughter that escapes me. "I was never a drug dealer. I just sort of ended up squatting in the wrong barn. It's a long story."

"Oh." Gabe frowns. "Yeah, that does sound complicated. Hey, are you going to take on more jobs at the Stock Tree Farm again? Because I thought we worked pretty well together, and—"

"Malachai?" Sam appears in the room suddenly, like an apparition conjured from my dreams—as per usual with him. "Oh, my apologies for interrupting. Hello, Gabe." His eyes narrow slightly as he looks back and forth between the two of us. "Is everything alright here?" he murmurs.

Oh my gosh; is he *worrying* about me right now? Worrying that Gabe might be messing with me or something after what happened last weekend?"

Hi, Dr. Evers!" Gabe beams at him. "I was just apologizing to Malachai for being a total jerk last weekend."

Sam's shoulders relax slightly. "A very good plan, Gabe," he murmurs. "I'm glad to hear it."

Gabe nods. "I was a butthead. Hey, um, I'm sorry to you as well. And your brother and friend. I'm sure I was really annoying that day."

Sam lifts an eyebrow. "Actually, Tom found you very amusing. He's already asked me if he'll see you again the next time he's in town."

Gabe's face immediately loses all color. "Tom asked about... me?"

"You certainly made an impression," Sam answers, his voice a little dry. "He'll be back in town for the leaf festival; possibly a little bit sooner. I'll tell him you said hello. Malachai, could I have a word with you?"

Shit. Did someone notice that I haven't finished my billing work yet?

"I'll take off," Gabe says. "See you later, Malachai. And Dr. Evers, thanks for telling your brother I said hi!" He rushes for the front door of the office and just misses running into the screen on his way out.

"He's an interesting character," Sam mutters. He turns to look at me, his gaze narrowing sharply again. "Marie said you looked like you were falling asleep at your desk earlier."

Fuck, I guess someone noticed I've been slacking on the job today. "I'm really sorry about that," I tell him. "Like, really sorry. I was up late last night finishing that lab assignment I was telling you about. But I'm working on the billing now." I manage to slyly close the textbook on the desk next to me. "I'll finish everything on schedule, I promise."

Sam frowns. "That's not why I was asking. Malachai, is this all becoming too much? Running the festival as well as the office while you're going to school? Marie's worried about you, you know."

Marie's worried? That's an interesting choice of words, given the way he's staring at me right now. I'm definitely blushing. Just a little.

"You already had such a full schedule before taking on the festival work," he goes on. "And—"

My phone buzzes on my desk. Shoot. It's the Stock Tree Farm. What could they want? I haven't done any work for them since I took the festival gig. "Hang on one second," I tell Sam. I quickly slide the button to accept the call. "Hello!"

"Hey, Malachai! It's Jeb Stock. How are things going?"

"Pretty good," I answer. Sam's eyebrow goes up again; he clearly doesn't believe me.

Fuck *me*, this protective vibe is turning me on a whole lot more than it should. I order my dick down and do my best to concentrate on Jeb. "Sorry I haven't been able to take on more hours at the farm," I tell him.

"Oh, no worries. We all heard about you taking over the festival management for Devon Falls and we figured you were busy. Listen, that's what I'm calling about, actually. You know how Henri finally got together the paperwork for Vermonica the cow to appear at the festival?"

Of course I know. Vermonica's basically royalty in Vermont; she's the state mascot, a cow born with the actual shape of a maple leaf on her stomach. Henri told me last year that she's been trying to get Vermonica to appear at the festival for years now, but it's apparently *very* hard to get on Vermonica's schedule. "A president of the United States was once denied the chance to see

Vermonica," Henri told me this past summer. "But this year, I'm making sure we get her." Right before she left, she passed over the paperwork for Vermonica and informed me that Vermonica should be one of my top and most important priorities for the festival.

"It's an absolute travesty that a cow born with a maple leaf on her stomach hasn't ever been to the Devon Falls Leaf Festival," Henri said solemnly as she passed over a manilla file labeled VERMONICA THE COW in large letters. "It's far past time that wrong was righted, Malachai."

"What's wrong with Vermonica?" I ask Jeb, doing everything I can to keep pure panic out of my voice.

"Nothing's *wrong* with her, exactly. It's just that her handlers were supposed to drop her off here at the farm the night before the festival—well, the festival wedding, I guess?"

Yup. Vermonica's even officially been scheduled to attend Benson and Jack's wedding. I wonder if anyone's told Benson yet.

"Yeah, that's the plan. And then we were going to have her go back to you every night until the festival is over. We don't really have a barn right on the festival grounds where she can stay comfortably at night."

"That's what Henri said. And we definitely don't mind having her—we're honored, actually."

"*Honored?*" I hear a voice say loudly and skeptically behind Jeb.

"She's famous, Embry," Jeb calls back to Embry, one of his two partners. "Well, here's the situation," Jeb goes on. "Her handlers just called and said that Vermonica can't stay at the Stock Tree Farm unless we can provide proof of all of our other animals' vaccinations, and that proof apparently needs to be dropped off in person to some office in Burlington. And they want it tonight or they say they're going to cancel Vermonica's visit."

"What? Shit! They can't do that!" I practically bellow out the words, and Sam rushes over to my side. Only now I'm too distracted to appreciate Dr. Sam Evers going all bodyguard on me.

"It's bullshit," Jeb agreed. "Someone dropped a ball somewhere for sure. We should have known about this weeks ago. But I know how badly Henri and Devon Falls want Vermonica at the festival this year, and we're swamped with visitors at the pumpkin patch over here right now. None of us can get away in the next few hours. So I was wondering if you could make a quick trip to Burlington?"

"Burlington. Burlington. Okay, I think I can go to Burlington. No problem, Jeb. The doctors' office closes in fifteen minutes anyway. As soon as the doors are locked, I'll run over there to grab the documents from you, and then I can head straight down to Burlington." We say our goodbyes and I hang up the phone as I start gathering papers off my desk and sweeping them into my bag. I stifle another yawn. *Shit.* I really needed time tonight to work on the office billing and catch up on calculus, and honestly I'm so very tired right now that a three-ish hour round trip drive to Burlington doesn't sound fun. But the entire town of Devon Falls will be so disappointed if I'm the reason their maple-leaf decorated cow isn't at the festival. I'm just going to have to power through the evening and make this all work.

I'm so busy packing up my desk that it takes me a few moments to notice Sam is still standing next to me, his arms crossed and his eyes narrowed again.

"Did I just overhear correctly that you're about to drive all the way to Burlington?"

"I guess so." I shake my head. "Well, with a side trip to La Fierte along the way."

"Absolutely not," he says firmly. And how is this level of bossiness *still so damn hot?*

"What do you mean, absolutely not?" I ask him. "I don't have a choice, Sam. I have to. You must have overheard Jeb. That paperwork needs to get to Burlington tonight."

Sam nods. "Yes, I heard that. But there's no way I'm allowing you to drive to Burlington on two hours of sleep." He walks across the room to our office coat closet and opens it quickly, then pulls out his large gray peacoat.

"I'll be driving you."

Chapter 16

23 Days to the Devon Falls Leaf Festival

"You're perfect exactly as you are," I whisper into his ear. "In any size, in any shape." —Sam Evers

"Your car is amazing," Malachai murmurs as he swipes his hand across the heated leather seat of the Land Rover and then runs his finger across its midnight black dashboard. "I've definitely never been in a car this nice before."

"It has excellent safety features and four wheel drive. I wanted to be sure I was prepared to drive in Vermont."

Malachai snorts. "I'm lucky my current car has front wheel drive. I had to spend a small fortune putting good snow tires on it last year or I never would have made it into the office during that big holiday snowstorm we had. Wow, I can control the temperature on my side of the car?"

His enthusiasm for a car I've spent approximately four minutes of my life thinking deeply about is contagious. "Yes, that's a nice feature. I'm very glad you like the car. You've never been in a Land Rover before?"

Malachai snorts and rolls his eyes. "Hell no. There aren't exactly dealerships for cars like this in Alcott. People get excited if someone drives a used Ford with less than thirty thousand miles on it. Do you have any idea what a magical life you have?" he says as he shakes his head. I steer the car out of the parking lot and down the Main Street of Devon Falls. "Your brother is a literal movie star and you own a car that costs more than a lot of the houses where I grew up."

"Oh, I'm aware I was born very lucky," I tell him. "My mothers worked hard and were lucky enough to inherit some wealth as well. That financial cushion allowed both Tom and I to follow our dreams in varied directions. Tom actually worked for some time as a cruise director while he was trying to find his place in Hollywood." I glance over at him. "I'd never deny that having money can make life much easier in so many ways. But it's also true what they say: there really are some things money can never buy."

Malachai nods. "I guess it couldn't save Christian," he murmurs softly, his eyes fixed on something outside of the passenger window. I frown at the large pickup truck in front of me that seems to have absolutely no working blinkers. The acts that Malachai and I engaged in earlier this week were significant for me on so many levels; I can only imagine how significant they must have been for him.

He trusted me with something so important: his first physical intimacy with another human. More and more over the past few days I've begun to feel like I owe him the same level of openness he showed me that day. And as hard as it will be to share my darker, more closely kept secrets with him, this feels like the time.

"I was very lucky to know Christian," I answer Malachai softly. "Very lucky. He was a wonderful friend to me. A best friend, if you will."

Malachai turns to look at me, his eyes brimming with curiosity and confusion.

I draw in a large breath of air. "Can I tell you something, Malachai? Something no one else knows?"

Malachai's eyes widen, but he nods.

"I thought I was in love with Christian when I married him. And I truly do believe we loved each other, always—but not in the way a married couple should love each other. Neither of us, I don't think, ever fully realized that. It wasn't until Christian died and I came to Vermont that I fully understood what it means to be *in love* with someone."

Malachai's mouth opens. Then closes. Then opens again. "I thought," he finally says, "that you were still in love with him."

I breathe out a sigh of relief as the troublesome pickup finally turns off in front of us. "No," I finally answer. "I'll always love Christian for who he was, and I'll always feel responsible for his death. I didn't care about him enough to join him on the roof at the pool that day. That's a burden I'll carry for the rest of my life. I'll mourn that loss. Always."

"Sam." Malachai slides as far to the left as he can in his bucket seat and places a hand on my shoulder. "You can't put that kind of blame on yourself. That's not fair."

I glance over at his wide, open expression. Malachai has so many moments like this, where his youth and innocence take me entirely by surprise. "Christian deserved so much better than a marriage to a good friend and a death in a rooftop pool," I finally say. "And only I can take responsibility for both of those things."

Malachai raises an eyebrow. "Sam, I'm pretty sure someone else shares equal responsibility here."

I bite at my lip. It's not as if I haven't thought the same thing myself in moments—but then I remember the truth. "Possibly. But only one of us is still here to do penance for those mistakes."

Malachai shakes his head. "You know what's weird? You're one of the few people—well, you and the Lancers and Benson—who are always telling me I need to stop taking responsibility for what happened here last year with that drug operation. You even told me, that day at the school carnival, that I did the best I could at the time."

"Yes," I agree. "I still hold to that."

"Well," he says, sitting up straight in his seat as he crosses his arms, "I could say the same to you, sir."

The word *sir* jolts me just as much as the rest of his words do. "The situations aren't the same," I mutter.

"Really? Because they seem awfully similar to me."

He goes back to looking out the window, and neither of us says anything else until we arrive in La Fierte to pick up the vaccination paperwork.

After we pick up the vaccination papers and I'm briefly introduced to the rudest, oddest goat I've ever encountered, the tense energy in the car seems to dissipate. Malachai, busy as always, works and reads on his phone for most of the drive. He tells me about the latest leaf festival planning debacles he's handling, and we quickly dissect the oddity of having a state cow invited to not only a leaf festival but also a marriage ceremony.

"I'm not going to be the one to confirm for Benson that Vermont's state cow is going to be at his wedding," Malachai announces. "That's got to be Jack's job. Benson's going to lose it, and then we're all going to have to listen to bad jokes about cow pies for days."

"He pretends to hate all this, but he secretly loves how much the town adores him now," I tell Malachai.

"That's what I thought!" Malachai shakes his head. "Honestly, I don't totally get why he complains so much. If Devon Falls liked me enough to want to plan my wedding, I'd be really honored."

I turn on my blinker as we come to a stoplight in the downtown area of Burlington, a city I've come to appreciate. Not every city which holds the honor of being the biggest in its state can carry a small-town energy the way Burlington does. "Has Benson told you anything about his childhood?" I ask Malachai.

"A little. I know it was pretty terrible. That's why he acts the way he does about the wedding, huh?"

"I think it's hard for him to accept that people truly care about him," I agree. "So he pushes care away first, just to make sure it can't be taken away."

Malachai snorts. "Like Jack would ever let anyone hurt Benson like that. He'd destroy anyone who even tried."

"He would," I mutter, shifting slightly in my seat. It's uncomfortable to remember that I feel exactly the same way about Malachai: as though I'd happily tear to shreds anyone who ever tried to do him harm. There was a moment in the office with Gabe today when I wondered if I was going to have to physically or verbally damage a man who wears cow print shoelaces.

It's uncomfortable to remember that I never, ever felt such protectiveness for Christian.

"Jack does the coolest things for Benson," Malachai goes on. "I'll never forget that time he bought out all of Thai for Two one night just so they could celebrate their three-month anniversary there alone. No one's ever even asked me to *go* to a restaurant with them, let alone bought one out for me!" Malachai laughs, but there's a wistfulness, a regret there I can't miss.

I pull into the parking lot of the state office Malachai punched into my phone's GPS earlier.

"I'll be right back," he tells me. "And thanks, Sam, for bringing me down here. It means a lot," he adds softly. "And I meant what

I said before, by the way. You're a great guy. Like, the best. I bet Christian knew that too. I'm sure that's why he married you... and I bet he wouldn't want you to feel as guilty as you do right now." He hops out of the car without another word and begins jogging toward the office entrance.

I frown as I sit in the car and wait, with so many of the words from our conversation echoing through my head. One line hangs heavier than the others.

No one's ever asked me to go to a restaurant with them.

And just then, I know where I need to bring him once we've completed our errand.

"What is this place? Where are we? I thought you said we were going to get something to eat."

Malachai stares around him in awe as I wind the Rover up a dirt road we turned onto about a half mile or so back. The gravely surface crunches below our wheels and the colors of the changing trees seem to grow brighter and even more vivid as we climb higher into the foothills of the Vermont mountains.

"We are," I answer him mildly as I guide the vehicle around a large pothole. "I'm taking you to the restaurant where Jack and Milo convinced me to come stay in Vermont."

Malachai turns to me, his eyes wide. "Sir, I thought you meant we'd pick up hamburgers."

I shrug. "They have excellent burgers, if that's what you prefer to eat tonight. Steakburgers, really. I think they may be wagyu? Tom is always better than me at remembering those details."

"I—sir, I—" Malachai's eyes are wide, his face almost pale with fear, and immediately I rush to assuage his concerns. I place my hand on his knee and rub it gently. "Don't worry about the money. Dinner tonight is on me. A thank you, if you will."

"Thank you? But I should be the one thanking you! You let me live in your house rent-free. You just drove me all the way to Burlington, and I haven't even given you gas money yet! You—"

"You do more for me than you can imagine," I tell him firmly, determined to end this conversation. The place I'm taking Malachai is special, and I would hate for his worries over debts—monetary or otherwise—to ruin this experience. "The restaurant I'm taking you to is owned by Imbari Olsson, a Nigerian-Swedish chef who moved to Vermont shortly before I did. She's Michelin-starred. Have you heard of her?" Malachai shakes his head.

"She says she got tired of the grind in New York City and wanted to start fresh. So she bought this property, not too far from Devon Falls, and she opened up a restaurant by the river here. She's open very few days a week, and right now her clientele is largely Burlington tourists who've followed her career, but I suspect she's about to have many, many more customers than that. She's selling her spicy jollof meatballs at the leaf festival this year." I guide the Rover up a driveway and park in front of a large barn with a sign that says *River's End Eating* above the door.

"Oh, wow." Malachai pushes his door open and steps out of the car, already entranced. I understand why: I, too, felt as though I'd stepped into the most magical part of Vermont when I first arrived at this place. Tables settled inside of long, tall tents line the edge of a rushing stream across the lawn from us. Twinkling fairy lights circle the barn and the top and sides of the tent covers, creating an ethereal, fairy-like vision in the falling twilight of the Vermont sky. The nearly-fallen sunset behind us only adds to the perfection of the moment, as though the world is falling into a trance of its own beauty and color.

"Dr. Evers." Malachai breathes the words more than says them. He takes another step closer toward the edge of the lawn, and I let myself swim in the awe and delight of his expression.

If I do nothing else good or important in my life, at least I will be able to say that I helped to place that expression upon Malachai Flynn's face.

I step up beside him and place a hand on the small of his back. "I was able to get us a table for two right there, right on the water," I tell him, pointing out a set place for two with a candle of some kind lighting the space between the two seats. "Now, let's go see about—"

I don't even finish the words before Malachai turns and grabs me around the middle, pushing himself up on his toes to push his lips into mine and take me in a nearly crushing kiss. I don't bother to pretend that I don't want to engage with him in this, and I kiss him back with equal strength, exploring more and more of his mouth with my own as the night and moment swirl about us in this clear and presently perfect moment.

And I do something I rarely do: I close off all the voices in my head and let myself enjoy it.

Eventually we break apart. I take Malachai's hand, letting the moment between us linger, and lead him to the host stand. We're shown to our table, and so begins the most perfect dinner I've had in a very, very long time.

"This is where you decided to come live in Vermont temporarily?" Malachai asks me as we engage in a soup that somehow combines flavors of Nigeria and northern Europe with, incredibly, maple syrup. "Holy shit, that's good."

"I keep waiting for your eyes to roll back in your head," I tell him, much more delighted than amused. "Yes, it is. I'd been hedging for quite some time, determined not to leave my apartment. My comfort zone, I suppose. Then, on one of my weekend trips here with Milo, Jack's father insisted we all try this new spot together."

Malachai nods as he slurps at his soup, his expression pure bliss. I know that expression. I understand it.

"I loved the food immediately, just as much as you are now. I loved the space, the sound of the rushing river, the feel of it all." I smile at the memory as Malachai devours the agege bread on the table. "I spoke to the chef afterward. She told me she came here for a fresh start. She'd been burnt out by the restaurant industry, the speed of it all. She came here, and for the first time, she said, she felt alive again." Malachai reaches across the table and takes my hand in his. "I felt that way too," I tell him softly. "I knew I could only come here for a short time, and Jack and Milo convinced me to try. I rented the farmhouse the next week."

Malachai frowns. "Why only a short time?" he asks. "You seem to like Devon Falls a lot, Sam. Why are you going to leave right after the wedding and the festival? I bet Jack and Marie would love to have you work at the office full time."

I push my spoon around in circles in my soup bowl. "Because some mistakes don't deserve to be forgiven that easily," I finally say softly.

Malachai's eyebrows go up.

"But I don't want to talk about that right now," I say quickly, determined not to ruin anything about the perfect evening I hope to give Malachai here. "Tell me what you like best about that bread."

Malachai presses his lips together for a moment before he finally nods. "Well, I think it's the texture I like best..."

The evening spirals from there in a spattering of so many tiny, perfect moments. Entrees that leave Malachai breathless with excitement; a dessert course which, he claims, is the best thing he's ever eaten. A short, quiet walk by the lights next to the river on the way back to the car, where we hold hands again and say nothing but small words that feel so large under a clear and starry sky. The rest of the drive back to Devon Falls is filled with easy, comfortable small talk of state cows and difficult patients. And then we find our way to my house—or our house, as it's certainly starting to feel like now—and Malachai laces his hand with mine as we walk up the driveway.

We step through the front door, and he says the words before I can: "Can we go to your bedroom together?"

After that, it's as though we're caught in a riptide of sensation and feeling and action. We trip up the stairs together, with him unbuttoning my shirt and me grabbing at the belt of his pants, until we're at the edge of my large, king-size bed and Malachai's gripping at the tails of my previously buttoned green collared shirt. "Sir." He whispers the word into the cool air drifting through the window: one syllable that latches to the swirling energy around us.

"You're mine tonight," I tell him. "Until you tell me to stop, you're mine."

He licks at his lips, a hint of something almost feral in his expression. "Yes, sir," he answers huskily.

I move him until he's standing between my legs, eyes staring up at me hungrily. I finish the work I began on the stairs, slipping my hand into the waistband of his pants and making quick work of his trousers and boxers, which are still far too holey and worn. I remind myself again that a shopping trip is in order but don't give the thought too much attention; there are more important things to take care of right now. I tug his polo shirt up over his head, and then he's standing there, in front of me, human perfection blinking rapidly in his nakedness while he looks around almost anxiously. I realize this is the first time I've seen him fully naked, and I suspect he's just had the same realization.

"I—uh, I know I'm kind of skinny and I don't have muscles like you, sir, and I don't—"

I take him into my arms. "You're perfect exactly as you are," I whisper into his ear. "In any size, in any shape." I push him gently down onto the bed and follow after him, cradling him in my arms and savoring the sensation of having every bit of his skin against me.

Malachai, however, clearly wants me unclothed. He wriggles against me as he works the rest of my shirt buttons open and shoves at the waistband of my pants. I let him undress me while I keep him close to my body, unable to fully let go of him in any way.

"Uh, wow. You're... kind of big." He gulps as I help him slide my boxer briefs down, and I catch the glint of something like fear in his eyes. I rub carefully at his cheek with my calloused skin, forcing him to look up and into my eyes.

"Malachai," I tell him. "We will never, ever do something you aren't ready for. And I will never, ever hurt you. I promise."

The corners of his mouth lift into something approaching a smile. "Yes, sir," he says softly.

"And tonight," I tell him, "your only job in this bed is to let me make you feel good. Do you understand? Can you do that for me?"

He nods rapidly, his hair brushing back and forth against my shoulder. "Yes sir."

"Good boy." I reach to my bedside table to find the lube I keep in the drawer there, quickly pouring some of it across my fingers. And then I grasp our cocks, both hard and straining, together in my hand.

Malachai gasps hard as our bodies come together, and I take advantage of his moment of surprise to capture his mouth with mine. I set a rhythm between us, like a boat rocking into a gentle wave, as I keep our lengths together with one hand and hold on tightly to him with the other. The energy between us is palpable in the space, lifting, as he hardens further in my hand and his lips quiver against mine in quick and light bursts. I pull back suddenly.

"Come for me," I tell him. "I want to see your face when you do." I flick my thumb across the top of his cock and then mine, and he yelps slightly as he arches up against me. "Come now," I order him.

And he does, spilling across my hand. The way he vibrates and shakes against me triggers my own orgasm in exactly the way I expected it to, and soon I'm arching back against him, grabbing on tight against the heightening waves, determined to make sure he stays safely on the boat of whatever it is we're riding together there.

When we finally collapse together in the soft, cool breeze of the space, I wrap him tighter in my arms. Thoughts of his safety and well-being are so ever-present in my mind that my first question for him is simple. "Are you okay?"

He lets out something like a snort. "Okay? Geez, Dr. Evers. I mean Sam? I mean Sir. I mean...fuck, yeah. I'm way more than okay."

He giggles. Then chuckles. Then begins to laugh into the room, and soon I'm joining him, because Malachai's lilting and quiet laughter is the kind that's impossible not to join.

"Oh man," Malachai finally says in between chortles. "Just imagine if we both weren't leaving Vermont so soon. The things you could teach me, sir..."

The words are like a sudden jolt of electricity through my body. *Just imagine.*

Chapter 17

15 Days to the Devon Falls Leaf Festival

This whiplash isn't exactly fun. In fact, I'd say it's the exact oppo-site of fun. —Malachai Flynn

"Malachai! You're here!"

Gabe beams at me from where he's sitting at the counter in Luis' Cafe and Bar, a large bowl of mashed potatoes in front of him. "Come sit with me!"

It's been a long day of Saturday classes and studying, mixed with taking endless phone calls about the festival that's somehow just over two weeks away, and honestly the last thing I feel like doing right now is making small talk with someone who managed to out my virgin status to my landlord/boss/crush, even if that outing of my virginity didn't exactly end badly for me. Still, I really need to grab a quick dinner, and I just found enough small bills in my pocket for one of Luis' amazing maple-turkey sandwiches. And I'm not sure how to say no to anyone who looks as hopeful as Gabe looks right now, even if he's the last person I wanted to see when I stepped into the cafe this evening.

I wave at Ellis Ryker, the red-headed waiter who's rushing frantically around the restaurant right now—the place looks pretty swamped—and make my way to the counter.

"Sit, sit." Gabe pats the seat next to him excitedly. "I'll get you pie! Like I promised. Unless you'd rather have cake or something? And Luis also makes that really good ice cream sometimes, and—"

"I'm just going to have a sandwich," I quickly interrupt him. "You know, as soon as Ellis is free. Then I've really got to go. I've got lots to do right now, what with the festival. And work. And school."

Gabe's face lights up. "You're in school? Where? The community college? Tell me all about it!" He leans on his elbows and stares at me as if I'm about to spill the details of my recent trip to Ibiza.

"Um, it's just community college," I finally say hesitantly. "Right now I'm taking chemistry and math. Have you been wanting to take some classes?" I ask, because it's impossible not to notice the dreamy, hopeful stare that's taken over his entire face.

"Me? Huh?" Gabe sits up quickly on his barstool. "Um, no. School's not for me, unfortunately. Hey," he goes on before I can ask why. "You're staying with Dr. Evers, right? Are you two, like, together now?"

Good thing Ellis hasn't gotten around to bringing me any water yet, because I'd definitely be choking on it right now. "Did you seriously just ask me that? Right off the bat?"

Gabe wrinkles his nose. "Too direct, huh? Sorry. I'm not always very good at knowing when I'm supposed to say certain stuff." He frowns. "It's just that I saw the way he was looking at you in the doctor's office the other day."

My face goes hot with the memory of the last time I saw Gabe: a little over a week ago, the day Sam brought me to Burlington.

The day we ended up in his bed together.

I wish I could say that a whole lot more has happened between us since then, but that's unfortunately not the case. Festival duties have *really* ramped up this past week, and I spent most of my weeknights this week on the phone with Devon Falls residents and vendors who suddenly seem to have endless questions, concerns, or bills that need to be paid.

Then I confirmed with Benson that Vermonica would definitely be at the wedding, and *that* conversation turned into an entire dinner with him and Jack where he basically pretended he hated the idea for two hours before finally admitting that it would be kind of cool to have the Vermont state cow at his marriage ceremony. I would have been more upset about the lost time I could've spent studying for my next calculus test, but the look on his face when he and Jack hugged me at the end of the meal and thanked me for all of my help lately definitely made up for that.

Well, mostly. I still got a B on the test, which was a little annoying. I would have liked an A.

I also would have liked a little more bedroom time with Sam this week, but he's been pretty up and down with me, honestly. Making me dinner and then disappearing into his room without a word. Bringing me coffee at the office in the morning and then barely looking at me for the rest of the day.

I get that whatever's happening between us right now has to be confusing for him. I mean, it's a lot for *me* to take in, and I'm not the one dealing with incredible levels of guilt and grief. I don't blame him for being a little intermittently distant.

Still, this whiplash isn't exactly fun. In fact, I'd say it's the exact opposite of fun.

"Sam's a really good guy," I finally tell Gabe. "Like, an amazing guy. But he's going back to New York City right after the festival. And then I'll be leaving for Boston not long after that, so..."

"Oh." Gabe nods. "I get it. Catching feelings would be pretty dangerous."

I'm definitely beyond catching feelings here. The feelings ship sailed long ago—it could have done a round-the-world tour by now. But I just nod in agreement. "Yup." I pop the P on the end of the word.

"Oh, fancy meeting you here."

I swear, just hearing that voice makes my entire body tense into concrete. "Hi, Avon," I say stiffly, determined to keep my cool around the guy who seems to enjoy nothing in life more than seeing me sweat. I turn slightly and there he is, standing next to me at the counter, wearing a sweater over a collared shirt along with his usual sneer.

"Hello. I'm so glad I found you here, Malachai. I've been looking all over town for you." He settles into the seat and slides a manilla folder across the counter to me.

I recoil from it, immediately wary. "What's that?" I ask him.

"I've had my lawyers—and I do mean *mine,* not these ridiculous town lawyers who are so fond of you—draw up some papers requesting public and open access to the Devon Falls Leaf Festival accounts. After seeing you all about the town with Dr. Evers, I decided I don't fully trust that he's looking out for the town's best interests here, so I've demanded more oversight."

I flip open the folder and glance through the documents there, but the words blur on the page in front of me. My dread is starting to pool in my lungs now, and there's a low-level pounding building inside my skull.

It's okay, I try to tell myself. *He can look all he wants; there's nothing to find.* I've been obsessively careful with every penny that's gone in and out of the festival accounts. Avon can ask for every document that exists relating to the festival; he won't find anything wrong.

But the town will know what he's done; he'll make sure of that. He'll make sure they all remember that there are plenty of reasons I don't deserve to be trusted with their festival.

"Why are you doing this?" I blurt out the words, softly into the background noise of the cafe. "Why? Why do you hate me so much?"

Avon sucks in a hard breath, the sneer on his lips curling even farther upward. "I don't hate anyone," he finally says stiffly. "I simply love Devon Falls and this festival. And I won't risk a criminal like you ruining it." He lets out a huff.

It's on the tip of my tongue to tell him that he can just take over the damn festival if he cares this much, but then I remember exactly how badly I need the stipend money that comes to me at the end of all this. Plus, there's the fact that Avon never actually even volunteered for this job when it was up on offer.

Some people, my grandma used to say, will complain to high heck about how you milk the cow but never shovel a piece of manure themselves.

"My lawyer will be sure those accounts are made public, and then everything that needs to be out in the open will be." Avon huffs out a breath while I'm trying to figure out exactly why he seems to hate or distrust me so much more than everyone else in this town. He picks up the manilla folder and strides back out of the cafe, confidence exuding from every pore of his body. Meanwhile, the pounding in my head has reached a rapid pace, and I'm having more and more trouble taking gasps of air.

I haven't done anything wrong. I haven't done anything wrong, I repeat to myself. And yet the idea that there are going to be even more debates in this town about my past, my work ethic, who I am as a person...

I'm not sure I can take it. I'm not sure I can do it all again.

"Malachai?" Gabe grabs for my arm. "Are you okay? You look really pale."

I'm having to fight for every inch of air I take in now. This panic attack doesn't look like it's going away on its own. I close my eyes and try the strategy my high school counselor used to suggest that always worked best: *picture a place where you feel safe.*

Immediately, my mind goes to Sam's house: to the warm, comforting sun-filled kitchen, to the bedroom with its absurdly high thread count sheets that I sleep on every night, to the den with its dark wood and crackling fireplace.

And then my mind reaches further: to Sam, to his room. To the moments he's wrapped me up in his arms, holding me close, his own breath against my ear.

For a moment the picture sends calm through me and I'm able to take one deep, diving breath—and then my mind sends the cruelest possible reminder.

He's leaving soon, you know. You're going to lose him. You're going to be alone again, without him, just like you always have been.

My breath catches in my chest, and now all I can think is *get the fuck out of this diner before the entire town sees me lose it.*

I lurch off the stool, ignoring Gabe's questions, and head right for the front door. I make it outside, still gasping to find any kind of breath I can, and I head in the only direction I could possibly imagine going in right now. The only place where I might hope I can feel safe, even when that safety is so incredibly precarious.

I head toward *him.*

Chapter 18
15 Days to the Devon Falls Leaf Festival

I've never fully felt the power of that science before—not until I met Malachai. —Sam Evers

There was a time when I had so many possible ways to spend a night off that I had to flip coins to decide which one to choose. Night clubs. Parties. Fancy restaurants. Club openings.

Christian loved them all. I tolerated them.

Perhaps the best aspect of moving to Devon Falls, Vermont, is that no one really expects me to be anywhere on a Saturday night. Jack and Benson did invite me to join them at Thai for Two tonight, but neither of them batted an eyelash when I said I'd rather stay in and work on my knitting projects.

I take a sip of my craft beer—Vermont's third largest export after maple syrup and dairy products, I'm told, and I'm still not sure whether Burt Busby was kidding or not—and frown down at the hat that continues to give me fits. I just can't seem to get the decrease rows at the top right. The fireplace behind me cracks softly, bouncing light off the corners of the den, and I try to ignore the fact that this perfect evening at home alone seems to be missing something.

It's perfectly natural that on some level I wish Malachai were here enjoying this evening with me. Isn't it? I've gotten very used to having him around. His company has become a natural part of this house, after all.

It's very reasonable that I would miss him right now. Totally and completely reasonable.

"Damn," I tell the hat. "I've pushed him away too much this past week, haven't I?" I've felt conflicted the entire last seven days as I wondered: should I let myself lean into my highly inappropriate feelings for my employee/tenant/inappropriate obsession, or should I reset my boundaries?

The answer remained elusive, so I essentially did neither. I hemmed and I hawed, moving in and out of his space at highly random moments. I hope I haven't confused Malachai into never coming back to this house again. I glance up at the large antique clock above the fireplace—seven p.m. Perhaps he's just out late studying?

A sudden, sharp noise rocks through the house; I recognize it immediately as the sound of the door being shoved harshly open. "Sam?" A voice, high and filled with panic, calls out. "Sam, are you home? Please be home!"

Malachai. I'm out of my chair so quickly that it rocks backward and hits the floor with a loud *thwack*.

I rush through the hallway and kitchen and into the entrance area, making it there in mere seconds. Malachai's on his knees on the tile floor, face down, breathing in harsh gasps. "I... can't..." he whispers to the floor.

He's having another panic attack. When did this start? I can only hope he didn't drive himself home in this state. I drop to my own knees at his side and run my hand through the waves of hair falling across his forehead. "You're okay." I tell him softly. "I'm here now." There are tear tracks on his face, and his skin looks especially pale in the front hall lighting. I wonder if he's going into shock.

My brain flashes to a sort of primordial demand: *take care of him. Now. Immediately.* I take a deep breath and force myself to find a mode of emotional clarity; one where I can focus fully on Malachai. "Don't worry, darling," I tell him, and I don't bother to worry or wonder about the boundaries I've now broken several times by calling him *darling.* There will be time to worry about details later. "I'm here. I'll take care of you. Let's get you upstairs and into a warm bath." I lift him from the ground and pull him up into my arms, holding him tightly against me. "Breathe with me," I whisper into his ear. "Just one breath at a time. In... out... in... out..."

At first his breath catches again as I make my way through the hallway and carry him toward the stairs. But I keep whispering the words, over and over, and soon he's pulling in longer breaths, his cadence nearly matching mine, as I bring him into the bathroom and settle down on the floor next to the tub with him in my arms. His skin is cold to the touch, and I reach around to turn on the tap, waiting until the water runs warm before I begin whispering again.

"Let's get you into the bath. Would you like me to get in with you?" When Malachai bites his lip and then nods in agreement, I've never been more glad that the owner of this house had a soaker tub installed as part of its remodel.

I undress him slowly, carefully, listening as his breath settles back down into something patterned and steady. He shudders underneath my hands when I lift his shirt over his head, then collapses against my chest when I remove my own.

I know all the science behind why there's power in skin-against-skin touch. I understand all the research about oxytocin and other chemicals that react when human bodies come into contact with other bodies.

Yet I know I've never fully felt the power of that science before—not until I met Malachai.

I drop a bath bomb into the tub that promises calming scents—another gift from the owner of the home; there was an entire basket of them when I moved in—and settle us into the warm water together, my body framing his under the soft, warm bathroom lights. Eventually he relaxes against me, his breaths coming in longer stints now, and I wrap my arms around him.

His body sinks perfectly into mine, the water molding to places where our limbs fit so gently together. For a moment I think that I could happily stay in this exact place, this exact tableau for the rest of my life.

I stop myself from thinking any further into all the ways that will never be. I sink back into the water, holding Malachai close. "Breathe," I whisper into his ear again. "Just breathe. That's all you ever have to do. That's all you need to worry about. I'll take care of the rest."He closes his eyes, and he breathes.

Eventually, we talk.

"I don't know why it's so easy for Avon to get to me like this," he says. "All he asked for is the festival's books, and I know there's nothing for him to find there. I haven't done anything wrong. But I just kept thinking about the town knowing he asked for them, and the way he was *looking* at me, and all of the sudden I couldn't breathe right."

"I understand." I run a wet hand over his hair, drawing him closer to me. "What Devon Falls thinks of you is important to you, and that's completely understandable. You have every right to care about a town you've invested so much in."

He leans harder against me, his naked body locked with mine. "I guess."

"Can I ask you something?"

"Sure, of course."

"Have you always had panic attacks like this? Or are these new?"

Malachai turns his face into my neck, warm water droplets moving from his hair into my skin. "Since sixth or seventh grade, I think. One day I got sick at school. My mom was at work and no one could get in touch with her to come pick me up. I waited in the nurse's office all day, throwing up." He swallows hard. "There was no emergency contact listed in my file, so no one else could come for me. When I realized there wasn't anybody coming to take me home, I started to have trouble breathing."

"Oh, darling." I drop a kiss into his hair. "That must have been so frightening."

"I mean, I wasn't in danger or anything," he hurries to add.

"But you were. Human beings are wired for connection. Loneliness, fear of loneliness, *is* its own danger. Of course a situation like that would create the kind of fear that stayed with you."

Malachai frowns. "I guess. I mean, I never thought about it that way. I had some friends in middle school and high school, you know? It's not like I was *completely* alone. And the attacks always kind of came and went. I saw my high school counselor about them for a little while, and she helped, but then I graduated and moved here. And our insurance at the office covers therapy, but I haven't had time to find anyone. And affording the copays is tough."

I pull him against me again, new guilt seeping through me like the water around us is driving it under my skin. The way I've acted this week, pushing him away and then pulling him back toward me, probably hasn't helped with any of his abandonment issues or fears. Not for the first time, I worry about just how much harm I'm doing Malachai by leaning further across so many boundary lines with him. "Why did you come here tonight?" I ask abruptly. "And how? Please tell me you didn't drive to the house while you were having a panic attack."

"It's just a few miles," he says, and I groan. "I went slowly," he assures me. "Super slowly. Maybe driving was a bad idea. But everything felt like it was closing in on me, and I just needed…"

He doesn't finish the sentence, and I don't ask him to. We're swimming into deeper, darker water now, and I think we both know it. The clock is ticking down toward the festival and my return to New York. I know I have to leave here alone. I've always known that would be the inevitable conclusion of my time with Malachai. But how the two of us will eventually make that break is becoming increasingly complicated.

I run a hand up and down his arm. I've never been particularly good at living in the moment: I tend to forever be thinking five steps ahead of the situation in front of me. Part of that comes with being a doctor, I suppose. But right now, nothing feels better than just enjoying this hour or so of time I have in this bathtub with Malachai, soothing out his hurts and reveling in the feeling of holding him in my arms.

"Breathe," I tell him. "It's all going to be okay, Malachai. Let's both just breathe."

Perhaps if I breathe long and hard enough I'll stop five steps past the end of my time with Malachai, and all the blackness that awaits me there.

Chapter 19
14 Days to the Devon Falls Leaf Festival

I wake up wrapped in blankets so soft that they seem to be cocooning me in a cloud. All the blankets in Sam's house are like this, but I open one eye and immediately recognize that I'm in his bedroom, drowning in the perfect mattress on his king-sized bed.

"Hello." He's lying next to me, reading something on a tablet, one arm wrapped carefully around my shoulder. "You seemed to sleep well last night. Would you like some coffee?" He gestures to two mugs sitting on the bedside table next to him.

"Yes, please." I sit up slowly. My body always feels a little bit like it's been run over by a truck the morning after a bad panic attack, and today's no exception. But that long, hot bath last night with Sam must have helped, because I don't feel quite as sore and achy as I sometimes do.

Last night, despite all the shittiness that kicked the evening off, ended kind of perfectly, honestly. After we cuddled in the bathtub, Sam carried me to his bed, dried me off, and held me until I fell asleep. I kept waiting and wondering if he'd get up and leave or bring me to my bedroom, but he never did. He just stayed there, wrapped around me, and the feeling of safety and security was so strong that eventually I drifted off.

And now, with a clear head and some truly delicious coffee on my tongue (because honestly I didn't even know coffee could taste this good until I moved in with Sam, who probably spends more on one container of coffee than I've ever spent on five), I feel more prepared than ever to deal with the situations in front of me.

Avon's going to audit the festival books. So what? I've done Henri proud. The finances are in good shape, and the festival's going to go off without a hitch in two weeks.

This time with Sam has been one of the best things to ever happen in my life. And my time with him ends with the festival. It's time I accepted that. Sam's got baggage he's clearly not ready to move on from, and I know that. So I'm waking up this morning with a new outlook: I'm going to enjoy the hell out of these last two weeks I have with him. And then I'll be ready to let go.

I've come to terms with this decision. I've accepted it. More than that, I've *embraced* it.

And that means that I'm ready to ask for something I want. And what I want is to ask Dr. Sam Evers to be the first person to ever... well, honestly, I'm not even sure how to say the words to myself without sounding like some safe-sex video. "Take my virginity" seems wrong, since "virginity" is a pretty non-specific term that can mean a whole lot of different things to different people. "Be inside of me" feels somehow overly specific and not specific enough all at the same time. Are you ready to ask someone to join you in a specific sexual act if you can't figure out how to even *say* the sexual act? Maybe this is all a sign that I'm not actually ready to ask Sam for what I want.

"Do you have any plans tonight?" Sam asks.

I wrinkle my nose as I think through that question. It's Sunday. I've got some more vendor stuff to deal with for the festival and another lab assignment due, but tonight I should actually be free.

Tension falls from my shoulders as I imagine having an actual night off. "I think I'm free," I tell him.

"Good. Then I'd like to cook you dinner." He's wearing reading glasses, and they're sliding down on his nose as he taps something on the tablet. He's not wearing anything but boxers, and he looks so damn hot in those glasses that the urge to dive under the blankets and start doing very inappropriate things to him is *strong*.

But I can be patient when I need to be. And Sam's question has led to a plan forming in my head.

I wait until dessert to make my move. Sam really went all out with this dinner—steak, potatoes, salad, blueberry pie. He probably didn't think twice about the price of these ingredients as he was loading up his grocery cart, but this is the kind of meal I dreamed about and drooled over back when I was living in my shitty apartment at Dairy Corners, or before that when I was living on a barn floor. I savor every bite, letting the buttery steak slip down my throat slowly as I imagine how it's going to feel when I have Sam in my mouth later.

I imagine, and I daydream. But I wait for the pie to make my move.

"And now Amelia's decided that the knitting group should learn to crochet multi-colored leaves so we can sell them at the festival as a town fundraiser." Sam shakes his head as he serves ice cream over the top of the pie's perfectly golden crust—he definitely bought this at Marion's bakery—and slides it across the table to me. "Luis is thrilled. Don't get me wrong, I'd like to learn to crochet, but do you know how long it's taken me to knit a hat? And the last one I made came apart at the top while Milo was wearing it! He sent the damn thing back for repairs! Learning to crochet is my next textile nightmare."

I'm barely listening. My whole attention is focused on his mouth as I drag my spoon to the ice cream, gathering some of it from the plate, and then slowly pulling it over and across my tongue, dragging out the motion carefully while the sweet vanilla flavor melts into my palate.

"I just—" Sam interrupts himself as his eyes travel to my spoon. "Malachai, what are you doing? Is something wrong with the ice cream?"

Okay, so much for my seduction techniques. "Uh, no." I sit up in my seat; it seems like it's time for me to be a little more direct. "Sam, I want us to have sex tonight," I blurt out. "Um, anal sex," I add, because it's not like we haven't had sex in plenty of ways already and I seem to be struggling with specificity of language right now. "Please. *Sir.*"

The last word of that sentence clearly has my desired effect, as Sam's entire jaw clenches and his eyes go strangely narrow. If we were in some sort of werewolf novel right now I'd think he was about to shift right in front of me. "What did you just say to me?" His voice is low and husky, the timbre hitting those notes that never fail to speak right to my dick. It's already rising to attention.

"I said, sir. Um. That. I'd like you to be... inside of me tonight. Um. Sir."

Sam drops the spoon he's holding onto a plate and sets down the pint of locally made ice cream. It probably cost more than my entire lunch budget for the week, and I have to fight the urge not to tell him to put it away before it melts onto the table. We have more important things to talk about right now. "Malachai," he says slowly. "Are you quite certain you understand what you're asking me?"

I lean across the table, nudging my finger against the top button of his polo shirt, letting it skirt against the blond hairs on his chest. He draws in a quick breath. "I am very, very certain, sir," I whisper.

He nods, and I watch his Adam's apple move as he swallows. "What you're asking me for," he says quietly. "It's something I take very seriously. I want you to know that, Malachai. Because I take you, and all that you offer me, very seriously." He takes my cheek in his hand. "You are too precious," he whispers, "too important, too good, for anyone *not* to take what you are offering right now with the utmost seriousness."

I blink back the tears that now seem to be spontaneously appearing in the corner of my eyes. "Sir," I finally say. "When you say things like that—well, that's exactly why I'm asking what I'm asking right now. Why I'm asking *you*, and not anybody else."

He pulls his hand away from my cheek and stands up from the table as he studies me carefully, his eyes washing over my frame.

And then, before I can react to that movement, he's circling the table, sweeping me up into his arms as if I weigh nothing, and carrying me toward the stairs.

Fuck, I think, as my chub hardens further and my heart speeds up. Did he actually just *sweep me up in his arms?*

I'm not interested in any waiting time that might result in Sam changing his mind about what he's just agreed to, so I get to work unbuttoning those buttons on his shirt, nipping and licking slightly at his chest while he practically jogs us up the stairs. And how much does this guy work out, anyway? I may be skinny, but I do weigh something, and he's been carrying me around an awful lot in the past twenty-four hours. Still, when we arrive in the bedroom, he sets me down gently on the bed as though the trip hasn't winded him at all.

He plants his arms on either side of me and leans forward. "I need you to know that we can stop this at absolutely any moment, Malachai. If you want this to stop," he says slowly, his voice that same low growl that goes directly to every nerve in my body, "all you have to do is say *ice cream.*"

It's on the tip of my tongue to ask why he picked ice cream when he leans farther over and swallows my mouth with his.

The intensity is immediate and almost overwhelming. He somehow keeps our bodies wrapped together, his mouth almost always against mine, as he slowly undresses me, item by item. Time seems to grind to a halt as he keeps me wrapped up in his arms, holding me closely. He's lost his shirt at some point, but his pants are still on, and the feel of his chest against mine is something I know I'll savor forever.

For some reason, I expected this time with him to be quick, urgent—maybe because that's how our moments like this have often felt before. But it's clear Sam is in no rush tonight, and I lean back away from any urgency I felt when I was first asking him for what I want.

I have what I want right now, and I won't have it for long. I'm determined to enjoy every single moment of this experience.

He arranges his body behind mine, his check nuzzling against mine, the weight of his stubble boring sweetly against my skin. "I'm going to ask you some questions," he says in a whisper. "And I expect you to answer them honestly. With *sir,* of course."

I shiver within his arms, even though I'm not the slightest bit cold. "Yes. Sir."

He runs a hand down my body, stopping to brush it against my cock, which seems to somehow harden more with each sensation. It's already purple and nearly painful, and I jump slightly when he pulls his hand away from it to circle my balls, tease my perineum, and then move to find the circle that no one's ever touched the way he has. He teases the puckered opening there, gently at first and then with a bit more pressure.

"What have you had inside of you here, Malachai?"

I hear a *pop* of a bottle behind me, and then something wet drips down my hole. Sam slides the tip of a finger inside of me, and I have to squeak out my answer. "Really just some fingers, sir. Yours. Mine. A dildo, once or twice."

"I see." It feels like he's almost performing surgery behind me right now as he carefully slides the finger back and forth, in and out. Another joins the first, and pressure and pain merge with pleasure in a way that sparks light all the way through my brain.

"What did you like best?" He whispers the words into my ear.

"The dildo, sir." No contest. The answer is easy.

"Why was that?"

"I liked... the thickness, sir. The size." I gulp as I think about that dildo, the one I saved and saved for. I still have it, hidden in the bottom of my duffel bag here. I wonder if Sam would ever use it with me, before our time here is up.

"I'm glad to hear that," Sam says. "We're going to spend some time preparing you, Malachai. Your only job is to tell me what you like most, because every part of this evening is about making you feel good. Do you understand?"

"Of course. That, sir! That!" My voice runs high as Sam slides a finger farther in, hitting a pleasure point that no one else but me and that one dildo have ever touched before. I go flying into the sensation, and it seems a long time before I come down.

And then Sam proceeds to destroy me with sensation.

One finger at a time, he opens me up, wets me down with liquid, presses at that spot over and over, all the while leaning across my body to kiss and tease me with his tongue and lips. He keeps bringing me to the edge, nearly dropping me off of it, and then grabbing me and pulling me back just as I'm desperate to fall. Over and over and over he takes me to that ledge, and it's not long before I'm begging, clutching at his arms. All I want is to have him inside of me, to feel all of him inside of all of me.

This may very well be, I know, the only time that Sam Evers and I will ever be as close as this. And I'm determined to savor every minute of it, no matter what.

"Are you certain you're ready? You must be certain, my darling." He whispers the words against my earlobe.

"I'm ready, sir."

"How do you feel? Be honest, please."

"Um, good. I feel really good, sir. Maybe just a little worried, if you really want honesty." I choke back a laugh as my gaze travels down his body. His pants are gone now too, and I gulp as I look down at the broad, wide length and girth below me. It's so much. *He's* so much. I can't imagine, exactly, what he's going to feel like inside of me, but I know for damn sure that I want to find out. "But also, I'm really, really fucking excited, sir."

Sam laughs as he flips me gently onto my back, brushing hair out of my eyes before he slides on a condom. For a few moments I just stare at him, memorizing every inch of his face as he places pillows carefully underneath my torso and lines my legs up over his shoulders. "I promise we'll take this slowly and carefully," he tells me. "We'll try this position first—I want to be able to look at you, to ensure you have everything you need and that I'm not hurting you. Remember: *ice cream* if you want me to stop."

There's no way I'm saying those words tonight. I don't care how much anything right now fucking hurts.

Sam leans over to kiss me gently on the earlobe. "*Ice cream, my darling,*" he whispers. And then he says the words that nearly undo me yet again: "I've got you, Malachai. I'll never let anything happen to you."

And then he eases gently inside of me.

And it does hurt, at first. I'm not stupid: I've known for a long time that porn isn't real, and I always knew my first time doing this would probably be at least a little bit painful. But Sam moves so slowly, so carefully, with such precision, that every stab of discomfort starts to blend with a million other sensations. When my erection starts to flag, he takes me in his hand, stroking me exactly the right way. "Push back against me, darling," he tells me.

I do. And then everything feels even more right.

He keeps moving, slowly and slightly, and the more of him my body gets, the more it adjusts, the more it wants. Then he's stroking me, faster, while he speeds up slightly inside of me. A pinging voice in my brain wonders what it would be like if he wasn't wearing a condom: what would it be like to feel him come inside of me, spilling into me with nothing between us? That fantasy rolls through my brain as it occurs to me that the pain is almost entirely gone now, washed away under the pops of pleasure that roll through me every time he moves against that spot, against the nerve endings that yell with excitement each time he moves back and forth, in and out, our bodies catching a rhythm together like nothing I've ever felt before.

"Faster, sir? Please?"

He looks down carefully at me, as if he's double-checking to be sure. But I've never been more sure of anything in my life. He begins to move faster, and then I lose time. For a moment I'm nothing but the feel of his body as it thrums into me, his cock buried in me, nudging at my prostate over and over, his fingers on my cock, teasing, and then his cock pushes even more deeply into me as he leans over my body to lay his forehead against mine.

"Sir!" That's the word I call out, loudly, as I come in his hand and all over his stomach, as I feel him jerk to a shuddering, pulsing halt within me. It's as though he grabs me in his arms and jumps over an edge with me, and both of us fall into some kind of abyss together, clinging tightly to one another.

We lay there for what feels like the longest time, his body curled around mine, the pulse of his heartbeat echoing upward into my ears. I count the seconds, determined to relish every single one.

After all, there may never be another moment like this.

"Oh, Malachai." Sam lets out a laugh as he collapses his face into my neck. "The gifts you keep giving me."

His words make no sense. Gifts I keep giving *him*? He just gave me one of the most perfect experiences of my life, and he's talking about me giving *him* gifts? But I'm tired now, worn out from all the endorphins and adrenaline coursing through my body, and I don't have the energy to study those words too carefully. All I want right now is more of Sam's body against mine. I snuggle into him, hard, making sure as much of his skin as possible is touching mine, and he pulls the covers up over us.

"You make me wonder," he says softly. "You make me wonder if..."

I fall asleep before I can let my mind run through all the different ways he could have finished that sentence.

Chapter 20

12 Days to the Devon Falls Leaf Festival

I seem to have kicked this trip off with a bang. —Sam Evers

Malachai always leans on the left side of his desk.

It's an observation I've made in near perpetuity since we began working closely together. When a patient comes into the office and he stands to speak with them, he always leans to his left. When a colleague approaches and he steps away from his chair to meet them, he does the same. Before or after breaks, when he stops next to the dark wood and stares off into his space, his eyes fixed on a spot in time none of the rest of us can see, he always leans on the left side of his desk.

Right now he's leaning gently, one hip pushing slightly into the wood's edge, smiles and laughter dancing across his lips as he talks to Benson about something. Probably the leaf festival; there's little else anyone in this town discusses this close to the festival's opening. There's a cold nip of fall fully in the town's grasp now, held just as tightly as the grip Malachai seems to have on me. His eyebrows dance together as he gestures toward the ceiling, mimicking something in a low tone that causes Benson to openly and loudly snort. I drop one hand into my pocket and grip the cloth there tightly, determined to look away from him.

"This office frowns on eye-stalking employees, you know."

"Shit, Jack!" I actually trip backward in the Lancer Family Medicine hallway, nearly spilling the contents of my afternoon coffee across both my shoes and his. I pull myself together and turn around, pushing past him as I stalk back into my office. "That was unnecessary."

"Was it?" Jack eyes me, a look I can't fully identify lingering across his face. This is unusual for me. Jack and I have known each other for years. We've been friends through residency hell, dating, and divorce. Death. There are very, very few expressions of his I do not automatically recognize.

"It sure was." I shuffle the two papers on my nearly immaculate desk. "I heard from Milo. He's driving up with Tom and Colin today. They're going to stay at the winery's new bed and breakfast through the wedding and the festival. I guess they all decided to take some time away from New York together."

Jack raises an eyebrow. "Holy shit. You just said five sentences in a row that didn't make me feel like I was in a British boarding school."

I run my wording back through my head. "I can choose whether to speak formally or informally anytime I like, Jack Fucking Lancer."

Jack snorts and rolls his eyes as he drops into a chair across from me. "Sure, but I think that's the first time I've heard you choose 'informally' since you came to Vermont." He smiles slightly. "Milo will be glad to hear it."

Jack, Milo, and I have been largely inseparable since residency, until Jack's move to Vermont and my subsequent trip following him a few years later. Milo is very fond of reminding us that our abandonment causes him nothing but pain and he's counting the days until my return trip.

A return trip that keeps sending sharp pains through my chest each time I think about it. All the more reason *not* to think about it, I've decided.

"I knew Milo was coming up for the next few weeks." Jack crosses his arms over his chest. "But Tom and Colin are coming up now too? That's an awful lot of time on the Canadian border for two people who just showed up in a recent edition of *People* magazine."

"They have rooms at the bed and breakfast attached to that new winery. They seem to have developed a minor obsession with it," I tell him wryly.

"Hmm." Jack frowns and arches an eyebrow. "I wonder..."

"What do you wonder?" I ask.

Jack sighs. "These wedding plans have gotten a little bit out of control. I just hope there's not another surprise Henri or someone else snuck in that Benson and I haven't discovered yet. But I think Malachai would tell us if that were the case."

I'd be worried if I didn't know that he and Benson were both fully caught up on the appearance from that state cow. But I know my best friend well enough to know this is just nerves. When the day of his wedding arrives, he'll be more than ready to embrace all the ridiculousness and absurdity it will likely have to offer.

He loves his fiance deeply. More deeply, I know, than he's ever loved anyone.

"Jack." I lean across my desk. "The wedding's going to be perfect, no matter what happens. Because it will be a wedding for you and Benson."

Jack smiles softly. "Thanks, Sammy. I think I needed to hear that today."

A burst of laughter comes from the front room, pushing itself through my doorway, and I instinctively lean forward.

Malachai. I would know that laughter almost anywhere now.

Jack falls back into his seat as he studies me carefully. "Hey, Sam? Mom was asking me again the other day if we need to have you sign paperwork. To disclose whatever's happening between you and Malachai. You know, protect everyone from lawsuits and all that."

Visions of the past weekend hit my brain like sharp shards of beautiful cut glass, pounding at me with flashes of memory. *Malachai, eyes wide, his face glued to mine as I knelt over him. His body, open before me, his hand, drifting up toward my face, slowly running over my cheek, across my beard—*

"That's not necessary." I cut the memories off, determined not to let them bore themselves any further into my skull today. "Nothing of significance is happening between me and Malachai. I'm leaving in less than two weeks, Jack. You know that."

"I do." Jack nods. "But I'm wondering if anything's changed that might be making you reconsider that decision."

I shake my head, averting my eyes to the computer screen at my left, away from Jack. "Nothing will change," I say carefully. "I'm going back to New York after the wedding and the festival."

Jack shakes his head. "Look, buddy, Milo and I have both talked about this. And we know how much you were in love with Christian, okay? We were there through your entire marriage, and—"

Something in his words breaks a dam inside of me, a dam that's been holding water for far, far too long. "You don't understand!" I hiss the words quietly but firmly as I stand up from my desk, desperately clawing into the wood beneath my fingernails. "The problem is that I wasn't in love with Christian! Not nearly enough! The problem is that I didn't even fucking love him enough to go a *damn pool party,* and he died! The problem is that I feel things for Malachai I never felt for Christian!"

The words hang in the air between us, and Jack's mouth drops open in shocked silence.

"Well," says another voice, and Jack and I both turn fast to face the doorway and the new visitor standing there. "I guess that clarifies some things."

I rub my hand over my face. "Hello, Tom," I say tiredly.

He nods. Behind him, Milo and Colin are as still as statues. Looks like the New York entourage has arrived for their sojourn in Vermont.

And I seem to have kicked this trip off with a bang.

"Maybe I always knew, on some level."

Tom takes a long drag of beer after he says the words, and then he tilts the bottle neck as he hands it to me. I grab it to take a sip myself, letting the dark amber liquid wiggle its way down my throat in time with the dancing flames in front of me.

The winery's bed and breakfast is equipped with many fantastic features, I've learned today—hot tubs, a dining room run by a friend of Luis', and several outdoor fire pits. After my revelation in the office this afternoon, I suppose it's only natural that Jack, Milo, Tom, Colin, and I would end up next to one of those fire pits with a large cooler of beer, wine, whisky, and tequila sitting between us.

I also suppose it was only a matter of time before the truth came out and Colin learned everything about my marriage to his brother. I guess I should just be grateful that Malachai was far enough away, in the front office, that he missed hearing the confessions I made in front of all and sundry today. He already knew the first part of that confession, of course: the part about the lies in my marriage. But I deeply, deeply doubt he's ever realized that my feelings for him are what helped me to fully see what was missing in my marriage.

He and Benson are off at dinner right now, talking through some final wedding details. So far Jack's phone isn't humming with text messages, so I assume it's going well.

"Did you really know?" I ask Tom mildly. "Because I don't think I did. I always thought we were happy. Life with Christian was so easy, for the most part. After the accident, I was certain I was as depressed as I was because I couldn't imagine life without him. But then I started therapy, and I realized that what I was feeling was something much more like..."

Guilt. But I can't bring myself to say the word in front of my dead husband's twin brother.

Milo sighs from across the fire. He's a large man, tall and imposing, not unlike me and Jack. He's also incredibly attractive. Christian used to take endless joy from making fun of how Jack, Milo, and I looked when we stood in scrubs together. "The cast of *Grey's Anatomy* isn't supposed to exist in real life," he used to tease us.

I've still never seen one episode of that show.

"I wish you'd said something then. Confided in us, Sam," Milo says quietly.

I shrug. "Confided what, exactly? That I was feeling like I hadn't loved my husband enough when he was alive? What difference would that have made? Anyhow, it wasn't until I came to Vermont that I really saw things as they were, I suppose."

Tom shakes his head. "That assistant of yours sure has made a premier appearance in our lives, hasn't he?"

"He's the office manager, actually," Jack says as he takes another sip of his own beer. "And yes, he's special." Jack glances over at Colin. "But so was Christian," he adds.

Colin nods and frowns as he sits upright in his seat. He hasn't said much of anything all evening, and he doesn't say anything now.

I lean toward him again, the fire crackling at my feet. "I need you to know this, Colin," I tell him urgently. "I'm not going to be with Malachai. I'm not going to be with anyone, ever again."

Someone pulls in a breath that sounds more like a gasp, and Colin looks at me sharply.

"Sam," Tom says gently, "Christian wouldn't have wanted—"

"Christian deserved the world," I interrupt him. "He was an amazing human being, and I was so very lucky to be married to him. I'll always know that. I owe his memory more than letting myself give into feelings for someone else that I could never give to him." I shake my head. "I'm going back to New York after the festival. Back to our apartment. I can spend the rest of my life there honoring him, as he rightfully deserves."

"Sam, for fuck's sake!" Milo's shaved brown head is illuminated sharply in the firelight now. "You can't actually mean that! Are you telling us you're planning to be alone for the rest of your life? Out of choice? I'm with Tom, man. Christian was family to us too, you know that. And there's no fucking way he would have wanted that kind of life for you."

Jack nods in steady agreement. Tom looks at Colin carefully, who's still staring at the fire, looking away from all of us. Then Tom's gaze finds its way back at me.

"You two never fought," he finally says. "Well, not really. You always seemed so peaceful and easy with each other."

"That's because we were," I tell him. And that, I don't add, was the problem. All we ever were was peaceful and easy: nothing more.

Colin stands and drains the rest of his beer. And then, without saying another word, he starts slowly walking away from the fire. I start to stand up, to go after him, but Tom glances over at me and gently shakes his head. Then he jumps up to follow Colin.

Milo comes around the fire to take Colin's place next to me. "Sam," he says softly. "Colin's just upset right now. You dropped a bomb on him, man. When he starts thinking clearly again, he'll realize that what we're telling you is right. You can't decide to be alone for the rest of your life." Jack nods in agreement.

"That's easy for you both to say," I tell them gently. "You don't wake up in the middle of the night, imagining Christian's face in that water. Imagining his cries for help—all the ones that went unheard."

Milo laces one hand over my right hand, and Jack does the same with my left. For a moment I'm reminded of our first year of residency together. The first time I lost a patient and the two of them sat with me in the on-call room for hours, holding my hands, holding all of me together through the rest of my shift.

But I'm not that young man anymore. I've seen so much more of life since then: what the world gives and what it takes away. Whatever Milo and Jack and Tom and even Colin may say, I know the truth: I'm not making any of the choices I'm making for Colin, not really. I'm making them for Christian. All that matters is honoring his memory.

And that's why I've got to start saying goodbye to Malachai and start really, truly letting him go. Someday he'll thank me. Malachai deserves so much more than someone who's as broken as I am. He'll move on and find someone who can give him real happiness—I'm sure of that.

I have to be.

Chapter 21
10 Days to the Devon Falls Leaf Festival

Now my heart's a hummingbird in my chest, threatening to beat itself into destruction at any moment. —Malachai Flynn

"Jeb? Jeb, are you here?"

Shadows are dancing through Jeb's barn in the evening light, popping magically against the dark wooden floor and walls. Someone moos—or bellows? I'm not really up on my animal-speak. As far as I can see, though, the barn's empty.

Fuck.

Not that this is an emergency, thank goodness. At least I don't think it is. I've just come from the town hall, where more paperwork has come through about Vermonica's care and handling during the festival. Since Vermonica's due to arrive in just over a week, I figured I should get it to Jeb and his partners right away. Given that we're in the high pumpkin season, I expected there to be more people around Stock Tree Farm when I arrived. But there's only one truck in the driveway, and I haven't seen a single person yet since I've started wandering about the property looking for Jeb.

Shit. I really needed to get these documents handed over in person so I could talk through the logistics of transporting Vermonica back and forth with him. Tomorrow I've got a long day at the office, and this weekend I really need to catch up on my reading for chem.

A noise that sounds something like a grunt rings through the barn, and just like that Sherbert's standing in front of me, fully drawn up on his hind legs. Is he *glaring?* Sure seems like it, but goats can't glare, right?

"Um, hi, Sherbert." I edge a hand toward him while I start glancing around for apples. "How are you, um, doing?"

Sherbert's eyes seem to narrow menacingly.

"Okay, okay, I'm looking for apples! Listen, if you'll just give me a minute, I—"

"I didn't know you worked with farm animals as well as drug dealers."

I whirl around at the sound of a voice that's familiar but completely out of the context of where I'm standing.

"Avon? What are you doing here?"

Avon's face is dark and almost haunted-looking under the fallen beams of light barely coming through the barn rafters and illuminating only half of the area around him.

"Jeb sells ice cream from our family's creamery," he says shortly. "I'm here dropping off a delivery."

"Oh." There's absolutely no chance of me hiding my surprise, so I don't try. My brain didn't connect Avon and his two hundred dollar shoes with making ice cream deliveries. "I was actually here to drop something off too. Have you seen Jeb?"

Avon shakes his head. "He and Embry and Adam took the night off. I believe they're at some town holiday planning event here in La Fierte. You should have messaged them before you came."

Clearly. I glance back and forth between Avon and Sherbert, who are starting to give new meaning to the term *between a rock and a hard place.*

"Oh, makes sense," I finally say. "I guess I'll just leave the paperwork under their front door, then. I can call Jeb in the morning." I take a few steps backward from Sherbert, toward the door, but stop when I realize Avon clearly has no intention of getting out of my way.

"Since we're both here, you might as well know that I've requested a town meeting for this weekend," he says, and there's a grittiness to his voice I haven't heard before. "I thought you might want to know."

"A town meeting?" My fears of Sherbert fall right out of my head as I turn to face him. "Why?"

Avon snorts. "Did you really think I wouldn't find out? I told you I had my lawyer looking at all of the festival's accounting."

"I know that," I tell him. "But there's nothing to find there. I double-checked all my figures, and then Sam triple-checked them."

Avon crosses his arms and stares at me incredulously. "Do you really think I'm that stupid? That Devon Falls is *that stupid?*" he shakes his head. "Honestly, Malachai, your cockiness will be your downfall."

My mouth definitely drops then, because nobody in my entire life has ever accused me of being cocky. "Avon, I swear," I say, with every ounce of patience I have in my voice, "I don't know what you're talking about right now." Now my heart's a hummingbird in my chest, threatening to beat itself into destruction at any moment. What the hell does he think he found? And *fuck,* now I'm starting to get a little short of breath. "Whatever you think you found, I can explain—"

"Explain what?" Avon asks calmly. "Explain why you did it?" He shakes his head again. "There's no justifying your actions, Malachai, and I think we both know that."

"Once again, I don't know what you're talking about!" I throw up my hands and take a step away from him, away from his words, only to remember that Sherbert's still behind me. But when I glance around, I realize that Sherbert's not looking at me anymore. His eyes are fixed on Avon, and he's drawing his front legs up like he's preparing for an attack.

Oh shit. "Avon," I tell him. "Whatever you think you found, it can wait, okay? Right now we have to find some apples, and—"

The sneer that's been on the tip of Avon's mouth is fully visible now as his lips curl unnervingly. "You really thought you were going to get away with it, didn't you?" He shakes his head back and forth and makes a mocking *tsk* sound with his tongue. "After all they've done for you," he murmurs.

"What are you *talking about?*" I hiss rather than shout the words, desperate not to upset Sherbert. "And what did I ever do to you, anyway? Why are you so determined to make my life miserable?"

Avon sucks in a hard breath, and Sherbert makes a low noise behind me. "You're everything that's wrong with Devon Falls!" he shouts. "Do you know how hard I've worked to try to fit in there? Do you know what it's like to be born in a town where you're immediately known as *the rich kid* before you're even out of your onesie*?* I've spent my whole life as an outsider in the place where *I was born.* I was sent to boarding schools, so I never had any friends. The other children made fun of our fancy clothes, or only wanted to play with us if it was to use our pool. I've worked my ass off every single day for my grandfather's company, but to those druggies you were friends with, I was never anything more than the stupid rich boy who lived up on the hill—and they made sure I never forgot it!"

His words stun me into silence, and behind me I hear another huffing noise right before I realize Sherbert's dropped back down to all four legs. He trots up beside me and tilts his head as he looks at Avon.

"You were bullied?" I finally say. "For having *too much* money?" His story is so very much the exact opposite of my childhood that his words stew in my brain for a long moment, waiting to be processed. At least, for whatever reason, all that processing has paused my panic attack.

He crosses his arms. "You're just like those criminal Fletcher brothers. A conman who clearly tried to cheat this town. I may not be a part of this community the way I wish I could be, but I still won't let anyone hurt the people of Devon Falls." He lets out a huff and finally turns around, away from me. "And at the town meeting tomorrow I'll make sure you can't hurt them anymore."

"I'm sorry all that happened to you, Avon," I call out to him as he starts to leave. "The Fletcher brothers are total assholes. No one knows that better than me! But I swear, I don't know what you think I did wrong!"

Avon ignores me as he stalks out the door. I watch through the barn window as he climbs into his Tesla, its perfect silence mocking me as Avon pulls away into the falling afternoon light.

Sherbert nudges his nose gently into my jeans, then lets out some kind of *bah* sound.

"Sorry, boy," I tell him. "I don't know where Jeb put your apples."

It *has got* to be my imagination, but for a moment I could swear he nods at me. Then he nudges me gently in the knee again before rubbing his hard head against my ankle and trotting back to his pen.

I stand there for a long time, staring at the walls of the darkening barn, shaking in its silence. When I finally go to leave, my right sneaker crunches down on something: a leaf, swirled in orange and reds, now half-crushed and falling apart. I must have tracked it into the barn under my shoe.

I lean over and pick it up, twirling it between my fingers. I think about Ken Davidson and the Fletcher brothers and Avon. I think about this town meeting he kept shouting about. I still can't figure out what the hell he thinks he found in the festival's books.

But mostly I think about Sam. I think about the way his eyes light up when he laughs. I think about how perfect the world feels when he holds me in his arms. I think about him going back to New York and sitting alone, silent and still with only his knitting to keep him company, in the apartment he once shared with Christian, who isn't there anymore. I think about what he told me the other night, about how real the fear of human loneliness is.

I wonder if any of us ever really belong anywhere.

Chapter 22

10 Days to the Devon Falls Leaf Festival

I'll take the best possible care of this butterfly I can while I have it. —Sam Evers

"Dr. Evers?"

I twirl around, away from the supply cabinet I'm standing in front of, at the sound of a voice that brings far too much comfort to my ears. Malachai is standing in the doorway of one of the exam rooms at Lancer Family Medicine, wringing his hands together, a look of pure despair upon his face.

"Malachai? What's wrong?" I rush over to him, taking his face in my hands and holding it carefully as I study him. "Did you have another panic attack?" I ask. I run my fingers over the soft skin of his cheeks and forehead as I wait for an answer. Luckily, nothing seems immediately amiss. Nothing except for the tears sitting at the corners of his eyes, poised as though they're waiting to fall.

"I... I..."

He can't seem to form full words, and now I'm worried he's in shock. I take Malachai's hand and guide him over to the exam table, sitting him down gently on it before I sit next to him and take his hands in mine. "Tell me what's wrong," I say urgently.

"Whatever it is, we'll fix it. You and I, together." I don't bother to parse my words or justify them. Malachai and I may not be headed down a path of long-time happiness together, but right now, he needs me. I'll do anything in my power to help him through whatever momentary difficulty he's facing. "Is something wrong with your mother?" I ask gently. I know very little about Malachai's family, but I do know his mother still lives alone in Alcott, and she's his only close relative.

Malachai shakes his head. "No. I mean, I don't think so. Nothing's wrong. Not exactly. Except maybe it is? I'm not sure."

"Then tell me," I say calmly. "Tell me the problem." I squeeze his hand up against mine. "Please, Malachai. You can trust me. I promise. I'll help you with whatever you need."

A sharp tingling in the back of my mind reminds me that this trust and support I've offered, however real it is, will always be short-lived. Colin's face flashes through my brain as I remember the promises I made to him only a few short days ago.

Malachai shakes his head slowly. Sadly. "Avon," he says quietly.

"What's Avon done?" I ask sharply.

Malachai drops his head into his hands. "I don't know, exactly. He says he's called a town meeting. He says there's something wrong with the festival books. But I swear I've checked everything twice, Sam, and you've looked at them too! There's nothing to find!"

"Okay, let's remain calm." I will not allow Malachai to sit here and suffer. "Malachai, I meant it when I vouched for you in the town hall that day. I'll vouch for you again if Avon raises some kind of trouble with the town. You've done nothing but take great care of this festival in Henri's absence. The town sees that. They know it."

Malachai sags against me. "Maybe you're right," he says softly. "But he kept saying the town was going to see me for who I really am, and he wouldn't tell me what he meant..."

"Hey, hey, hey." I grab his hands, pulling him back toward me. At least he's breathing, and no panic attacks seem to be on the horizon. That's progress. "There are a lot of people in this town who care about you, Malachai. I care about you. If Avon wants to start trouble, we'll be ready for him."

Malachai shakes his head again, pursing his lips together as he stares up at me. "All I've ever wanted," he says softly, "is somebody who would be there for me when I really, really needed them. Somebody who could help when things got really, truly fucked up. That was why I always knew I never *could* fuck up. My mom wasn't going to be able to rescue me. There wasn't anyone else to do it." He blinks more tears back into the corners of his eyes. "That's how I ended up living in that barn," he goes on miserably. "And now you're here, offering me help like this, and I don't know what I did to deserve it."

"You didn't ever have to do anything," I say as I run my fingers gently through his hair. "Being yourself has always been more than enough." I move a strand of hair out of his eyes. "I only wish I could be there for you for more than just another week," I finally add.

He bites at his lower lip. This is a habit he has, I've noticed, something he only ever does when he's thinking very hard. "I understand, sir," he says. "You have to know that I understand."

I reach for him, pulling him up against me, in a hug that I hope I can carry with me long after I've left him behind and gone back to New York. "All I ever want for you," I tell him, "is to have people in your life who support you unconditionally. You deserve that from this world, darling."

He deserves better than me, quite honestly. He deserves better than a boss who developed a highly unhealthy relationship with their employee. He deserves better than a partner tied to a mistake they can never, ever undo. I understand, deep in my soul, that I don't deserve someone as good and wonderful as Malachai: he'll forever be a butterfly flitting on my fingers, one that I will eventually have to release, no matter how much I desperately want to stare at its beauty.

So, then: I'll take the best possible care of this butterfly I can while I have it.

I brush more strands of sweaty hair away from his forehead. "We'll deal with Avon together," I tell him. "In the meantime, is there something I can do to make you feel better? How can I take care of you? We could go back home and have another bath if that would help."

He takes a long gulp of air before he leans over and takes my mouth against his. His kisses are harsh and demanding at first and then soft and lyrical, a dance between the two of us, a fluttering of emotion, space and time. Eventually, he pulls away slightly. "Um," he says. "This might sound weird, but are you working right now? Or just closing up the office?"

"I have some paperwork to finish up before I leave," I tell him. "And I'm just doing some cleanup around the exam rooms. Jack and Marie have been very kind, putting up with my moods lately. I thought I'd return the favor since I'll be leaving them even more short-staffed very soon, as you know. Why do you ask?"

"Well." He hesitates, biting his lip again. "I don't know. I mean, there is something? Something I've kind of always kind of thought might help me feel, um, better when I freak out about stuff. But I've never tried it before for really obvious reasons and I'm guessing it's kind of unusual and it probably isn't your thing and just—never mind, forget I said anything!" He starts to jump down from the exam table, but I hold him in place.

"Malachai, you can ask me for anything you need," I tell him. "Anything at all. You never have to feel any kind of shame about asking me for what you want or need." Malachai tries to look away from me, but I take his chin in my hand, forcing him to hold my gaze. "I promise, my darling. You can always be honest with me."

Malachai draws in a long breath, lets it out slowly, and then closes his eyes before he starts speaking again. "I, um, saw it in this video once? A guy was just, um, like, holding another guy's dick in his mouth. He looked really calm and at peace and relaxed. And for some reason, I kept thinking that I might feel that same way if I ever tried that. With, like, the right person or whatever." His eyes drift down to my crotch, where his gaze against the zipper of my pants immediately has me hardening within them. "Never mind, it's weird! So weird that I even asked. Forget it!" He moves to jump up off of the table again, but I quickly grab at his arm, holding him in place once more. "Malachai," I ask, before he panics his way into a stroke. "Are you talking about cockwarming?"

His eyes widen. "I think so. Maybe? I'm not sure what it was called."

I kiss him on the cheek and wait until his muscles relax slightly against my hand before I say anything more. "Well, first of all, there's no shame in asking for anything you want sexually, as long as it's safe and consensual," I remind him.

Malachai blushes. "I guess I know that in theory. It just seems kind of weird, you know? That something like that might relax me or whatever."

"I detest the word *weird*." I lean over slightly to nibble at his earlobe with my teeth, and he shivers against me. "It implies that there's some exact line of correctness that everyone's tastes and preferences should align perfectly with. And that simply isn't the case. I've never cockwarmed myself, but believe me, I'm more than willing to try it. Especially if you think it might help you to relax." I stand and lift him up into my arms, because I've learned that giving Malachai too much time to overthink any decision or course of action will only lead him to greater panic. And really, there's nothing to worry or panic over here.

I'd give him the moon if I could. Some time with his mouth wrapped around my dick? That's a much easier—and frankly very appealing—ask.

Malachai lets out a squeak as I carry him from the exam room, but he doesn't protest. I carry him out of the exam room and through an empty hallway into my office, where I set him down gently before I quickly close and lock the door.

I situate myself in my very comfortable rolling chair. "First of all," I tell him, "never be afraid to ask for anything you want from me. You will never be *weird,* and the things you want will never be *weird.* You're exactly as you're supposed to be. Now. Take me in your mouth," I order him. "And please be sure to call me *sir* for the rest of the evening."

"Yes, sir." He says the words breathlessly. Gently. I unzip my pants and take out my cock, which has only hardened further in response to Malachai's quick response to my orders.

"I'm going to work on paperwork," I tell him. "Should you feel uncomfortable or want to stop at any time, you only need to say the words *ice cream.* Do you know what you need to do?"

"Yes. Yes, sir." He breathes out heavily. Then he kneels down and walks on his knees a few steps before coming to stop in between my legs. He falls into a curled position there and drops his head into my lap, laying it against my right knee before taking my cock into his mouth and letting it rest against the side of his cheek. He lets out a slight sigh that appears to be filled with all the content I'd hoped he would when he first asked for this and I offered to try it with him.

The feeling of his mouth, holding me deeply in this gesture of near-innocence, almost undoes me. Christian and I were never exactly the sort of folk to cockwarm together, so as I told Malachai, this is a new experience for me in every possible way. And yet, something about it feels so familiar. So *right.* I turn on the computer in front of me and do my best to finish up some patient paperwork that's been hanging over my head. But my hand keeps drifting down to Malachai's head, my eyes hitting that place where his hair rests against my thigh. And all I can think about is how right this feels, how normal and regular this has become in mere moments: particularly considering that neither one of us has ever done this before. I can feel Malachai relaxing into me, and I wish I understood better exactly why this is an activity that he finds comforting.

But I also know some people's releases are hard for others to understand—including our own. As I told Malachai, *weird* is a word that has little to no meaning in its judgment. All that matters right now, today, is that I am offering Malachai some level of comfort he needs when it seems I can offer him little else. At some point between my notes about a whooping cough case and a fatty liver, I begin to recognize that this moment is one I will appreciate and treasure forever: largely because Malachai allowed me to give this moment to him.

Then something shifts, and by *something* I mean my cock. Malachai has begun rolling it slightly in his mouth, pulling it gently back and forth.

"Malachai," I say, my tone high with amusement. "Did I give you permission to do that?"

His eyes go wide as he pulls back from me. "No, sir. I'm sorry, sir. But my mouth started to cramp up a bit, sir, and I..."

"Well," I say, my voice mimicking disappointment. "We can't have you in pain. I suppose I'll just have to give you another order, then." His eyes widen as he stares up at me. I lean over, now harder than I've possibly ever been in my life, as I say my next words.

"Strip and prepare yourself in front of me. Then warm me with your hole."

I'm watching him carefully. I must be certain this isn't too much, that I haven't pushed him too far with this most recent order. But

Malachai leaps to his feet with more energy than I've seen from him since he first stepped into this space with me earlier.

He undresses in record time, and soon he's on display for me, his lithe body trembling slightly in the chilly air of the office. I draw him closer to me, offering some warmth, as I reach into my desk drawer to find a small tube of medical-grade lube I placed there after our last encounter together in this office. I dislike being unprepared for something twice. "Get yourself ready," I tell him as I hand him the lube. "Lean against my shoulders if you need to."

The next few minutes are so highly erotic that I consider it an absolute miracle I don't come right in my own office chair like a fifteen-year-old watching his first porno. Malachai's eyes stay wide as he sets his left hand carefully against my shirt and uses his other hand to begin stretching himself. He moans and writhes and occasionally jumps back against his own fingers, his eyes drifting back into his head as he works, and my sudden bark of "Are you prepared now?" is more out of necessity to preserve my sanity than anything else.

He nods and gulps loudly. "Sir, permission to ask a question?"

"Of course."

"Well, um, you know you're my first... there. And I've been tested, and I thought you said you've been too, so I was wondering if maybe we could... not use anything? If you're comfortable with that," he adds.

Go bare? With Malachai? I've only ever been bare with one person in my life, and I suspect Malachai knows this. Doctors aren't supposed to play with risks this way, but my mouth spits out an answer my heart firmly agrees with: "Yes, I've been tested. We can. Sit in my lap, Malachai, and lower yourself down on me. And then," I add, whispering the words in the dark growl Jack likes me to tamper down that I know Malachai loves, "please us both."

The next few minutes seem to pass in a blur of spectacular plea-sure as Malachai follows my orders to the letter. The practicalities of the chair are a bit difficult to navigate at first, but it's a large chair, and soon I find myself with a lapful of Malachai Flynn as he lowers himself onto me, taking my bare cock into his body. He drives himself down onto me slowly, his naked body hitting every inch of my clothed one, as he calls out into the silence of the room and I clutch at him.

And then he begins to *move.*

Perhaps it's the scene around us, the intensity of it, the fact that every nerve of my cock is hitting every nerve inside of him—but it's immediately clear that neither of us will last long. Within only a few strokes I can already feel him quivering steadily, and my own body isn't far behind his reactions. "Come when I tell you to," I order him. I grasp his cock in my hands, listening to the aching desperation in his calls, and I relish in the flighty sensations rushing through my entire body. And then—

My cock feels as though it flares inside of him. "Come for me now," I order. I release into him, nothing between us, jerking up into him as I brush my fingers over the top of his cock. He screams into the room as he follows my release, painting my hand with a flourish as he writhes on top of me.

When we both come down from the high of the moment, he wraps his arms around me, holding onto my neck as though he craves stability.

"Thank you, sir," he tells me. "That was... wow. Yeah. Wow."

I hold tight to him, this ball of light and joy in my arms. I know I will never be able to give Malachai what he truly deserves, and that's something I will regret for the rest of my life.

But at least I was able to give him this: some modicum of comfort, I hope, in the middle of the storm he finds himself in right now.

Chapter 23
8 Days to the Devon Falls Leaf Festival

I'm starting to think we're all a lot more fragile than we like to let on to other people. —Malachai Flynn

"Tell me again why your entire town is sitting on these ridiculously hard chairs in the middle of a historical society?" Milo, Jack and Sam's other giant, way-too-good-looking friend, shifts against the stubborn wood underneath him as he peers around the Devon Falls town hall meeting area.

"Mostly just to mess with your back," Jack answers him evenly. "Actually, to be honest, I have no idea why Amelia called this meeting. She just said it was about the festival. Malachai, do you know what's going on?" He looks over at me from his seat between me and Benson, and I shake my head frantically.

"Um, no, not really. Avon has some concerns about the festival's finances or something." I twist my hands into each other as I think of Avon's face in the barn, and Sam reaches over to gently rub my arm with one hand. My whole body instantly relaxes.

"Malachai and I went over the books together again three times last night," Sam says smoothly. "We found absolutely nothing to be concerned about. Everything's in order. The festival's set to go off without a hitch. Even the part where you two get married," he says to Benson and Jack.

"Assuming the state cow doesn't shit all over the wedding," Benson mumbles. He rolls his eyes. "If this whole meeting is just Avon Loseff trying to one-up me as town asshole, I'm going to be pissed. I've got due diligence documents to fall asleep on and a reputation as Biggest Jerk in Devon Falls to keep up." He nudges me slightly in the side with his elbow. "If he tries something, we've got your back," he whispers to me.

Sam sends me another quick nod, as if he's seconding what Benson just said. "Breathe," he whispers. "Everything's going to be fine, Malachai."

I start breathing in time. *Four... two... six. Four... two... six. Sam says everything's going to be fine, so it's going to be fine.*

Tom comes rushing through a crowd of people who are looking for seats. "Excuse me, pardon me, emergency!" He nearly shouts the words. He shows up at the end of our row, and I swear he looks like he's going to cry when he sees us all together.

"Colin's not here?" he asks frantically.

"Colin?" Sam frowns. "I thought the two of you were sitting this meeting out and staying at the winery."

"Yes, that's what I thought too." Tom runs his hands through his hair, clearly frustrated. "We had big plans to play drinking games with their new vintage and watch as many *The Fast and the Furious* movies as we could before we passed out. Vin Diesel's abs may have been involved. But Colin wasn't at the winery when I woke up this morning. I've been looking for him all day, and I can't seem to find him anywhere, and I..."

Sam shoots up in his seat. "Fuck," he whispers softly. "Is this because of what I said? The other day?"

What the hell did he say the other day that could have upset Colin enough to make the guy just disappear? I don't know Colin all that well, but someone who regularly drives cars at speeds of two hundred miles per hour doesn't exactly seem like the fragile type.

Then again, I'm starting to think we're all a lot more fragile than we like to let on to other people. *Oh, shit.* One look at Sam, and I think I realize what Sam must have said: he told Colin the truth about his marriage to Christian.

Shit. Shit shit shit shit shit. Now all I want to do is jump into Sam's lap and hug him hard, but this probably isn't the best place to make that kind of gesture. I settle for resting my hand on Sam's leg and squeezing it gently. Benson notices and sends me a raised eyebrow, but I manage to ignore him.

Tom shakes his head. "I'm not sure why he left. He hasn't wanted to discuss what you told us, Sam. All I know is when I got up this morning he was gone—left a note saying not to worry about him. I figured I could find him on my own, but it's late afternoon now, and there's still no sign of him." Tom runs his hand through his hair. "So, naturally, I'm panicking. And, because he's an utter asshole, Colin's not answering his phone."

Sam stands up and walks over to set his hands on Tom's shoulders. "Take a breath, okay? We'll find him." He turns around to look at me, Jack, and Benson. "Who can go look for Colin while I hold down the fort here with Malachai?"

The town hall blurs around me for a moment as I process what he's saying: is he actually offering to stay with me while his brother-in-law is missing? *Holy. Fucking. Shit.* But one look at Sam's expression, tight and perplexed as he frowns at Tom, tells me that however much I might want Sam here with me right now, I can't agree to that plan.

I swallow. Hard. "You should go look for Colin," I blurt out. I have to fight to push the words out of my body. I've been a nervous wreck about this meeting for days, and the only thing that's kept me from constant, perpetual panic attacks has been Sam—his strong, careful presence, his constant assurances that everything would be okay.

But I'm not Sam's priority, and I've always known that. Christian's memory is his priority. And Colin's arguably the greatest part of the memory. I don't have any right to ask Sam to choose me over Colin right now and stay here as my support. We're not partners. And in just a little over a week, we probably won't even know each other anymore.

I zip up my lips tightly. I've definitely gotten too dependent on Sam, I realize. This might be as good a time as any to finally start to let go.

"Malachai?" Sam fixes his eyes on mine. "Are you sure? I can stay here, and the others can look without me. Will you be okay if I leave?" he asks gently.

That question settles any doubts I had about suggesting he leave. He *wants* to leave—of course he does. This is Colin, after all. Colin's important.

Me? I'm never the important one. Not yet, anyway. But that's okay. I can take the power and strength Sam's gifted me these last few days, weeks, and months, and I can use that to power through whatever Avon Loseff has in store for me. And then, well, then it will be time for both Sam and I to leave this place.

I draw in a deep, long breath, the kind I always try to pull in when I'm staving off a panic attack. "I'll be okay," I finally say. "I can handle this. Whatever it is." I send Sam the best smile I can come up with. He looks back and forth for a moment between me and Tom before he finally nods. "Okay," he says quickly. "Let's go. Milo, can you come with us? Benson and Jack, can you stay here as backup in case Malachai needs it?"

"Of course," Jack says, his eyes narrowing thoughtfully as he looks back and forth between me and Sam.

Benson lifts an eyebrow at me as I clutch the sides of my seat. "You know Jack and I have got your back, right?" he asks carefully.

I nod. "Yup. Yup. Thank you both." But I'm too busy keeping up my breathing to say more than that.

I know Benson and Jack will support me through whatever... *this* turns out to be. But the truth is that they're not Sam.

And suddenly, I'm more than a little terrified of all the days I have ahead of me without Sam anywhere in sight.

The meeting starts out okay, actually. Amelia gives Avon the floor, and he tells everyone in the overly-packed room—and the size of the crowd here today is definitely not terrifying at all—that he decided to ask his lawyers to look over the festival's books, just as a safety precaution.

There are some murmurs when he says that, and a few raised eyebrows are pointed in my direction. But it's nothing I can't handle, especially when Benson squeezes my shoulder slightly.

"At first everything looked to be on the level," Avon goes on.

At first? What the hell is he talking about? I sit up straight in my chair and will myself to keep breathing. *In... out... in... out.*

"Then I found something." Avon whirls around in front of the podium to face me. "And I thought it best we discuss what I found as an entire town, as this finding affects all of us."

Heat's rising in my cheeks as everyone turns to look at me.

"Malachai Flynn," Avon says evenly, "can you please explain why your stipend for festival management is twice what the stipend was last year for someone managing the festival? And why are you receiving that amount even though you've only managed the festival for a few short weeks?" He holds up a piece of paper.

There are a few gasps from the crowd. Amelia stands up and jogs across the front of the room to snatch the paper out of Avon's hand. She narrows her eyes as she reads it, then looks up.

Curiosity is written all over her face. And confusion.

My heart's pounding faster and faster in my chest, and I force myself to draw in one breath after the other while I answer. "I didn't—I didn't know what last year's stipend was, not exactly. The stipend amount for this year was the number in the spreadsheets I got from Henri, so I just—"

"You really expect us to believe that?" Avon snatches the papers back from Amelia and holds them up, as if the entire town might be able to read the tiny numbers etched there. I can't make them out, but I don't need to.

All that matters is what that piece of paper represents: me, somehow failing this town yet again. Yet another moment of criminal activity and harm from Malachai Flynn, the outsider. The loser.

"We can call Henri," I burst out. "She can explain! I didn't change this year's stipend amount, I swear!"

"Henri's daughter just had her baby, hun," Amelia says, frowning. "She's asked us all not to disturb her right now, remember? But yes, we clearly need to talk to her. Let's just pause this conversation for a bit. In a few days we can call Henri and get this all straightened out. I'm sure it's all just a misunderstanding. And not what needed to be brought up in front of the entire community before we did our research." She levels a hard look at Avon, who remains completely nonplussed.

There's a long, low murmur through the crowd, and it's clear not everyone's happy with that solution.

"Malachai, keep your cool," Jack whispers. "Benson, you too. I see you curling those fists. Just stay calm, both of you." He stands up. "Listen, everyone, you all know that Mom and I trust Malachai Flyn with our entire medical practice. He takes excellent care of our finances; he's one hundred percent trustworthy. You also know that Sam Evers has been supporting Malachai through the festival planning process, and Sam has also said that everything is in good shape." He flashes the room the same smile he gives little kids right before a shot. "This is just a simple misunderstanding, and it probably has to do with Henri leaving in such a rush. Let's all stay calm. There's no need to jump to any conclusions."

There's another murmur throughout the room. Then someone calls out, "Say, where is Dr. Evers? Why isn't he here?"

My heart's beating so fast now that I'm starting to think I might actually know what a heart attack feels like. This isn't a heart attack, right? Can the stress of a stupid town meeting actually cause a person to have a heart attack?

More mumbling and grumbling. "Oh, for fuck's sake," Benson mutters. He stands up suddenly. "Seriously, everyone? You're actually listening to this crap? And Avon, you actually called an entire *town meeting* about this?" He shakes his head. "This could have been a quick phone call with Henri and the town council. But no. Clearly you just wanted a show here today."

"This isn't a show!" Avon shouts the words as he throws up his hands. "This is embezzlement! Well-hidden embezzlement, I'll give you that, but still embezzlement. The numbers I have show that last year's stipend was a fraction of what you've budgeted this year." He points the piece of paper he's still holding directly at me.

I throw up my arms like I'm surrendering to him. "I swear, I don't know what you're talking about! I didn't review any of the previous stipend amounts. Henri already had this year's amount in the budget when she left! This all must just be a mistake!"

But something in my stomach curls slightly, because now I remember: when I first looked at that stipend number, I thought for a moment that it seemed high, or higher than what I thought I remembered it being, anyway. But I wasn't sure, and I wanted that number to be right. I desperately *needed* that number to be right.

So I didn't say anything to anyone. And now I'm living with the consequences of that choice.

My face must read something of what I'm thinking right now, because Avon tilts his head slightly as he glares at me. "Well, there we have it," he announces to the town. "I think we can all see the guilt on his face. It's written right there for us. And we all know how desperate Malachai Flynn is to make extra money at any job he can. What more evidence do you all need? I think we all know exactly what happened here."

The world around me goes fuzzy. I vaguely hear someone shouting—Benson, I think—and there's more murmuring and grumbling from the crowd, and then I'm pretty sure other people are saying things but I can't seem to make them out. "Let's just call Henri now! She'll understand why we had to interrupt her," someone says loudly.

I let my eyes drift toward Sam's empty chair. As much as I appreciate Benson and Jack and Amelia all coming to my defense, it's clear to me as I fight for another breath that the only person I want here with me right now, as the entire town of Devon Falls debates my potential crimes, is Sam Evers. All I want is him by my side, wrapping his arms around me, making promises that everything will be alright, his strength reminding me that I can find my own strength.

But he isn't here. He can't be. He has a past life that matters more to him than I ever will, and that's okay. I understand that.

The noises around me get louder, more dissonant.

Breathe in. Breathe out.

It's okay, I tell myself. *You always knew you needed to leave. You've known for a long time that you're not meant for Vermont. You can do this.*

I stand up from my seat. "Everyone?" I say. The word comes out as a small squeak, but the room goes quiet as heads turn toward me.

"I promise you all," I tell them. "I promise that I never, ever tried to cheat anyone. I didn't know that stipend was more than the usual stipend. I'm sure Henri can explain what happened there." I draw myself up as I face Avon. "But this meeting makes it pretty clear that a lot of you in Devon Falls will never, ever trust me, and I understand that. So I resign as festival manager. There's no need to pay me the stipend."

Loud murmurs flow through the crowd again. "Malachai, seriously?" Benson hisses next to me. "This is just going to make you look more guilty to that asshole!" But I keep going.

"Dr. Evers—or maybe Amelia, if he's not here—can make sure the festival runs the way it's supposed to next week. At this point, everything's set up and ready to go. I think it's probably time I got out of Devon Falls." I glance back at Sam's empty chair and let out a chortled laugh that doesn't even sound like it comes from my body. "I mean, let's face it. I never really belonged here anyway. It's time I left."

And honestly? I don't care if leaving makes me look like the guiltiest person in the world. I just want to get the hell away from this place. From this town—this town where I was so, so very close to being happy for the first time in my entire life. Even if only for a moment.

I push back my chair and take off out of the room, ignoring Benson and Jack's calls behind me.

Breathe in, breathe out.

By the time I find my car, tears are already flowing down my face. I tell myself that's just because I'll miss so many parts of Devon Falls—Jack and Marie and Benson and Luis' sandwiches and the poop emoji statue. So many, many things.

But that's not what you'll miss the most.

I turn the ignition and let myself cry harder and harder over the sound of the engine.

Breathe in. Breathe out.

For the first time, I find myself wishing I'd never even met Dr. Sam Evers. Because leaving him behind feels like a thousand tiny pieces of glass are slowly shredding my heart, one inch of muscle at a time. I wonder what will be left of me when they're finally finished.

Chapter 24

7 Days to the Devon Falls Leaf Festival

I close my eyes and imagine Malachai, curled up in my bed against me, hair matted against the sheets, breathing softly around me.
—Sam Evers

I may not exactly have a reputation as the "life of a party," so to speak, but I can confirm I have been drunk in numerous unexpected places—many of them with Christian. I have been inebriated in, amongst other locations, a high school gymnasium, the back of a pickup truck, two invitation-only clubs in New York City, and a restaurant so fancy and expensive that their waitlist is eight months long.

Oh, and during a poolside orgy in Monaco. I didn't participate, but I did get *very* wasted. That was the night Colin unexpectedly won the Monaco Grand Prix.

Still, I do have to say that lying on the grass next to the tomato patch in Jack and Benson's backyard might be the strangest place I have ever been drunk.

How did I get here, exactly? That part's a bit unclear. I know it started with me coming back here from the winery after several failed hours of contacting everyone Colin knows. I know Jack and

Benson told me what happened at the town hall and I immediately tried to go after Avon and test my years of boxing skills on him, but they convinced me to look for Malachai first. I know all our attempts to find Malachai failed, and at some point Milo brought over beer.

I can't recall much of what happened after that.

"Sam, we're going to find them. You know that, right? Both of them."

I shake my head as I settle it back against my hands and stare down the stars populating the dark sky above me. Milo's words echo through my lightly pounding skull. "You don't know that. No one has seen or heard from Malachai since he ran out of the town hall, and he packed up everything he had at my house. And neither of them will fucking answer their phones, and you assholes won't even let me kill that asshole Avon Loseff!" I howl my final words at the sky.

Jack sighs. "We should have gone after Malachai right away. We screwed up, Sam, and I'm so sorry for that. But Benson was on the verge of a fistfight with Avon, and I was trying to keep that crowd calm." He shakes his head. "I thought Malachai needed some time to cool off. I didn't think he'd just pack up his things and disappear. I mean, hell, tomorrow's a work day at the office, and Malachai never no-shows at work. Plus he's halfway through the semester with his classes here..."

Jack goes on and on, and I manage to sit myself up on my elbows, still only half-listening as the world spins oddly around me. It's suddenly clear to me how well I understand Malachai in contrast to others. I would have run after Malachai immediately if I had stayed for the town hall meeting. I would have immediately known and understood how the accusations being thrown at him would trigger all the deep pain and abandonment that live within him. I would never have let him leave alone with his thoughts and his panic and his fears.

But you did leave him alone, a nasty voice reminds me. I cannot argue with it. I wasn't there for Malachai when he truly needed me the most. I knew that meeting had every potential to wreak havoc on Malachai's soul, and yet I chose to go looking for Colin instead of staying by his side.

At the time, the decision felt as though it made sense. I'll leave Devon Falls so soon—in less than a week. Staying with Malachai through difficult times won't be a long-term option for me no matter what. Leaving yesterday almost seemed like a natural progression of things, especially given Colin's fragile mental state after what I shared with him the other day.

Only now Malachai's alone, out somewhere with only his car and whatever small amount of money he has at the moment. I'm fully aware of Malachai's ability to take care of himself, of course. But the thought of him suffering as he must be right now, by himself and without anyone to comfort him...

That thought is a parasite living within me, slowly chewing me alive from the inside out.

"He has panic attacks," I finally say softly. "Bad ones."

Jack and Milo both turn to look at me. "Fuck," says Milo. He shakes his head.

Jack's eyes are wide. "How did I never know that?"

"I doubt anyone does. Malachai's very good at hiding his pain." I sink back down onto the ground, laying my head back on my arms. The massive amount of alcohol I drank earlier is starting to wear off now. I should find more, I think. Sobriety sounds downright repulsive right now. "Jack," I ask, "can you find us another bottle of that nice ice wine Tom loves so much? The one with the maple leaf label and the—"

"Samuel Lewis Evers!"

I sit up straight as a voice I know all too well makes contact with my slightly pounding head. "Mother?"

"Moms!" Milo leaps to his feet to hug Dr. Francis Evers while Jack shouts "Evelyn and Francis!" and quickly stands to embrace Evelyn Evers. I, meanwhile, stay put on the grass, my bottom all but melded to the ground.

"Why are you two here?" I finally manage to ask. Then my stomach catches up with me quite suddenly, and I turn to vomit into the tomatoes.

"You're supposed to be in Italy," I mutter as Mom, aka Evelyn, presses a cold washcloth to my head and holds up tea for me to sip.

Mother, aka Francis, snorts. "As if we were going to miss Benson and Jack's wedding. Especially once Marie told us about the spectacle it's become. Did you know the Vermont state cow's going to attend?"

"I heard something about that, yes," I murmur, as I inwardly curse the day that Jack and I introduced our parents to each other. They quickly became fast friends, and in my opinion they've held far too much collective power over us ever since.

"Then we heard from Tom that there was a crisis with Colin," Mom adds as she scoots into Jack's guest bed next to me and nudges me slightly. Her long, brown cornrows rustle against my skin, and somehow I'm immediately transported back to my days as a very young child when I was ill. Mom was the caretaker of our family, and she'd often lie in bed with me when I was sick, singing soft songs or reading me stories while I waited for the nausea or ear pain or fever to loosen its hold.

If only she had the power to make my feelings for Malachai loosen their hold. If only I was certain I wanted that.

Tom, who's sitting in a chair in the corner of the room next to Mother, groans. "Don't put your long-distance travel on me," he says. "All I did was tell you what was going on here when you asked. A simple text doesn't mean you have to hop on a transcontinental flight."

"Of course it did. Our boys were in trouble." Mother leans over to kiss Tom lightly on the forehead. She's the one who carried both me and Tom, using the same sperm donor each time, and Tom in particular looks very much like her. As she rubs her hand through his hair, it's impossible not to notice how nearly identical it is to her own blond hair, at least in the sections that aren't graying. Their eyes are a matched set, and I know my eyes match them both equally. She takes one of Tom's hands in hers. "Now. Catch us up on what the hell is going on here. Why is Colin missing? And who's this Malachai person everyone's so concerned with?"

Tom and I glance at each other. We don't have the same level of sibling telepathy that Christian and Colin have always seemed to share, but at that moment I know exactly what he's thinking. *Are you going to tell them?*

I close my eyes against the thoughts of Malachai that have crowded my brain so constantly for the past twenty-four hours. Where he is. What he's doing. Fears that he might be curled up in his car somewhere, alone and struggling to breathe. The types of worries, desperate and all-encompassing, that I never felt for Christian.

And for the first time, telling someone the truth about my marriage feels easy. Right. "Mom," I say. "And Mother. I need to tell you both something. About my marriage to Christian."

They let me talk for a long time, never interrupting. The two of them have always been good at that. I tell them about how our connection in our marriage dissipated more and more as time went on, and how easy it was to simply ignore the way whatever passion we once felt for each other slowly slipped away from us. I tell them about how we began spending more and more time apart, and about how I refused to go to the pool party that day—and I tell them about the guilt I may forever carry for what happened after that.

And then I begin telling them about Malachai.

"I know you both think, sometimes, that I've avoided you in the last few years. That's because it was just too hard to see the way you love each other." Mom glances over at Mother when I say that, and the two of them match their facial expressions in a short, sweet, very sad and personal smile—the kind I've been used to looking at since I was a child. "Yes, that," I add impatiently. "Exactly like that."

"It's nauseating sometimes, how much you two like each other," Tom says easily as he takes a sip from his water glass.

"Hey!" Mom sticks her tongue out at him and winks before she wraps her arms tightly around mine. "Go on, baby."

"Watching you two together just made it all the more obvious that something had been missing from my own marriage." I shake my head. "You all remember how fucked up I was after Christian passed."

Tom raises an eyebrow. "Swearing again, Sammy? I'm taking this as a good sign that you might finally break out of British headmaster mode." He tilts his head and frowns. "But yes, we remember."

"We were so frightened for you," Mother murmurs. "You were almost catatonic at times."

I remember that. I remember them taking turns with Milo and Jack and Colin to sit with me almost around the clock. "I was grieving," I tell them. "But not the way everyone thought. I think I was grieving..." I trail off, because even after all this time I still can't find quite the way to explain it.

"You were grieving what might have been and never was," Mom says softly.

She's so exactly right that I have to swallow against the rush of emotions her words send through my body. "Yes. That's it."

"Oh. Fuck," Tom whispers softly.

"And then I came to Vermont," I tell them. "And I saw Malachai. And within one conversation, every emotion I'd been grieving never having with Christian—well, there it was."

"Oh, hon." Mom gives me a tight hug, and the next thing I know Tom and Mother have joined us on the bed. The four of us barely fit on the full-size mattress, of course, but I'm suddenly so grateful to have my family surrounding me that I don't even care when Tom ends up nearly knocking the rest of us to the floor.

For a long time the four of us are silent, more or less just curled around each other in some strange Evers family puppy pile. Finally Mom says something. "Sammy, baby, you know that love looks a lot of different ways."

Tom sighs. "Oh, not the 'anyone of any gender can love anyone of any gender' talk again. Pretty sure we did that in elementary school and Sammy here took notes."

Mother snorts and smacks him in the arm. "I don't understand why all those movie executives put up with your sarcasm."

"It's part of my charm," he says sweetly.

"Anyway," Mom goes on as she rolls her eyes at Tom, "if you'll stop interrupting, son, what I'm trying to say is that not all love is the kind of all-encompassing passion your mother and I have—and we haven't had that for every single day and moment of our marriage. Love shifts. It changes. It moves and grows and adjusts, and sometimes it drifts and sometimes it returns."

Mother nods. "Baby, the three of us were all at your wedding. None of us ever doubted, not for one second, the love you felt when you stood up at that altar and married Christian. Maybe it wasn't exactly the love you thought it was. Maybe it changed over time. But you did love that man, sweetie. I'm sure of that. And I'm sure of another thing too." She leans across my legs, over Tom, and squeezes my hand. "Whatever your love looked like at the end, you were so important to Christian. And now that he's gone, he truly would want you to be happy."

Tears are running down my face now, foreign on my cheeks. I never cried much after Christian died; I never cry much at all, really. But now these tears are flowing like a force that feels as though I'll never get control of it again.

"For what it's worth, brother," Tom says, "You know I agree. Maybe Colin isn't ready to see what really matters now, but I do." He frowns. "Christian was a complicated man sometimes. But he cared about you, always. And the idea of you sitting alone in that apartment the two of you owned, punishing yourself for his death for the rest of your life..."

"He would never, ever want that," Mom finishes, and the three of them nod together.

I shake my head, gasping at the force and speed of tears that seem to be taking over my body. "Maybe you're right. Maybe you are. But Malachai... whatever's between us feels so much bigger than what Christian and I had. What if I've already lost any chance to see what we could be together? I've spent so much time telling him there can never be anything between the two of us." I can't even find the words to explain the depths of regret I feel for making someone like Malachai, someone so beautiful and bright in the world, possibly feel even less worthy of love than he already does. "I wouldn't blame him if he never wanted to see me the fuck again. And what if I do find him, and convince him to give me a second chance—and what if I screw things up again and end up hurting him as badly as I may have hurt Christian?"

Mom squeezes my other hand, and Tom grabs my shoulder, and now everyone in our family is holding onto me, grasping, like they're holding me together.

"There's always the chance you will hurt him," she says softly. "And always the chance he'll hurt you too, Sammy. Love is the greatest risk we ever take as humans," she adds. "Always. And like anything else, you'll both have to decide if the risk is worth the potential cost."

I close my eyes and imagine Malachai, curled up in my bed against me, hair matted against the sheets, breathing softly around me. Malachai, wide-eyed and deer like in his office chair. Malachai, flushed and panicky as he rushes from one place to another, determined to bring his best to every task he encounters.

Malachai, reaching his hands up to wrap them around my neck, whispering *sir* as he gives over all his trust to me.

I close my eyes against the tears. I grip my mothers' hands and send Tom a quick nod of thanks as he releases my shoulder.

"I think," I tell them, "that I've got to find my office manager. And then someone needs to let me murder the person who hurt him."

Chapter 25

5 Days to the Devon Falls Leaf Festival

The human touch I'm really craving is permanently off-limits. Forbidden. —Malachai Flynn

"You know, this isn't really where I'm supposed to be right now," I tell Sherbert as I muck out the stall next to his. "Not that there's anything wrong with mucking out stalls, of course. It's just that this actually isn't how I was planning to spend my day, so if you could at least get off your hind legs and stop staring at me while I shovel cow shit, I'd really appreciate it."

Sherbert stays right where he is, up on his hind legs as he eyes the large bucket of apples behind me.

"Fine. Whatever. Do what you want." I go back to shoveling crap and trying not to think too hard about the places I was supposed to be today before that disaster of a town hall knocked my plans for a one hundred and eighty degree loop.

I should be at Lancer Family Medicine. Or at the Devon Falls Leaf Festival grounds area, helping with setup.

I should be in Sam's house. Sam's kitchen. Sam's den. Sam's bedroom...

I blink hard as yet another image of him—very possibly the tenth one this hour—fills my vision. *Stop thinking,* I will myself one more time. Maybe this time my self-orders will stick. *Stop thinking about him and the way he'd pick you up in his arms, and the way he'd look at you across the table over a dinner that he'd cooked for you and—*

"Hey, are you doing okay there? You've been staring at our demon baby for quite some time now." I spin around to find Adam, one of Jeb's two partners, staring at me with a half smile on his face. "People generally don't find Sherbert comforting," he teases me gently.

I choke out a laugh. I like Adam. Like Jeb and Embry, he's easy to get along with. Calm. Cool. Well, Embry might not like to hear himself described as *cool.* He does a lot more grunting and grumbling than the other two. But all told, there's this general soft, calm sweetness about the three owners of the Stock Tree Farm, especially when they're together.

They've been nothing but kind to me since I showed up on their doorstep two days ago, asking if I could maybe start picking up extra work from them again. And when they realized that I'd found myself homeless yet *again*, they offered me their guest room. They're really good people. I was more than grateful when I took them up on the offer.

It's not like I had anywhere else to go or anywhere else to stay. By walking out of the town hall the way I had, I've essentially stuck myself between all the rocks and hard places imaginable. I don't have the money to make my down payment for nursing school because I gave up the festival stipend. I know I can never go back to Lancer Family Medicine. After what happened at that town hall meeting, working and living in Devon Falls again would be like standing permanently under one of those deadly icicles that lurk beneath window sills during Vermont winters. The kind that can take you out at any moment if you step the wrong way and it's got just enough melt to fall.

And I know I definitely can't stay with Sam anymore. That temptation is too large, and the potential payoff is too small. The risk of having him near me just isn't worth the reward anymore, and I finally understand that.

But I still have half a semester left in my community college classes, and I need those credits if I am ever going to get to Boston or another nursing school. I need money to live, and I barely had the gas money to get out of Devon Falls after making my last tuition payment.

So I didn't have a lot of options. Right now I'm feeling beyond lucky that Stock Tree Farm is in the heart of their fall pumpkin season and was more than excited to have some extra help corralling small children in their corn maze and shoveling the crap created by the menagerie of animals they collect and board in their many outbuildings.

"Sherbert and I are trying to come to an understanding," I tell Adam wryly, and he laughs loudly. Adam's some kind of PR guy from California, I'm told, and he somehow manages to look chic just standing in the middle of some animal pens. I find myself wondering how much his navy overalls and fur-lined boots cost and then quickly let go of that line of thought.

At some point, I'm just going to have to accept that some people are destined to have nice things, and I'm not one of them. That time I spent in Sam's rented farmhouse, with his bazillion thread count sheets and organic bacon and eggs and crackling fireplace, was probably as close as I'll ever come to living in luxury. At least I'll always have the memories of those days, however short they were.

"An understanding, huh?" Adam picks an apple out of the bucket and then eyes Sherbert patiently with one eyebrow lifted. For a moment it looks like he and Sherbert are locked in a permanent staring contest—but then Sherbert drops all four feet to the ground, batting his eyelashes at Adam, and Adam smiles as he tosses him the apple.

"Wow. Impressive," I tell Adam. "Now *that's* an understanding. My understanding with Sherbert is more like him temporarily deciding not to kill me and me appreciating the gesture."

Adam bursts out laughing again. "Fair enough," he eventually says. "Hey, do you want to come inside and join us for dinner?" He glances outside the barn window, where light is starting to fall through a bright Vermont sunset. "Embry's making burgers. And his semi-famous macaroni and cheese."

I shake my head and pick my shovel back up. "Thanks, but I'm okay. I've still got a lot of clean up to do here. And honestly, I'm not that hungry." The truth is that I don't think I've actually been actively hungry since that town hall meeting. Eating just feels like a chore right now.

So does sleeping. And waking up in the morning. And going to class. Existing in the world right now is like walking through hardening mud, and every step seems to get more and more difficult.

Adam purses lips together. "You know," he says slowly. "Jeb and Embry and me, we don't like to pry. And you're welcome to stay here as long as you like, Malachai, whether you want to keep working for us or not. We all understand what it's like to find yourself... well, at loose ends, I guess. We all know what it's like to need a little help."

The kindness in his voice is so clear, so strong, that I almost drop the shovel and rush him for a hug. I'm starting to wonder if I was maybe a little touch-starved before I met Sam Evers, because after the events of the past few weeks I find myself craving another human's skin against mine.

Too bad the human touch I'm really craving is permanently off-limits. Forbidden.

"Thanks," I tell Adam. "The three of you have been so great to me since I showed up here. I really can't thank you enough." I'm just about to say something about how I'm not used to this much kindness from other people—but that's not true at all, I realize quickly. There was so much kindness in Devon Falls before I set the wheels in motion to destroy my relationships there.

Especially from the Lancers. And Benson. Especially from Sam. My stomach jolts again as I think about how I've left them in the lurch. I couldn't even give the Lancers official notice. I just left a quick message on their office answering machine telling them thanks for everything, but I wouldn't be coming back. They always knew, of course, that it was likely I'd be leaving at the semester, but now I'd left them completely high and dry. Who are they even going to get to answer the phones while they hire a new office manager? I can't imagine how pissed they must be.

And Sam? There's no way I could possibly say goodbye to him, even after all he's done for me. That kind of thinking is too dangerous—another icicle threatening to murder me just because I've stepped in the wrong direction.

"Anyways," Adam says again. "We're not going to pry. But the three of us are here to listen if you ever want to talk. And we couldn't help but notice that some, um, gossip has been coming through the Devon Falls grapevine about you."

I groan and cover my face. "It's okay if you need to fire me," I whisper through my dirty work gloves.

"Jesus, no." Adam rolls his eyes as I drop my arms back by my side. "Listen, I know Avon Loseff, okay? We sell his family's products here, and I do branding work for them too. I don't think he's a bad guy. But I do think he's got some serious fucking trauma he never worked through, and sometimes walking around like that will make a person lash out."

I shrug. "Maybe. Or maybe he was just trying to protect the good people of Devon Falls from a con artist and career criminal."

Adam scoffs. "Malachai, anyone who's spent more than five minutes with you knows damn well that you're not some kind of career criminal." He shrugs. "You just got painted into a wall by life and started jumping on the paint to get out, and then you tracked some paint with you when you left the room. It's happened to a lot of us and no one ever knows when it might happen to them next. People like Avon sometimes forget that." Sherbert comes trotting back over to us, sending the apple bucket more side-eye.

"I don't know." I shake my head. "I can't stop thinking that I deserve everything that's happened to me. I put the town in danger last year. I guess I was an idiot for thinking a mistake like that would ever go away."

Another image of Sam's face flashes through my brain. *And I was an idiot for thinking I could have any small part of Dr. Evers—even a part without strings.*

Adam purses his lips. "Did you know that Embry and Jeb and I actually all went to college together?" he eventually asks.

"No," I tell him. It doesn't exactly surprise me, though. With the kind of closeness these three have, it only makes sense that they've known each other for years.

"Yup. We spent all of college basically cuddling in bed together every night. And the entire time all three of us thought the other two were straight."

"Seriously?" I say. I still don't see where he's going with this story, but at least it's taking my mind off my all-rocks-and-hard-places situation for a minute.

"Seriously," Adam says with a grin. Then his facial expression settles into something wistful and sad. "But something went down between me and Embry. I'll spare you the details; let's just say we hurt each other. Badly. And there were a lot of years where I thought I'd never ever speak to him again. A lot of years where I thought I'd messed up one of the best friendships I could ever have in my life."

"No way." I can't even bother to try and hide my surprise. Embry and Adam, as much as they appear to be polar opposites, are basically attached at the hip. The two of them and Jeb seem like some sort of unique three-piece puzzle that could never possibly exist with one piece missing. It's hard for me to even imagine Jeb without Embry or Adam, and vice versa. "I'm sorry," I say. "That must have been awful."

"Oh yeah, it sucked balls. Anyway," he goes on, "I'm not sure exactly why I'm telling you all this. Except that Jeb just picked this message up off the farm's voicemail." He hands me a piece of paper, folded up in quarters. I take my time pulling off my barn gloves and reaching for it, and then I take even more time slowly unfolding it.

The message there is short and simple. *I'm looking for Malachai Flynn. If you've seen him, please have him call me immediately. And tell him I'll be taking care of his problems with Avon Loseff. Sam Evers.*

I sink down onto a hay bale behind me, trying to ignore the hard straw that immediately pokes up through my threadbare jeans. Another picture of Sam flashes into my head, and it's as though I can hear his voice through the piece of paper, all orders and directness and power. I close my eyes against the searing pain that seems to follow from that hard piece of straw down through my body.

"There were a few other messages too," Adam goes on. "I guess we were prime suspects as parties that might be hiding you. Benson Lewis' message was a little more pointed than some of the others."

I choke back a laugh, imagining what kind of message Benson might have left on the Stock Tree Farm voicemail.

"But that message." Adam shrugs. "That's the one that seemed the most important." Adam steps over to one of the pigs and pats it gently on the head. The pig squeals, and I try for a moment to remember its name—something with food. Stock Tree Farm seems to house a lot of pets with edible monikers.

But asking Adam about that trend is the furthest thing from my mind right now. All I can think about is that message. Why would Sam be reaching out to me now? He's leaving the state in less than a week. And then I realize what this message is really about: he wants to say goodbye. He'll talk to Avon Loseff to make up for not being at the town hall. Then in his perfect, dark tone with all his perfect formal language, he'll remind me again why we can never be together and why he has to leave. And then he'll climb into his million dollar car and drive off into the distance, and I'll still be stuck here with no future, with no one to look forward to seeing at the end of a long day, with no one to hold me or remind me to breathe.

The most dangerous part of letting yourself finally be important to someone is what happens when they decide you aren't important to them anymore. I didn't understand that before, but I do now. I hand the piece of paper back to Adam.

"You don't need to worry about taking down any more messages for me," I tell him. "There's no one I need to talk to." I swallow hard, and then I pick up the shovel I've been holding and go back to moving shit from one pile to another. Back and forth, over and over again.

Behind me. Adam sighs. "I get it," he finally says. "I really do. But listen, there's one more thing you should know, okay?"

I don't answer.

"Those years that Embry and I weren't speaking," he says. "I'd do anything in the whole world to get them back."

He leaves, and the light keeps falling down the barn windows until I'm finally standing in pitch-black darkness.

Chapter 26

4 Days to the Devon Falls Leaf Festival

I'll leave if you want me to. —Sam Evers

"So you've finally gone full-on stalker, then?"

My brother's voice is high and light on the other end of the phone, but his words are a terrible reminder of just how dire my own situation has become. I lean back against the Rover's hood and sigh. "I'm not stalking Malachai, Tom. I'm simply waiting outside of the community college for his evening class to be over."

"Sure sounds like stalking to me." Tom sighs. "I get it, though. You haven't had any luck getting ahold of him at Stock Tree Farm? Gabe swears he's working there."

"You spend an awful lot of time talking to Gabe," I muse as I stare at the tiny industrial building that makes up the entirety of the Devon Falls Community College campus.

"Well, I'm staying at the winery, and he's working the front desk. Anyway, Gabe promised me he just saw Malachai there yesterday."

"Then he's certainly ignoring my messages. And Jack's, and Marie's, and Benson's." I frown as I consider the ramifications of that statement. It's not exactly surprising that Malachai would be distancing himself from all of us after everything that I'm told happened in the town hall meeting the other day. But the fact that he's working so very hard to avoid us—he even gave notice at Lancer Family Medicine without directly speaking to anyone—is concerning.

The large glass-and-metal door at the front of the building swings open, and a handful of people start to spill out of it. "Tom, I need to go," I tell him.

"Good luck! Have fun storming the castle!" he calls out as I end the call and slide the phone into my pocket. I study the crowd of departing students, faculty, and staff carefully. The Vermont evening has already fallen into darkness, and it's difficult to discern exact faces in the thin, yellowing light falling from the campus' parking lot lamps. I squint at the crowd, catching the moments of hope in my breath. What if he isn't here? What if he's dropped out of school? What if he's decided to leave Vermont altogether, and I missed any chance I might have had to see him again at the Stock Tree Farm? What if—

And then his face appears, set aglow by the shadows of perfectly cast lamplight. *Malachai.*

He waves to someone he's walking out with and then sets off across the parking lot. I didn't see his car parked here earlier, and I wonder where it might be. He's moving faster over the pavement now, toward a bus stop near the bottom of the campus' driveway, and I realize that the clock is ticking back against my chances to speak to him.

I pull in a long breath, eschewing the panic I feel over the importance of this moment, and I start following him. I don't want to startle him with my presence, and the parking lot is already emptying quickly around us, so I call his name when I'm still several feet away.

"Malachai."

He whirls around, something like fear falling over his facial features. Then he sees me, and his eyes go wide with shock.

"You're not supposed to be here," he whispers.

I take a step closer to him. "I'm not?" I ask casually. "I was under the impression this was a public campus." I take a step closer, quickly cataloging every inch of him. He looks thinner than when I last saw him days ago, his cheekbones slightly more sunken. The circles that seem to rest under his eyes in perpetuity are even darker than usual. I take another step closer to him, and then I pause when he steps back.

"I'll leave if you want me to," I tell him in a soft whisper. "I promise you that. If you want me to leave, just say the word. I'll go."

He doesn't speak.

"But if you're amenable to a conversation, I'd really like to talk to you, Malachai."

He purses his lips and takes a step back away from me again, and then another one towards me, almost like he's dancing back and forth. Closer, then away. Away, and then closer. He shakes his head. "I can't," he finally whispers. "I told you no strings, Sam. I promised you that. But after what happened at the town hall I realized I can't actually do that, not the way I thought I could, and I know we can never be together like that, and—"

I cross the pavement in three easy steps and lift him off the ground and into my arms as I capture his mouth against mine.

For several long, slow moments after that the world is nothing but the touch of his lips against mine, the feeling of his tongue swirling in rhythm with my own, the sensation of his breath and skin and nerves coming together against mine. Every cell in my body is on heightened alert, as they so often are when Malachai and I are in any kind of contact. He pushes and pulls against me, writhing in my arms, and then eventually pulls back from me, panting and clinging to me as his head falls against my shoulder.

"I can't do this," he whispers against my wool sweater. "You can't do this. Forbidden, remember?"

I nuzzle my lips against his ear. "What if... what if it wasn't?"

Malachai jerks up in my arms stiffly. I gently drop him to the ground, where he stares at me, baffled, as he clutches his backpack straps.

"What are you talking about?" he asks.

I run my hand under his chin, the way I like to do, studying how his hair falls against his forehead in the soft light of the moon and the lamps. "I think you and I need to talk," I tell him. "May I take you home? To my home?" To *our* home, I desperately want to add, but Malachai seems so very close to some kind of edge right now—I fear spooking him and sending him off to a place I cannot reach, either physically or emotionally.

Malachai shakes his head. "This campus is as far as I'll go into Devon Falls right now," he mumbles, his eyes on the parking lot beneath us.

I shouldn't be surprised, I suppose, that he's avoiding the town that so recently and abruptly rejected him. Still, he hasn't refused to come with me; I must take advantage of that. "I know where we'll go," I tell him. "Your car's not here?"

He shakes his head and shuffles his feet. "Not enough gas money right now. Someone gave me a ride from La Fierte. I figured I'd take a bus or hitchhike back."

I manage not to growl aloud at the idea of him hitchhiking.

I hold out my hand. "Come with me?" It's a question, not an order.

He tilts his head carefully up at me, as though he's deeply studying and considering my words. Then, just as the breath I'm holding begins to catch in my throat, he reaches out his own hand and drops it into mine.

"Okay," he says. "We can talk."

"Um, what are we doing at the winery?" Malachai squints up at the large converted farmhouse I've parked in front of and then frowns. "This is still in Devon Falls, Sam," he reminds me wryly.

"I know that." I smile over at him in the driver's seat. There's little light in the winery's driveway, just the shadow of pathway lamps mixed with those from the outbuildings around the inn. "But if the community college is safe territory, I assumed this was as well. They're both on the outskirts."

Malachai raises an eyebrow and studies me, and my heart beats ever so slightly faster in my chest as he makes his decision. "I'll allow it," he finally says.

I swallow down my relief. "Very good," I tell him. My phone pings with a text, which I check as Malachai unbuckles his seat belt.

Tom: Operation room-switch is a go. Moms and I are at your place. I left you a key for my room at the front desk. Enjoy!

Tom: Oh, and don't fuck this up, big brother.

My brother has his own very unique style of encouragement.

I step out of the Rover and stand next to Malachai in the driveway. "I can't stay that long," he tells me. "I have to work at the—I have to work in the morning."

I wonder if he knows that I already know where he's working. And does that make me a stalker? Even if it does, I can't regret it. Not knowing where he is, what he's doing... I've quickly realized in the past few days how much that lack of knowledge can unsettle me.

"Where do you want to talk?" Malachai asks unsteadily.

I understand, then, exactly how much rests on the conversation we're about to have. And I know what I need to do with this moment of time Malachai is giving me: I need to prove to him that he's become the most important thing in the world to me and that I'm ready to show him exactly what place he holds in my heart.

"Follow me," I tell him, in the gruff, demanding voice I know he can't resist. His eyes widen slightly, but he follows my lead up a few steps to the wraparound porch and then through the front door into the inviting space of the winery's front room. Soft jazz music plays in the background, and the rustic farmhouse decor is accented with tasteful reminders of the winery right next door. The front desk is being watched by Gabe.

"Malachai!" he blurts out. "I didn't expect to see you here! Does this mean you two are—"

Something in one of our faces must send him the right message, because he quickly closes his mouth. "Here's the room key, Dr. Evers." He hands over an actual key, attached to a mauve keychain shaped, of course, like a bottle of wine. He leans across the desk. "Listen, your brother told me to give it a quick clean, and, um do that other stuff you wanted? I hope I got it all right."

I have no idea what Tom might have requested he do, but I'm not particularly interested in stopping to chat just now. So I simply nod.

Malachai's silent behind me as he follows me up to the room. I'm not surprised to see him staring wide-eyed around us. This inn is all the town of Devon Falls seems to be talking about now that it's finally open: it's been fully remodeled and expanded, designed to appeal to both local clients and out-of-towners searching for a luxury Vermont luxury experience. Subtly expensive furniture dots corners, historical photos and paintings on the wall hit the right mark of tasteful yet intriguing, and all the creams and grays and whites that color the walls and carpets manage to be soft and soothing without being dull.

"It's like your house," Malachai mumbles. I'm not sure if intended for me to hear that, and I'm tempted to ask him exactly what he meant—but we arrive at the Room 8, just off the top of the stairs, and I choose to focus on unlocking the door and ushering him inside before he can change his mind about coming with me tonight in the first place.

I gesture for Malachai to step inside. He frowns, nods, walks in, and immediately gasps loudly.

I follow after him and close the door behind me, and then I immediately begin cursing my brother internally. *Fucking Tom.*

"Is this... real?" Malachai asks.

I'm somewhat tempted to ask the same thing. The jetted tub up on a raised platform in the corner of the room is certainly real, and exactly the kind of feature my brother would request in a room for a long-term stay. The giant four-poster bed, complete with hanging sheer curtains and a mound of pillows as big as my arm, is also certainly real.

The rose petals dotting every inch of space? The battery-operated candles casting light from all the surfaces of the room? The bottle of sparkling wine that sits on top of the room's sideboard table, carefully flanked by two glasses and a bottle opener? Those all look like they could be something out of a child's prank.

And given that my brother basically *is* a child, I suppose in some way they are.

I grab Malachai's hand. "I'm sorry if this upsets you right now," I tell him carefully. "This is my brother's room, and I—"

Malachai twists on his feet as he finally looks away from the rose petals and candles to study me. "Why would you think this would upset me?" he asks carefully.

"Because," I tell him. "Because I—"

I stop as I lose the words. But Malachai waits. Of course he does; he's always so very patient with me. He waits. And eventually, the words come back to me.

"Because I was wrong," I finally manage to say. I pull his hands into mine and tug them against my chest. "I was wrong to think that my feelings for you were ever something to be ignored. I was wrong to ever make you feel like anything other than the superbly wonderful and brilliant human being you are. I was wrong to think that my past needed to prevent us from having a future together. And I was wrong to leave you alone with Avon Loseff that day." I can't stop the growl that escapes me then as my eyes narrow. "I've scheduled a meeting with him, by the way. I'll make certain he doesn't bother you ever again."

Malachai's eyes are growing larger, saucers of white shock against his pale skin. He clutches at my hand, and that's somehow all the encouragement I need.

"And because," I tell him. "Because I put my past and my issues above your needs. Because I abandoned you when you needed me the most, and you deserved better. But no amount of rose petals and candles and booze can ever possibly right that wrong."

Malachai's studying me carefully now, almost the way someone studies a Sudoku puzzle or word search they can't quite solve. He tilts himself up on his tiptoes.

"I want to believe this is real," he says, his voice hoarse with some kind of emotion that I worry I don't fully understand. "I want to believe you mean everything you're saying right now." He shakes his head. "But I don't get too many good things coming to me, Sam. And when I do? I always seem to fuck them up somehow."

I pull my hand from his and ghost it across his face. "My mother says that love is the greatest risk we ever take as humans," I tell him. "I'd understand if you felt I wasn't worth that risk after everything I've put you through. But I came to find you tonight because *you* are worth any risk in the world. I'm in love with you, Malachai. And I'm done trying to tell myself, and my ghosts, and the rest of the world, that I'm not."

"Sir," Malachai whispers. And just as it always does, that word sends me across the edge of the cliff I'm forever trodding next to with Malachai.

He leans up as I lean down, and we fall against each other.

Chapter 27

4 Days to the Devon Falls Leaf Festival

Any order he gives me right now? I'm taking it. —Malachai Flynn

Did I have "sleep with my estranged former boss and landlord in the most romantic hotel room in all of Vermont" on my bingo card today? No, I certainly did not. My entire to-do list for the day consisted of fishing crying children out of a corn maze, working on a chemistry lab assignment, and then probably crying into one of Jeb Stock's pillows. But here I am, somehow, in the middle of yet another fantasy enacted by the man who seems to conjure my fantasies out of thin air at will.

It's hard to think about what this day was supposed to look like, though, when Dr. Sam Ever's body is *this fucking close* to mine once again, and every nerve is my body feels stretched so tightly that it could snap at any moment.

I pull away from him, panting. "Sir, I—"

His eyes darken, dangerously. "Oh, you should not have said that," he growls. The hard, commanding tone of his voice does exactly what it always does to me: brings my dick to attention while shattering every single one of my fucking inhibitions and better judgements. He begins to unbuckle his belt. "Safe word is still ice cream, yes?"

I nod so hard I'm kind of amazed I don't give myself whiplash. My thoughts are a wind tunnel of everything Sam's said to me in the last few minutes and the scene in front of me. I can't even start to process what he just told me—that he wants to be with me? That he's in love with me? That he plans to take down Avon Loseff for me? But there's no room to process any of that right now, not while Dr. Fucking Sam Evers is tossing his belt to the floor and demanding to know what my safe word is.

Hormones now, thinking later.

"Take your clothes off," Sam whispers as he begins to unbutton his shirt. "And then get on your knees."

The darker undertones of his voice have me actually shaking as I manage to get out of my clothes and kneel before him. My cock is already half-hard, ready for whatever this evening is going to turn into, and soon the warm room is like a blanket wrapping Sam and me closer and closer together. He takes my hand and leads me backward, with me walking on my knees, until he reaches an antique armchair patterned in—what else?—roses.

He drops his pants and boxers to his shoes and sinks down into it. "Cockwarm me, Malachai," he orders.

"Yes, sir." I drop my head into his lap and take his half-hard dick in my mouth, and what happens then is so hard to categorize or explain: it's like my head just *empties.* Like all my anxiety and worry and the thoughts of everything I'm supposed to be doing and should be doing and the past and future just ooze out of my skull, until all that exists is Sam stroking my hair, his cock settled warmly in my mouth. This is the job I need right now, and focusing on it is just so fucking *peaceful.*

"Such a good boy," Sam whispers as he runs his hands back and forth between my forehead, neck, and over my skull. "Such a good boy for me."

I swear, my cock instantly fucking hardens at the words *good boy.*

"I've missed you," he whispers. "I've missed every part of you since you left, Malachai. The sound of your laughter echoing through the house. The feeling of your skin against mine in the middle of the night. Our dinner conversations. And I've missed the way your body feels when it's wrapped around mine, the way you hold me so tightly inside of you..."

I groan around his cock, and he laughs softly as he moves his hands down my neck and begins to massage my shoulders.

"I'm so sorry it took me so long to get my head out of my ass, Malachai. You leaving was a wake-up call I clearly needed. But I promise that I'm here now. Ready to be yours. Forever, or for as long as you'll have me."

I'm so fucking high on adrenaline and endorphins that I feel like I'm only half-processing what he's saying, and the words swirl together confusingly in my brain. Is Sam really offering this to me? A future? A new beginning?

He drives powerful thumbs into my shoulder blades, and his cock hardens further in my mouth. I groan again.

"I could be your Sir forever. Order you to do this for me every single night," he whispers. "And then so much more..." he traces a finger down my cheek, and I shiver involuntarily. "Are you ready for more now, Malachai? Are you ready for more of my orders?"

I nod hard against his thigh. He gently lifts my head from his cock, holding my face in his hard hands.

"Then I order you," he says, "to take what you want from me. And the entire time you're taking what you want, what you need, I order you to tell me exactly what you want from me when we have a life together—what you need from me as your partner."

The order's so big, so much bigger than what I'm expecting, that I can feel tears running down my cheeks as I nod in agreement. It's like every emotion I've been holding tightly within my body is losing its tension all at once. But there's no way I'd ever have the capacity to say no to Dr. Evers right now. Any order he gives me right now? I'm taking it.

He helps me up from the floor as he kicks off his pants and shoes and then sheds his unbuttoned shirt behind him. He scoops me up in his arms, my skin tingling more with each and every moment that it makes more contact against his, and he carries me over to the large bed in the center of the room.

He lays me down gently on the bed before lying down next to me, arms stretched over his head, then stops and frowns for a moment as he sits back up. "Just a second," he mutters. He rummages in the bedside drawers and then suddenly laughs and he pulls out a bottle of lube and a box of condoms. "My brother, always prepared." He lays back down again as he runs another hand over my cheek. "Take what you want, Malachai. That's an order. The lube is required; the condoms are your choice. You know I trust you implicitly. And as you take what you want from me here, now, tell me what you want from me forever. What you *need.*"

"Yes, sir," I whisper. His first order? I'm more than fucking certain I can do that right now. Sam's cock is on full display in front of me, hard and ready, and all I want at this moment is to feel him inside my body.

But the second thing he's asking me to do? I'm not so sure I can do that. I guess we'll just have to see.

"If you want what I think you want," Sam growls in a low tone, "you better start getting yourself ready."

His words spur me to action. "Yes, sir!" I lean over to find the lube where he's dropped it on the bed, and then I straddle him as I take my time prepping myself, first with one finger, then two, then three. This whole anal sex thing is still *really* new to me, and I want to enjoy myself when I sink down onto Sam in a few moments.

Because what if this really is the last time I get that chance? That thought jolts through me. He's lying here, swearing that he wants more... swearing he wants everything with me. But it all feels too good to be true or real.

I'm not the kind of guy whose dreams come true. I'm just not. That thought is like a cloud of black ink running through my sex-addled brain, but at least now I think I know what to tell him about what I really want from him in the future.

He's stroking his cock back and forth, up and down, with one hand. "Sir, please lube yourself up. But no condoms," I tell him, because I do trust him and I don't want anything between us right now. He takes care of dripping lube down his cock and then stroking it over himself, and I nearly come just watching the movement of his long fingers.

If I'm not careful, I'm not going to last much longer and I know it. So I straddle him, placing my hands down on his chest, and I lower myself onto his body.

The movement definitely burns at first. My body's still not quite used to this sensation, this fullness. But I push down and breathe out, and it isn't long before he's inside of me and I'm whimpering against the fucking *fullness* of it all.

"Sir," I whisper, stuck in place on this cock. "Oh, sir..."

He runs his hands up and down my hips, then up to my chest. He teases my nipples, drifting fingers back and forth over them, and I cry out.

"Move, Malachai," he orders. "Move for me. Take what you need, and tell me what you need forever."

Sparks are flying through my head, and there's almost a buzzing sound running in my brain, as I begin to move up and down on him—slowly at first, but then his cock starts pushing harder against me, against that spot—every single nerve in my body is at attention and demanding me to go faster, so I do, moving up and down, more and more quickly as I brace myself against his chest with my hands.

"Tell me," he urges as he holds onto my hips. "Tell me everything you need from me."

"I need this!" I blurt out. "I need you to be in control of me, to take care of me, because no one else ever fucking has, okay? Because I always had to take care of myself, and I like when you do it!"

"Yes." He growls the word. "Keep fucking going, Malachai."

"I need to belong to you. I know Christian will always matter to you, and I love that about you. But I need to believe that I belong to you now, that I belong with you—I've never belonged with anyone before."

He thrusts up inside of me and moans, and I almost come, but he gives the tip of my cock a quick pinch, making me howl. "No coming yet," he orders. "Keep talking, Malachai."

"Yes, sir." I rock myself up and down, back and forth, barely aware of the sounds I'm making as I take everything he's giving me. "I want... a safe space. A place I can finally be where no one's telling me I'm shit, where someone's always there to take care of me if I need it. A place where I can screw up and know it's not going to be the end of the fucking world, okay? Where I'm not going to end up sleeping in my car or on some barn floor."

I'm crying now, I realize, as Sam reaches up to wipe a tear from my face with his thumb. "Oh, Malachai," he says softly. "Oh, my darling."

That word undoes me. I come all over his stomach as well as mine, and I scream so loudly that other people in the inn definitely have to hear, but I don't care. Every fear, every hope, every dream I've ever had feels like it's rushing out of me as I come across my own body and Sam's, and then he's coming too, shaking and shouting and he holds down my hips and loses himself in me.

I lift myself off of him, fast, and I fall across his chest, still crying. He wraps his arms around me, holding my body firmly against his.

"Oh my darling," he says again. "Oh my good, sweet, boy. You'll never, ever have to be alone again. I promise."

Every ounce of energy has been drained out of me, and I lay there like a log as he cleans us both up and runs a bath with oils and bath salts in the jetted tub that sits in the corner of the room. He carries me over to it, sinking me onto his lap inside of the warm water, and we sit there for a long time, silently.

Finally, Sam speaks again. "Will you stay with me?" He whispers. "Will you accept my apology, Malachai? Will you let me be everything you need?"

I gulp down the urge to say yes. It would be so easy to agree, to nod and try to move forward and just hope that for once I can somehow hold tight to the gift I've always wanted as it's handed to me.

But I've believed in dreams like that before. I thought when I came to Devon Falls that I'd finally found someplace safe. Someplace where I even mattered, maybe? And it didn't take me long to wreck that.

Whatever this is? I'll wreck it too. Or something will go wrong. Maybe he'll change his mind about letting go and moving on from Christian. I don't know. He hasn't mentioned anything about Colin. Is Colin still missing? What if he comes back? What if he reminds Sam of everything he's fully letting go of to be with me?

It takes me a long time to answer Sam, but I finally do.

"I know you said love is a risk," I finally tell him. "And I think you're right."

He tightens his arms around me.

"I've taken a lot of risks in my life," I go on. "They haven't really panned out for me. My mom took a lot of risks too, once, or so she tells me. They didn't really pan out for her either."

"Oh, Malachai." Sam buries his head into my neck.

"I guess I'm just worried this will be one more risk that blows up in my face. I believe everything you're saying, Sam. But you've spent a lot of time telling me that you can never be with me, and I've never doubted that. So everything you're offering right now feels like a really massive, massive risk. And one more failed risk... well, I don't know what that would do to me. I don't know if I want to find out, you know?"

"I understand," he says quickly as he kisses my neck in rapid-fire bursts. "I completely understand, my darling. I have a lot to make up for with you. I have a lot of work in front of me to prove that I will never, ever put your heart at risk again."

"No, you don't." I shake my head, sending droplets of water across the tub. "I know you'd never try to hurt me, Sam. And you needed time to deal with losing Christian. I understand all that. I guess I'm just saying that I trust *you,* but I'm not sure I'm ready to trust *this*. Or myself."

Sam wraps his arms harder around me. "I'll do whatever it takes," he says. "To prove to you that you can believe in this. Believe in *us*, Malachai."

I settle back into his arms, because more than anything, I want to believe he's right—that he can cast another one of his spells over me and I'll stop feeling like this is all a fever-dream. One I know I'll wake up from at any moment.

We go to bed together, and I do my best to fall asleep. But sleep won't come. So I lay there, for hours, listening to Sam's breath and watching the moonlight cast shadows across his body.

And finally, I know what I need to do. I get up, I get dressed, and I find a pad of paper on the dresser. I write a note.

Dear Sam,

Sorry about taking off like this. I'm not leaving the state or anything. I just need some time to think. In La Fierte, though. I'm really not sure if I can come back to Devon Falls anymore, except when I have to, for class. If you're still here after Benson and Jack's wedding and the festival, I think you know where to find me.

Thank you for tonight. Thank you for the roses and the bath and thank you for everything else you've done for me. You gave me so much more than I think you'll ever realize, Sam. I hope you know that.

I'm sorry I might be too much of a chickenshit to take this risk. I hope you understand.

For what it's worth, I think I've loved you since the first moment I saw you.

Love,

Malachai

P.S. Please tell Jack and Benson I'm really sorry I'll miss their wedding. And I'm sorry for everything else, too.

I set the note down on the table next to Sam, and I watch his chest rise and fall in the moonlight for a long time. Eventually, I creep out of the room, half-hoping he hears me and wakes.

But when I finally push the door of the room open, he never stirs.

Chapter 28
2 Days to the Devon Falls Leaf Festival

Milo's just given me an idea. —Sam Evers

"This is a pretty gangster plan, Sam." Benson glances around the office we're standing in, studying the walls covered with gold-plated awards and photos of happy farmers standing next to happy cows. I guess one does want to celebrate when one wins The Best Rocky Road in New England honor four times in a row.

"Gangster?" I snort. "We're standing in the office of a man who oversees the making of ice cream for a living, and you're carrying a manilla folder and wearing a flannel shirt."

Benson sighs. "Yeah. Wow, it's amazing how much Devon Falls can tighten up your perspective on the world, huh?" He nudges me in the arm with his elbow. "Still, this plan is pretty badass. You making an appointment to see Avon at his office so you can scare the fuck out of him."

I adjust the collar of my button-up shirt. "I've got no exact plans to 'scare the fuck' out of anyone. I'm just going to make it clear that Avon better make sure he never, ever harms Malachai Flynn again. Ever."

Benson laughs out loud and claps me on the back. "See? Gangster!"

Thankfully, his ridiculous enthusiasm is interrupted when the door behind us opens and Avon Loseff comes strolling into the office. He's wearing khakis and a polo shirt with the words LOSEFF CREAMERY emblazoned on the upper right hand chest area, and his ridiculous haircut is bouncing around his forehead, just as it always seems to be. His eyes narrow when he sees the two of us standing in front of his desk. "My secretary said two members of the town wanted to see me. He neglected to mention who they were."

I smirk, because that's my doing. I diagnosed Tim Fabro's tonsillitis last month. He owed me.

"How unfortunate," I tell Avon. "Did you not wish to see us today?"

Avon snorts and looks back and forth between me and Benson with that same sneer of derision I'm beginning to think he might have a patent on. "I don't associate with thieves," he says as he saunters by us and falls into his desk chair. "So get out of my office now before I call the police and have you both arrested for trespassing."

"Oh, there's bad news on that plan," Benson tells him, deadpan. "For one thing, the local sheriff loves me. She says my humor is a breath of fresh air or something? I don't get it, exactly, but there we are. And for another thing, we're not trespassing and Malachai Flynn isn't a thief." He tosses the folder he's carrying down on Avon's desk, looking triumphant.

Avon's eyes somehow manage to narrow further. "What the hell is that?" he asks.

"Actual research," I tell him. "Research which took Benson and I approximately thirty minutes to do. Research you could have easily done yourself if you hadn't decided to needlessly destroy another human. That's a signed affidavit from Henri confirming that she raised the festival manager stipend this year in accordance with a town council ordinance passed three years ago saying that the festival stipend should be raised regularly according to inflation rates."

Avon grabs the folder from the desk and throws it open. "You're lying." He practically hisses the words as he begins reading.

"Nope, not even a little," Benson tells him cheerfully. "Oh, and that she did add some additional funds to Malachai's stipend for taking on the work so last-minute, but that was also in accordance with a town ordinance that I'm sure you never bothered to check. Everything about Malachai's stipend was completely on the level, and Henri's pissed as hell about what you did, Avon."

"Normally, this is about the time we'd all be demanding that you apologize." I cross my arms and walk around to the side of Avon's desk, careful to place myself just far enough into his personal space. "But Malachai's determined not to return to Devon Falls ever again. Thanks to you."

Avon's face seems to be getting progressively paler as he reads the affidavit. "This isn't—I didn't—" he stutters.

I've heard enough. I slam my hand down on his desk, enjoying the way he jumps in his seat, drops the folder and leans away from me. Fear is written into his eyes now, and I won't deny that it makes me feel good. "You did!" I shout. "You did all of it! You made an accusation with no research or evidence behind it, in front of an entire town, and you drove a good, kind, young man away from the place he called home!"

And I didn't stop you, or stop him from leaving me. But that's my guilt to live with, guilt I'll spend the rest of my life making up for, should Malachai decide to let me. But this moment, this confrontation, isn't about my guilt. It's about Avon Fucking Loseff.

He harmed Malachai, and I will not let that stand.

Benson's standing at the other side of the desk, arms crossed and mouth turned upward in a hint of amusement. I'm not remotely surprised he's enjoying this scene. Avon's cheeks are turning a shade of pink now. "He's a criminal," Avon whispers, more to the desk than to me or Benson. "He spent all that time with those criminals, and they're awful people! They made my life a living hell the entire time they were here! They deserved everything they got last year, and Malachai—"

I've heard enough. I grab Avon by the shirt and jerk him up out of his chair. "Malachai deserved *none of what you did*, because he did nothing wrong!" I shout. "Are you hearing yourself right now, Avon? You cannot decide to make someone else's life hell simply because yours was! You cannot project your past pain onto your present with another person!"

That sentence rings in my ears slightly, another reminder of the wrongs I, too, have committed where Malachai is concerned. I step back quickly, letting go of Avon's shirt. He falls into his desk chair, looking like a wilted plant as he stares blankly at his desk.

Still, I have more to say. "Should this town ever be lucky enough to have Malachai back in its borders, I better never, ever see or hear you attempt to hurt him in any way again," I hiss. "*Ever.* Or I cannot be responsible for what the fuck I might do to you." I slam my hand down on the desk one last time.

"Gangster," Benson mumbles. He snorts. "And for what it's worth, Avon," he says "the Norton brothers didn't exactly throw me a picnic when they were still here last year, and you don't see me stomping all over other people because of what they did to me. That's because if there's one thing I can tell you I've learned over the years, it's that the bullshit from your past doesn't go away when you try to treat everyone else like shit. Therapy works a hell of a lot better. Trust me on that."

Avon jerks his head up, bringing his gaze back to the two of us. His eyes are sunken, almost red-rimmed, and he looks very much like he's trying not to cry. "I was just trying to protect the town," he says, his voice hollow. "That's all I was trying to do."

I snort. "When you finally tell yourself the truth about why you did what you did," I tell him, "maybe you'll finally be able to make it right."

I slam the door so hard when we leave the office that Benson swears he hears at least three awards fall from the walls.

"Badass. He was a fucking badass." Benson holds up his coffee mug in the gesture of a toast. "Gangster. Fucking. Badass."

I sigh. "I think what Benson's trying to say is that the message seemed to get through to Avon. Not that it may have mattered in the larger sense. I texted Malachai to tell him that Avon wouldn't be bothering him again if he returns to Devon Falls, but Malachai said that he still needs time to think about what he wants his future to be."

Jack frowns across from me from where he sits in one of Luis' booths. Benson, who's sitting next to him, sets down his coffee mug and crosses his arms over his chest. And next to me, Milo just sighs.

"For what it's worth," Milo says, "however all this turns out, I'm really happy for you, Sam. You know how much we've worried about you since Christian died. Whatever goes on now, maybe this means you can move on."

I push a pancake from one side of my plate to another. "I'm not sure," I tell them. "I haven't felt this alive since Christian died. I'm not sure what that means, exactly."

Benson frowns. "Look, Malachai's still right down the road," he says abruptly. "He's not gone. He's not refusing to answer his phone like Colin. He's in La Fierte playing with trees and pumpkins and that fucking terrifying goat."

"Someone's still a little bitter about our last visit to the Stock Tree Farm," Jack murmurs.

"I just think that if you're going to have some animal standing on his hind legs glaring at everyone you should warn people so they don't end up screaming in front of crowds of small children, okay? *Anyway,* my point is that you've still got the chance to prove to Malachai that what you want—what he wants—can be real." He bangs his hand down on the table. "Ow, that hurt. But I stand by my point. You've just got to stop talking and *show* Malachai you mean what you say."

"Aww, babe." Jack leans over to kiss him on the cheek. "You've been watching teen rom-coms again, haven't you?"

"All I'm saying is that if you finish *Heartstopper* without crying, you have no soul. And honestly, my new taste in television is this stupid town's fault for turning me into such a cheesy romantic."

"Well," says Milo, "in your defense, your wedding is tomorrow."

"That's not really an excuse." Benson groans and drops his head into his hands. "Jeremy and Aaron are going to have a fucking field day when they see all the cheese at the ceremony. Both literal and figurative cheese."

I still haven't met Jeremy and Aaron, two people Benson enjoys waxing poetic about from his former internship in Burlington. I've been assured I'll meet them at the wedding tomorrow.

Which is a wedding I'm now dreading, unfortunately. Sitting there alone, next to a seat that should certainly belong to Malachai. It's going to be so very, very painful.

"I thought again today about going over to Stock Tree Farm," I tell the table. "But I know I can't fully imagine the life Malachai had before he met me. And after the way I've behaved the past month... well, if he needs space and processing time, maybe I owe that to him."

"To be fair," says Jack, "I don't think you're the only reason he needs processing time away from Devon Falls right now." He sighs.

"We all know this town meant something to Malachai, and that town hall clearly destroyed him. You may have gone to see Avon, Sam, but we all know Malachai's problems aren't just about Avon. Mom and I were talking the other day, about just how inside of himself Malachai was when he came to work for us. But he really opened up over time, even before you got here. It clearly takes a lot for him to trust people. He let himself trust us, and we all let him down at Avon's meeting that day. All of us."

"You should have murdered Avon Loseff instead of just telling him off," Benson says darkly as he rips apart a piece of bacon with his teeth.

Milo shrugs. "I don't know, guys. I was at that town hall. I saw how everyone there was acting. I don't think Avon and Sam are the only people around here who owe Malachai some apologies."

"Maybe not, but mine are certainly still the biggest." I push the jug of maple syrup toward Milo. "When I think of all the time I spent pushing him away this past month, essentially telling him that he could never be enough for me..."

"I don't know that I'd put it like that," Jack says.

"I would." Milo crosses his arms. "Well, obviously, I don't know Malachai that well. Not like the three of you do. But listen, here's the thing. Sam, you asked him to take a risk the other night, right? The kind of risk that you yourself haven't been ready to take. And he's surrounded by a town that was too afraid, really, to take a risk on him. So maybe this is really about showing him what kind of risk he is worth taking." He shrugs and stuffs a quarter of his pancake into his mouth with a fork.

"That's a good point." I sigh and lean back again. "I guess I just wish I'd have fucking done that the first day I ever brought Malachai to my house."

Milo raises an eyebrow. "Hey, now, are you finally letting go of the headmaster voice? I swear, you've been talking normally this whole breakfast."

I snort. "I don't have time to dissect my own vocal patterns right now," I tell him. And I mean it; I don't.

Because Milo's just given me an idea. One that's slowly coming together in my head the same way Jack's nephew builds a song chord by chord.

I stand up and step out of the booth. "I need you all to have the town assembled at my house at five-thirty p.m. today. Get Marie on the message boards, and make sure everyone's there. And meet me at my place in two hours to get things ready. Malachai needs to see something."

"How are you going to get Malachai to your house?" Benson calls after me.

"I'm not sure, but I'm guessing I might have to get an overly enthusiastic winery front desk manager involved. And possibly a goat," I call back.

I can't put together the exact event I had in mind in the space of seven hours, but I do come very close, actually. It's amazing what money, a collection of overly enthusiastic friends whose businesses just happened to be closed for a wedding, and a trio of mothers—mine and Marie—with dedicated organizational skills and commanding voices can achieve. By the time we're all waiting for Malachai to arrive, things are fully in order and ready for him.

"Are we all set?" I ask the crowd that's assembled on the front lawn underneath the very large banner they've managed to construct together. The table underneath it contains dishes with every single one of Malachai's favorite foods, encompassing everything from Luis' empanadas to the lasagna I used to often make for us to eat together. His face lit up whenever he saw it on the dinner table;

he once told me that he'd only ever had lasagna from a microwave before he met me. That homemade lasagna was a staple in my childhood, a food I actually once became so tired of that I would groan when my mothers announced we were having it.

There was something about seeing the things I took for granted in my childhood reflected back to me through Malachai's eyes. Something that made me want to wrap him up in my arms and show him every single thing the world has to offer that he may not have tried or seen yet.

"Ready!" Mom shouts from where she's standing next to Mother holding a large cow bell. I didn't bother asking her what the cow bell is for or what she plans to do with it. Mom is above such questions.

"Good. Here they come!" I clap my hands, and everyone falls into place, lining up around and against the table. A rusted, canary-yellow truck rumbles up the dirt road toward my house, crackling and groaning as it pulls into the driveway. The brakes screech as it comes to a halt, and I see Tom flinch at the noise. "Can't believe he drives that thing," Tom mutters as Gabe spills out of the driver seat, beaming when he sees us. For a moment I worry Gabe's going to give us away by shouting with excitement. But he quickly mimes zipping his lips and then rushes around to open up the passenger side door as he helps down a blindfolded, slightly annoyed-looking Malachai.

"Gabe, none of this makes any sense," he says grouchily. "What the hell has Sherbert gotten into now that you needed to blindfold me to surprise me with? And we've been driving forever. Are we even still on the farm? I—"

Gabe pulls the blindfold off of Malachai's head and yells "Surprise!" cuing the large group of Devon Falls residents standing behind me to shout "We're sorry!" in unison.

Malachai just stares for several long moments. First at the large group of people standing in front of him. Then at Gabe. Then at the banner we stretched across the front of my farmhouse, which reads in very large letters: WE'RE SO SORRY, MALACHAI!

And then, finally, he stares at me. "Sam," he whispers. "What did you do?"

I come forward and take his hands in my own. "I didn't do very much," I tell him. "Henri straightened everything out. I've spoken to Avon again. Devon Falls owed you an apology, Malachai. All I did was offer a space to share it."

"We were jerks!" Burt Busby calls out across the lawn. "You've done a great job with the festival, Malachai. Sorry we doubted you!"

"I've arranged for the leaf dancers to dedicate their final medley to you at the festival performance this weekend!" Irene Cooley adds loudly.

"I've named the maple cotton candy special this year The Malachai!" someone else says.

"The band's playing a song for you in the parade!"

"The first leaf hike we lead on Sunday is in honor of you!"

And on and on they go. Malachai looks completely over-whelmed. "But I owe all of you an apology!" he finally yells at them. "What I did last year..." he shakes his head. "It was unforgivable. I understood why you didn't trust me after that."

"Oh, fu—forget that." Benson comes forward, waving his arms like some kind of traffic controller. "People make mistakes, Malachai. You made one. You said you were sorry, over and over again. Then Devon Falls made one. This is us, saying we're sorry."

He grins and grabs Jack's hand in his. "And if there's one thing I've learned about people in Devon Falls, when they say some-thing, they mean it."

"Darn right!" Alan Lancer, Jack's father, says cheerfully. "So, Malachai," he asks. "Can you forgive us?"

There's a chorus of loud begging from the audience, and Malachai laughs before he looks over at me. He shakes his head, and then he says the words I want to hear as he looks directly at me.

"I forgive you. Life's for second chances, right?"

Chapter 29
2 Days to the Devon Falls Leaf Festival

He brought an entire town together for me. —Malachai Flynn

"This is a whole lot of celebrations, you know," I tell Sam as we sit in camping chairs on one side of his lawn. Off to the left of us, Elijah and Pat are leading a group of kids in a sing-along, and to our right a larger group of Devon Falls residents are assembled together on the grass eating and talking loudly. Sam pours some red wine into a plastic cup and passes it to me.

"I guess it is. This, then the wedding tomorrow, then the festival the day after that." He shrugs. "Devon Falls does love a party, though. And they clearly love you, Malachai."

I blush hard as I look around at the crowd that's gathered. The crowd of people that came today to make a banner and bring all my favorite things to eat—and yes, I've had five empanadas already and I don't regret it—and tell *me*, little, meaningless me, that I'm important enough to them for an apology like this.

I think back on Ken Davidson and the rest of my tormentors in Alcott. If I showed up on Ken's doorstep tomorrow demanding an apology, I'm not sure he'd even know what I was asking him to apologize for. But here, in Devon Falls, things aren't like that.

People here noticed when I was in pain. People cared enough to fix it.

Sam noticed. He's always noticed, of course. I realize that now more than ever. "I still can't believe you did all this," I tell him.

He takes a sip from his own wine and smacks his lips. "I'm not sure I'll ever get used to the propensity this town has for drinking wine from plastic," he says, frowning as he studies his neon orange cup. "And I did it because I could, and because I needed to. You deserve everything you want in the world, Malachai. So I did something else, too." He sits back in his seat and smiles as he sets the cup in a holder on the chair and leans over to take my hand.

My stomach swirls slightly. "What else is there that you could have done besides this?" I ask incredulously.

Sam gestures at the house. "I bought that. For you. You own that house now, Malachai."

For a moment it's as though everything stops around me—the sound, the movement, the people. Everything freezes in place except for the man in front of me. "Excuse me?" I ask him.

Sam smiles and leans over to kiss my cheek. "The house. It's yours, completely in your name to do whatever you like with. You can sell it and go to nursing school. You can keep it and be a part of the Devon Falls community forever. You love that house, Malachai, and I love you. More than I ever realized I could love anyone. All I want in this world is for you to be happy, and I know I won't always be able to give you perfect happiness. But I can promise that I will always try my best. And today my best is buying you a house that I know makes you smile every single time you walk into it."

Tears are running down my face now, and I'm gasping a little as the world seems to come back online and I begin to hear and see and sense the world around us again. "You can't... you can't buy me a house!" I tell him in between tears.

"Why not?" He shrugs and kisses me again, this time on the lips. "I told you, if you don't want it, you can sell it. I trust you in every single way, Malachai, and I always will. I trust you to do what you want and what you think is right with that house. And I'll love you no matter what choice you make."

I'm gasping with sobs as I somehow end up in his lap, wrapped around him like who-the-fuck-knows-what in front of most of Devon Falls. *He actually bought me a house?*

I can't keep it, of course. That's fucking ridiculous. But still...

Then Tom screams "Way to not mess this up, brother!" at the same time Benson yells "Get it, Malachai!" and everyone on the lawn bursts into applause at once.

The sky starts to get dark soon after that, and I feel like I'm floating through the crowd and the hugs people offer as we clean up and put away lawn furniture and everyone waves and leaves, ready to get some rest and prepare for the big celebration to-morrow—the wedding tomorrow night, which is the official town kickoff for the Devon Falls Leaf Festival. I'm told that Sam, Ben-son, and Amelia have been finishing up the final set-up details since I left, but I'm looking forward to stepping back in tomorrow, with Sam at my side. It only feels right, somehow, that the two of us will be the ones who make his best friend's wedding happen.

And maybe one of my best friends, too, I think as I look over at Benson, who's complaining loudly to Jack about how they should have only had Luis' empanadas and meatloaf at the wedding, because they are clearly the best food in the world and Jack's dislike of meatloaf is ridiculous.

"Malachai."

The sound of an all-too familiar voice sinks like a pit in my stomach, and I turn slowly to see the person I already know is standing behind me: Avon Fucking Loseff.

Next to me, Sam *growls*. He actually, full-on growls. Like a damn wolf.

Avon holds up his hands in surrender. "Whoa, hang on. I'm not looking for a fight, okay? I talked to Henri, and now I'm just here to talk to Malachai."

I'm determined not to look as thrown off as I feel. "Hi, Avon," I say cooly.

"You should leave," Sam says testily. "You weren't invited here today."

"Sam." I turn to face him. "Look, I appreciate you going all bodyguard on me here. It's really fucking cute, actually." I press up on my tiptoes to kiss his cheek. "But I think I need to handle this conversation myself, okay? Can you give us a minute?"

Sam nods grudgingly and then slowly slinks away. But it's clear he only plans to stand about five feet off to the side as he watches us.

I won't even try to figure out why that's so damn hot.

"So why are you here?" I ask Avon. "I know Sam talked to you, and you said you talked to Henri. Did you come here to apologize?"

Avon shoves his hands into his pockets and drops his gaze to the ground. "I won't apologize for caring about this place and looking out for these people," he says evenly. "But the way I handled things—I owe you a big apology for that. Confronting you like that in front of the town was wrong." He shakes his head. "Especially when I hadn't done my due diligence first."

When I don't say anything right away, Avon sighs. "I think I've told you that in the past I've often struggled to feel like I fit in here, and I—"

It's like that's the only statement I'll ever need to hear from him. "I forgive you," I blurt out.

Avon raises his eyebrows in surprise, and I shrug.

"I probably understand you better than anyone else here, Avon. What you went through as a kid with the Fletcher brothers, wanting to be a part of this place so badly—I understand it all." I hold out my hand. "So, I forgive you. But try not to be such an asshole if something like this ever happens again, okay?"

A slow smile spreads across Avon's face as he reaches out to shake my hand. "I can try," he finally says.

"I still can't believe this belongs to *me*." I run my hand over the ever-so-slightly textured wall above Sam's bed. "I mean, I can't accept it. You know that, right? I didn't earn it, and—"

"I didn't earn it either." Sam rolls over and pulls me into his arms. "This whole concept that everything we come to own in this world is something we've *earned* is highly overstated, in both my opinion and Tom's. Colin and Christian always agreed with us. The four of us certainly all worked hard, and we took pride in our accomplishments. But we were all always highly aware that the circumstances we were born into were those of luck, and that luck gifted us different things than it gifted other people." He nuzzles me under his chin, against his chest. "I understand not wanting to accept something you feel like you haven't earned, though. I treated my mothers' offers that way for quite some time when I officially became an adult. If you're not in a place to accept this house, I understand that. I'll never force anything on you, Malachai. I'll watch out for the house. Just know that it will always be here, waiting for you."

Like you? I'm tempted to ask. But I think I already know the answer to that question.

He bought me a house. He brought an entire town together for me. Everything that was holding Sam so far away from me before clearly isn't there anymore. At all.

"Where is Colin?" I ask him. "You haven't mentioned him since that day you went looking for him and…"

"Abandoned you," he grumbles to himself as he pulls me even more tightly against him. I can't complain, but I can protest. "You didn't exactly abandon me," I remind him.

"I did." He sighs. "You may not see it that way, but I do."

"I told you to leave. And Benson and Jack tried to stand up for me."

"I'm sure they did. But I was the one who should have been there to stand up *with* you, not for you."

My heart swells so strongly in my chest I'm a little afraid it might burst.

"But no," Sam says. "We haven't seen or heard from Colin." He sighs. "Tom's worried, of course. So am I. We're hoping he'll appear for Jack and Benson's wedding tomorrow. Colin has a soft spot for the story of those two, though he'd never admit it."

I can believe that. Benson and Jack have a pretty incredible story—Benson arriving in town to destroy the leaf festival and then somehow offering to fake-date Jack to save Elijah from a terrible custody situation—but I'm still not sure Sam's optimism is fair. "Colin's pissed, isn't he?" I ask. "Because you told him the truth about your marriage to Christian."

"I think he might be." Sam pulls me tightly against his bare skin and sighs. "But if he is, I can't do anything about that. My mothers both reminded me—well, and Tom for that matter—what Christian would have really wanted for me. I'm going to trust that they're right. That I'm right." He sighs against my hair. "I won't ever be able to forget him, as a person. He truly was one of my best friends. Are you comfortable with me keeping his memory alive in the future?"I turn in his arms so I can completely face him to say my next words, because that feels important. "I wouldn't ever, ever want you to forget Christian," I tell Sam. "He mattered to you.

He helped make you the man who's here with me now. He needs to be celebrated and never, *ever* forgotten."

Sam hugs my naked body to his. Hard.

My cock tenses slightly as it makes contact with his

"Do you remember," he whispers against my ear, "the first time you were ever in my bed?"

I think I gulp more than answer.

"Do you remember feeling your body against mine?" he whispers, his voice harder, heartier. I nod against his neck.

"I think I'll always wonder," he says into my skin, "if I've stolen you from the world, somehow, by being the first to find you in so many, many ways. The first to see how responsive you are."

He draws our cocks together in his hand, and I shake in his arms.

"The first to hear what you sound like when you let go of all your fears." He's dropped lube into his hand at some point, I realize, as he begins to stroke us together, all at once. I whine against him.

"The first to know how incredibly pure, perfect, and real your heart is," he says as he begins to move his hand up and down, slower and then faster, in time with the sounds that keep escaping me, over and over again."

"Sir?" The word escapes me like a murmur, or an echo, or maybe a desperate cry, I'm not sure which.

"Tell me what you want," he demands, and now, finally, I can look him in the eye and tell him exactly what I need to say without stuttering or losing a single syllable.

"I want everything, sir," I tell him clearly. "I want the whole world."

And then he gives it to me. Stars, sun, moon, and all.

Chapter 30
1 Day to the Devon Falls Leaf Festival

The world has shrunk to a wonderfully sized bubble that belongs only to me and Malachai. —Sam Evers

"Okay, do we have Vermonica at the top of the stage? And are the dancers a go?"

Malachai will never stop being addictively attractive to me, but he's particularly attractive right now, as he clutches a tablet in one hand and a walkie-talkie in the other, hair hanging recklessly across his forehead and cheeks flushed. A cacophony of response comes through the walkie-talkie, and Malachai rolls his eyes and groans. "What do you *mean* one of the dancers can't find his left shoe? The dancers lead off the ceremony! Barefoot or not, they're on in thirty!"

I choke back a laugh as I cross the area behind the large, temporary stage that currently takes up a great deal of Vermont real estate dedicated to the Devon Falls Leaf Festival. "Hello, darling," I murmur as I step behind Malachai and drop a kiss on top of his head."

"Hi. Just give me one minute to—hey, stop that! I'm trying to put on a wedding here!" he says, giggling as I start nibbling at his neck. "There's no time for vampire activity right before a wedding."

"I don't know; I've met Jack and Benson. They're a little kinky. I think they'd find it quite fitting, actually."

Malachai moans slightly as I hit the area where his neck and shoulder meet. "Okay, I guess we can—no, stop that!" he interrupts himself, laughing and slapping at my hand as I start moving it back and forth over his hip muscle. "We don't have time for this!"

"Well, I certainly hope you have time to change." Tom pushes through the curtain, appearing in front of us in a blue linen suit that's perfectly pressed and carrying a garment bag.

Malachai's eyebrows go up at the sight of the bag. "Um, I'm already dressed?" He peeks down at his khakis and button up shirt, both garments I'm intimately familiar with from the office, as if he's worried he might suddenly find himself naked in front of both me and my brother.

Tom should be so lucky. I'm not the sharing type.

"Yes, and I do love the green in that shirt; it brings out your eyes," Tom tells him as he passes the garment bag to me. "But I had to go to Burlington recently to pick up some accessories I forgot in New York—can you even believe I traveled for a wedding without my Tom Ford loafers?—and Sammy here asked me to pick this suit up for you. Luckily, I have an eye for sizes."

Malachai drops the walkie-talkie into his pocket and whirls around to face me. "You bought me a suit? You already bought me a house, for crying out loud!"

"Of the two, I honestly expected the house to upset you more," I tell him mildly. I rub a hand across his soft, flushed cheek. "You certainly don't have to accept the suit, darling. But Tom was already at the tailor, and I thought you might want something new for this special day, to celebrate everything you've accomplished for our friends. You've put together a whole wedding, Malachai."

Malachai blushes against my palm. "Henri did most of it, and you know how much the town helped. Really, I just—"

"Stop that." I interrupt him with a quick kiss. "Stop talking down your accomplishments. From now on that's not allowed. It's a rule I'm making. There will be consequences for breaking it."

"Oh, really?" Malachai's eyebrow goes up.

"Yes, and—"

"Okay, enough!" Tom throws up his hands. "I love a good peep show as much as the next person, but I really didn't come back here for one. I've got to get back to Mother and Mom; they're eating themselves sick on the appetizers Luis has circling."

"Tell them I said hi," Malachai says meekly. He's definitely still a little intimidated by my mothers, who threw themselves at him yesterday with pure excitement and promises to spend lots of time "getting to know him better" in the coming days. I would have suggested they back off, but neither of them would actually know how to take that note. And Malachai doesn't need my help with them anyway. Anyone who's spent as long as he has working for the Lancers and living in Devon Falls can handle my mothers. He and I have already talked about taking them on one of the scheduled leaf peeping hikes that are part of the festival's regular programming this weekend. They'll enjoy the experience, and the activity will give Malachai a chance to get to know them without the entire town observing.

"I'll tell them," Tom says cheerfully. "Now, I do have one question before we start."

"Sure, go for it," says Malachai as he starts to unzip the garment bag Tom handed to me.

"Why, exactly, is a cow dressed in a leaf-patterned cape at a wedding?"

Malachai looks him in the eye as he answers, completely deadpan. "What else would she wear?"

Tom, for once in his life, seems entirely speechless as I burst out laughing.

Malachai truly doesn't give himself enough credit for his organizational skills, and the wedding goes off without a hitch.

Vermonica stands tall and proud off to the side of the stage where the ceremony is performed by Amelia. A small troupe of dancers from Irene Cooley's dance studio prance up the aisle first, throwing yellow and orange and red leaves every which way as Elijah and Pat's band plays the Rolling Stones song "Wild Horses." Then Jack's parents walk him up the aisle, one on either side of him, and Benson's father and stepmother do the same. I spot Benson's younger brother and sister in front seats across from where Malachai and I are sitting.

Benson's father is crying when he stops at the top of the aisle with Benson, and he whispers something in Benson's ear that has Benson tearing up too before he lets go and finds his place by Jack's side.

And then Malachai and I hold hands and watch our friends each marry the love of their life.

"I promise," Jack tells Benson, "to love every prickly piece of you, my perfect porcupine." The audience laughs and Benson answers with exactly the right jab: "I promise to love you for exactly who you are, you overbearing pile of romance."

The crowd sends out a loud simultaneous *awww* just then.

The ceremony is short, likely because Benson has no patience for these sorts of things, and it isn't long before Amelia is pronouncing them husband and husband. "Now kiss each other, you darn fools!" she shouts loudly as Jack pulls Benson against him and smothers him in a kiss that's just on the other side of PG.

"And now it's time for the party," Malachai whispers in my ear.

This time of October isn't exactly warm in Devon Falls, but Malachai and the team organizing the wedding are well-prepared for that. The large tents near the stage that host the wedding reception have heaters spaced comfortably throughout the tables, and even the giant dance floor at one end of the setup is adorned with four large heating towers. Fairy lights whirl through the entire setup, a mixture of traditional white and orange leaf-shaped glowing objects, and every type of leaf decoration imaginable is somewhere in the vicinity.

And then, of course, there's the real thing, the pieces of nature that bring an entire town so fully together every year: the trees that dot the leaf festival land and the woods that run for miles behind it. The crew putting on the festival has twined more fairy lights through them, showing off a spectacle of painted leaves in the midst of turning colors and becoming something new. Different.

Malachai is too busy to eat with me at first. He and his walkie-talkie are everywhere in the space making sure the meal goes off without a hitch, but eventually I manage to grab hold of him and place him in my lap to make sure he nibbles on something. "Just three empanadas," I tell him. "Then you can go back to running the world."

Malachai blushes scarlett.

"Oh, there's no need to blush on our account, honey," Mom tells him. "He learned that bossiness from me."

"Darn right," Mother mumbles as she rolls her eyes.

Malachai laughs and doesn't argue as I feed him an empanada with my fingers.

The reception relaxes into more and more of a party, with the dance floor getting livelier and livelier, particularly as more alcohol is consumed. Jack and Benson smear cake on each other's faces at one point; Benson pretends to hate it but clearly enjoys the experience. Then Pat, Elijah's band mate, announces from the stage that it's time for the couple to complete their first dance. The sounds of Sinead O'Connor's "Nothing Compares 2 U" rumble from Pat and Elijah's instruments, and Elijah begins to sing the familiar lyrics. Malachai leans over from where he's standing next to me at the side of the dance floor.

"Wait, *this* is their first dance song? This is like one of the most depressing break-up songs ever written!"

I pull him up against my hip, treasuring the warmth of his body against mine in the chilly Vermont air. "Strange choice, isn't it? Elijah apparently stumbled upon it during his recent obsession with Prince—you know Prince wrote this song?"

"No, I didn't." Malachai shakes his head. "Geez, just when you think you know the end of that guy's range."

"I know," I agree, pressing my nose into his hair to take a breath of his all-too familiar shampoo. I'm so very glad he smells like my bathroom again. "Anyway, Elijah and Pat decided to learn it in honor of Prince, who is now Pat's favorite musician of all time, apparently, and they were playing it for Jack and Benson one day. Benson told Jack that this song is every reason he never, ever wants them to be apart, and every time he listens to it from now on he'll remember why Jack is the only person he wants to love for the rest of his life."

"Wow. Okay, maybe that makes sense. For them." Malachai sighs into my chest and for several long moments of instrumental break we watch Jack and Benson dance together, arms twined around each other and foreheads touching. Jack looks so comfortable with himself; so at peace. "But this wouldn't be my choice for our wedding song," Malachai says softly.

"No?" I ask him, trying to keep my heart at a simmering pace despite Malachai's words. *Our wedding song.* Already in my head

I'm imagining that day, what it might be like, what it would feel like to speak a vow to be with Malachai forever.

"No. It's a great song, and all, but I've already known what it would be like to think I'll be apart from you forever." Malachai hugs me then, hard. "I don't need any song to remind me how much I never want to feel that way again."

"God, me neither," I whisper into his hair, and then Tom has to interrupt us with a joke about wedding propriety when I can't stop myself from pulling Malachai in for a kiss.

"There are small children here!" he hisses loudly.

The reception goes on for hours, with music echoing off the trees and children falling asleep across chairs. Vermonica the cow is led on a short walk through the wedding venue to the truck that will take her back to Stock Tree Farm for the night, and the crowd applauds her loudly while children rush to try and touch the famed maple leaf marking on her stomach. "Frankly, I still don't get what the big deal is," Embry, one of Malachai's bosses—former boss, possibly? We haven't discussed that detail—at Stock Tree Farm tells me and Malachai as his partner Jeb takes her away. "I mean, don't get me wrong, she's a great cow. Really good temperament; solid eater. But honestly, I'd rather spend time with Sherbert."

"Me too," Malachai agrees. "As long as there's a bucket of apples around."

Having spent very little time with the nearly mythological Sherbert, I can't say yet whether I agree or disagree, and I don't much care either way right now. At the moment I'm far too busy holding Malachai against my body, breathing in the scent and feel of him, feeling *whole* for the very first time in so long, to wonder or worry about goats or cows or any of the other magical oddities of this place I'm surrounded by. The world has shrunk to a wonderfully sized bubble that belongs only to me and Malachai, even if it is fully surrounded by others.

"Just wait until we get home," I tell him as I nibble at his ear. "The first thing I'm going to do is order you to—"

"Sam! Malachai!" Gabe, wearing a brightly colored leaf-patterned sweater and khaki pants, comes running up to us, breathing heavily. "Oh my gosh, I had to find you first and tell you! Oh my gosh, you won't believe it!"

"Gabe?" Malachai looks as shocked and mystified as I feel. "Is everything okay? What's going on?"

"Colin came back! He's here!"

Malachai looks at me, eyes wide. I tug him against me. "Breathe," I whisper into his ear. "Whatever happens, promise me you'll keep breathing." Malachai nods into my neck.

"Yes, sir," he says softly.

"Good. Because no matter what goes on the rest of this evening, just remember: you have nothing to worry about. I am never, ever letting go of you again."

Malachai relaxes slightly into me, but his eyes are still wide as he looks at Gabe.

Chapter 31
0 Days to the Devon Falls Leaf Festival

And then we're off to the festival to celebrate leaves and eat cotton candy and maybe bury the hatchet—or dredge it up—with my new boyfriend's deceased husband's doppelganger. —Malachai Flynn

Am I one hundred percent terrified to hear whatever Colin has to say now that he's come back to Devon Falls? Yes, I absolutely am. Do I just want to stay curled up with Sam in bed all morning the day after the wedding and completely avoid the festival, where we're supposed to meet up with Colin and Tom in less than an hour? Yes, I definitely do.

But I'm not the same terrified kid who first came to work at Lancer Family Medicine a little over a year ago. And I'm not the same person who used to cower at any kind of danger or at the idea of standing up for what I really want. I know we're always changing, always evolving, like the leaves that shift and revise themselves and ready themselves for a new chapter every autumn here in Devon Falls. And I've realized that if someone like Sam can love me for who I am, at my core, maybe I'm ready to do the same.

I hold onto that thought tightly as Sam wakes up and decides we should start the day with blow jobs—no complaints here—and then borderline leers at me while I dress in jeans and a black sweater of his that's way too big for me but smells so much like him there's no way I'm not going to wear it when he offers. And then we're off to the festival to celebrate leaves and eat cotton candy and maybe bury the hatchet—or dredge it up—with my new boyfriend's deceased husband's doppelganger.

Not a sentence I ever thought I'd find myself using, but here we are.

The first hours of the festival go off without a hitch, actually. All the vendors are in the place, and ticket sales are going smoothly. The leaf walks that start every hour and are led by local guides are as popular as ever. Irene's dance troupe is on stage doing a complicated routine involving three children in leaf costumes so gigantic that I'm worried they'll topple over when someone's shadow falls into the space next to me.

"Hey, Malachai."

I whirl around to see Colin there—and *fuck,* if I can't look at him without seeing Christian, what does looking at him do to Sam? I gulp and wait for Sam's words to patter through my head.

Breathe. Just breathe. Just breathe.

I do.

"I'm really glad you're back," I tell him honestly, because we've all been worried about him, especially Sam and Tom. I can't even imagine what Colin's gone through since Sam talked to him about his relationship with Christian. "Have you seen Sam?" I ask him anxiously. Sam left a few minutes ago to get some cotton candy and corn dogs for us. "He should be back any minute now, and—"

Colin holds up his hand. "I just ran into him a few minutes ago, actually. He's still getting the food, but I told him I wanted to talk to you alone for a minute."

Breathe. Just breathe. Sam wouldn't have told Colin where to find you if he thought Colin was going to lace into you. "Okay," I tell him hesitantly.

Onstage, a dancer misses a step and takes a quick stumble onto the stage, but he's back up and beaming a moment later, and the audience applauds. Colin frowns.

"I owe you an apology for just taking off like that. I owe everyone an apology, of course, but especially you."

"Me?" I would honestly be less surprised if he'd come here to angrily douse my head in maple syrup. "Uh, why would you need to apologize to me?"

"Because you love Sam," he says simply. "And I think Sam might need my blessing to like, love you all the way or some shit." He shrugs and kicks at a brown leaf beneath his foot. "I don't know, I'm not very good at talking about shit like this. I'm better with cars, you know?"

Having only ever driven a fifteen-year-old Mazda, I can't say that I do, but I nod.

"So, yeah, I shouldn't have just taken off like that. It was shitty, especially to you."

I'm still working on processing what he's saying when he starts talking again.

"Here's the thing." Colin puts his hands on his hips and stands up straight to face me, fully. "I loved my brother so damn much, and he loved Sam. Sam loved him. Their relationship wasn't perfect; I think now that maybe I always knew that. But they were good together in a lot of ways. The night they got married, I remember both of them telling me that there's nothing more comfortable than marrying your best friend."

"I understand that," I tell him, because I'm still not sure I see where he's going with this.

"Anyway, after what Sam told me, I was kind of fucked up, you know? Maybe I'm not supposed to tell you that, but I was. I needed to drive, so I rented this killer '42 Aston Martin from some place in Burlington and I drove back to New York. But I kept thinking about something Christian wrote me in a text once, back when I was still racing and I was overseas and he was here in the states."

"Oh," I say, because what else am I supposed to say to that? I'm not even sure exactly what an Aston Martin is. A car brand, I'm guessing?

"Anyhow, I couldn't remember the text exactly, and I knew it was on an old phone of mine. So I went back to my apartment in New York to find it."

He rummages in his pocket for a minute and pulls out a phone that looks brand-new to me, honestly. He touches the screen until something comes up and then passes the phone over to me.

Christian: Bro, you know how you said once that you'll never fall in love? NEVER TELL SAM I SAID THIS but sometimes I'm not sure i've ever been in love either. Not exactly. But I do love Sam, and if that's not the same thing i'm okay with that. Because Sam's so fucking good. He makes the world better. He makes me better, i think.

Christian: if anything ever happens to me you have to make sure Sam keeps making the world better, okay? Whatever that looks like.

Colin: Okay, I guess, but this is a weirdly maudlin way to talk right before I jump in a car to race at 200 mph

Christian: Please. We both know I'm dying first. I just don't care about shit the way you do lol!!!

Colin: Fuck i hate when you talk like this

Christian: You know you're bored when i try to act normal. Now go have fun driving around the same exact track a bazillion times in a row!

Colin takes the phone gently out of my hand while I'm *still* trying to figure out how to respond to what he's just shown me.

"Sam needs to keep making the world better," he says softly. "And you're going to help him do it, aren't you?"

When I don't answer, he nods, leans over, and kisses my cheek gently. "Maybe don't tell him I did that," he says as he stands up straight again. "Sam's always been a possessive little shit. Didn't even like sharing his toys when he was younger. But listen: not that you need it, but you two have my blessing. I told Sam the same thing."

Then he disappears into the crowd of people in front of me.

It's either two minutes or two hours later when someone pushes cotton candy into my hand. "Are you okay?" Sam asks me.

I twirl the maple spun sugar around in front of me. "You didn't need to have Colin show that to me," I tell Sam.

"I know that," he says as he leads me over to one of the park benches to sit down. He rips a piece of the candy from the cone and pushes it against my lips, feeding me gently. "But he wanted to show you. He wanted you to know that he's okay now. That he supports us. Telling us both mattered to him."

"Are you okay?" I ask as I pull a piece of the candy, which is spun in colors of brown and white, away from its home and hand it to Sam. "What Colin just showed me... that was a lot."

Sam frowns and accepts the candy, letting it melt on his fingers as he answers me. "Honestly? A few months ago seeing that text would have undone me completely. But not now. I knew before I ever saw that text what my next steps were, and that text only makes them even easier than they already were." He licks the melted sugar off his fingers and then leans over to kiss me with his sweetened lips. "Malachai, I want to follow you wherever you go next. Anywhere. Any nursing school in the world. I hope you'll let me help you pay for whatever schooling you want to do, because I want to be your partner from here on out. And if you're not comfortable with that, we'll find another solution. All that matters to me is being with you. I'm not sure I've ever truly believed that

I make the world better, but I would like to keep living up to that ideal Christian seemed to have of me. And you *do* make the world better; I've already seen you make me better in so many ways." He presses another kiss against my lips. "So how about if we live up to that legacy he had in mind together?"

I come up from another long kiss with him to take a breath and look around at dancers and leaves and people I was once so certain hated me, who now wave and smile and call my name happily. *Home,* my heart shouts.

"I don't want to leave," I burst out. "I want to stay here, in Devon Falls, with you. We can do that here, right? I'll go to nursing school in Burlington and commute or something, and we can work together at Lancer Family Medicine. And I don't *want* to own that house alone, Sam. I want the two of us to own it together. So maybe we can change the deed to have both of our names on it?"

Sam's laughing now, almost hysterically, as he sets the cotton candy down on the bench and pulls me into a hug. "Yes, Malachai. Oh, for fuck's sake, yes."

I almost do a double take. "Did you just *swear*?"

He laughs and shrugs. "Maybe. I have to say, I'm not certain I'm ready to leave highly formal Sam behind again—he's the Sam who fell in love with you. But maybe this is the beginning of you seeing a slightly less formal side of me." He wraps his arms tightly around me. "My greatest hope for us is that we both show each other more and more of who we are every single day," he murmurs.

I nod into his shoulder and realize what that means. "I should invite my mother here," I tell him. "Maybe even see if she could stay with us for a little bit. She needs a vacation. And she and I don't know each other very well, like I told you. I think I might like to change that."

"Oh, darling." Sam kisses the top of my head. "There's nothing I'd like better than to get to know your mother with you."

We sit together, Sam feeding me cotton candy and making gentle jokes about dancing leaves, as the fall sun fills the sky and brightens all the small and large festival moments that this town—this town and *I*—worked hard to make possible. This festival, which is so full of pasts and futures, of memories and possibilities.

I breathe, I fall against Sam's body, and I let myself sink into the kind of happiness I once was so certain could never, ever belong to me.

I breathe, and I live.

Epilogue

39 Days after the Devon Falls Leaf Festival

Today, we celebrate this new beginning Devon Falls is gifting us.
—Malachai Flynn

"Wow, baby. You really made this all happen, huh?" Mom reaches over to pat my shoulder. "I always knew you had something like this in you." She goes back to flipping through the pages of the scrapbook Benson made showcasing the wedding and the leaf festival—because apparently Benson Lewis scrapbooks now—in between taking sips of coffee from the mug Sam keeps refilling for her. "Thank you, Dr. Evers," she says as he tops her off yet again. Her mug was already more than halfway full, and now coffee's so close to the edge of it that I'm glad my mother serves warm beverages for a living. She knows how to balance a too-full mug in her hands.

It turns out that my boyfriend—and yeah, it's still kind of weird calling him that in my head—actually is physically capable of getting nervous in the right situations, and one of those right situations just happens to be meeting my mother for the first time.

"Please, Jody, call me Sam." He finally puts the coffee pot down on a coaster and settles next to me on the couch, wrapping his arm around my shoulder. "And yes, the festival was quite a hit this year. Malachai's been the talk of Devon Falls since then."

I'm definitely blushing now. "The festival was barely over a month ago," I remind them both.

Sam shakes his head. "No downplaying your achievements. You put on a celebration everyone's still chattering about. I can barely get them to shut up about how this was the best festival the town's ever had while I'm trying to give physicals."

Mom laughs out loud. "You two are so funny together! And you seem so happy here." She glances around us, at the bright paint and soft lighting and mahogany furniture of the room we're sitting in, and I know she's thinking the same thing I once thought when I moved here: *this is everything I always wanted.* "I'm really, really happy for you, baby," she says as she sets her mug down on the table and runs her hands across a page of the scrapbook almost reverently. "No one deserves to be happy more than you."

"That's what I say too," Sam says. He leans over to kiss me on the cheek, leaving me blushing again.

"I'm glad you could come visit for Thanksgiving," I tell Mom. "I didn't think you were going to be able to get the time off." She's only been here for a few hours, and I'm already a little worried that we're running out of things to say. There's only so much you can discuss about the weather and the drive between Alcott and Devon Falls and a leaf festival. I clutch at Sam's hand, and he squeezes it tightly. Whatever rising panic was moving through my throat seems to sink backward, away and down through my body.

Sam has that effect on me and my panic attacks. It's come in very handy several times during the last few weeks, especially with the success of the wedding and the festival. Between those wins and Devon Fall's determination to show me how sorry they are for everything that happened with Avon, I've been the center of attention around here in ways I'm not used to. And it turns out that being the center of attention, even for very positive reasons, isn't something I always handle very well.

But Sam's been there for every single lost breath, always with a hot bath or a breathing exercise or a quick touch that somehow makes everything better. Will I always have panic attacks? Maybe, and that's okay. Sam and I have talked about me seeing a therapist and how much that experience helped him, and one of things he told me was that therapy wasn't about him becoming someone different or new, it was about him getting more comfortable with accepting who he already is. And that's something he's obviously still working on, he also said as we talked and he held me tight.

We're talking about going to therapy together, too. I like that idea a lot. I like the idea of starting our relationship together with pure honesty. That's another reason I wanted to invite my mother to come for Thanksgiving. I want to be open with Sam about everything I can, including where I come from. And I'm not ready to go back to Alcott yet, so bringing Mom here was the next best thing.

"Oh, I didn't get the time off from work." Mom closes the scrapbook and sets it on the table while Sam and I both stare at her.

"What do you mean?" I finally ask. "How are you here?"

"I got fired." She takes a sip of her coffee and shrugs as she sets her mug down again. "Baby, I never once asked for a Thanksgiving off the entire time you were growing up. I've worked that holiday every year for almost two decades. This year, I wanted to come see my son in his new home with his new boyfriend, and those fuckers I work for—pardon my language, Sam—couldn't be bothered to help me out. So I told them I wasn't working Thanksgiving, and they fired me."

"Mom! I—uh—what—" I can't even figure out how to respond to that. Every question running through my head is laced with panic. Where's she going to work now? Alcott's not exactly swimming in jobs. Does she have something else lined up yet? How is she going to keep paying rent on her trailer? Is—

"Baby, don't worry." Mom pats my hand. "I've got it all figured out!"

"You do?" I ask in a strangled voice.

Mom beams. Her face, lined with wrinkles from years of stress and too-little sleep, looks brighter than I've ever seen it, I realize. She looks brighter. More content than I've ever seen her. She has since she got here actually. "Well, you see, I called the doctor's office my son works in to tell him what had happened after I got canned, and it just so happened that his boss answered the phone."

I whirl around to look at Sam, but he shakes his head as he smiles. "Not me," he says. "Marie."

"Yup," Mom goes on. "And she mentioned that her office manager is leaving his position at the end of the semester, because he'll be commuting to nursing school in Burlington." Mom grins proudly as I blush again. "And then," Mom goes on, "she mentioned that she and her husband—Alan's his name, right?—are leaving to do some traveling around the world in a few months after she fully retires and Dr. Evers here takes her place. So it turns out she was looking for someone to watch her house while she's gone." Mom sits back in her seat on the couch, a wide smile now on her face.

"Wait—are you telling me what I think you're telling me?" I set down my own coffee mug and lean across the couch to stare at her. "Are you *moving to Devon Falls?*"

"Yup!" Mom claps her hands together. "Took everything I cared about and threw it in the back of my car before I came here. Marie and I've done all sorts of planning, baby! You can start training me in how to take care of the office, and I'm going to stay in her guest room and learn how to take care of all her animals before she leaves to go traveling. I'll keep saving up money, and I should be able to get my own place before she gets back. It all works out perfectly!"

I whirl back around in Sam's arms to stare at him. "Did you know about this?"

He laughs. "I knew Marie was talking to your mother an awful lot, but I wasn't sure why. And Jody, I hope you know that you'd always be welcome to stay with me and Malachai if you ever needed to."

"Oh, I couldn't." She shakes her head. "You two just barely got together! You need your space." She grabs one of my hands. "Malachai, hon, are you okay with this? Because if you're not, I can turn right around and go home, and I—"

I pull her into a hug before I even realize I'm doing it. "It's perfect!" I blurt out.

I didn't want to tell anyone how worried I was about leaving the office at the end of the semester, especially with Marie about to retire. But I know I can teach my mother to take care of Sam and Jack and Lancer Family Medicine the right way, just like Henri once did for me. I even think Benson's going to like her.

Of course, this means we're going to be spending an awful lot of time together in the next few months and maybe even years. I'm going to have to figure out how to talk to her about things besides the weather and driving conditions. But it's probably far past time the two of us had the space and time to learn how to talk to each other about things that really matter.

Maybe someday I'll even be able to tell her about Ken and Emily. About crying in the nurse's office, sick and alone. About taking care of my own burn wounds while she worked all those long hours.

But not today. Today, we celebrate this new beginning Devon Falls is gifting us.

"I'm so happy," I tell her as I finally let go of our hug. "Really, really happy. This town—there's something weirdly magic about it, I swear. I think you're going to really like living here."

"I know I will, baby." She pats me on the cheek. "Because *you're* here."

"Okay, I'm giving the toast this year."

Benson stands at the head of the long, decorative table the entire Lancer-Evers-and-now-Flynn clan has taken over in the winery's dining room for Thanksgiving dinner. Jack clinks a knife against his glass. "Hear, hear," he calls out.

"Thanks, babe," Benson calls back. "The rest of you, shut up, okay?"

The table titters with laughter and the chatter around the table finally comes to a slow stop. Benson levels us all with a look that I bet wins him plenty of court cases.

"Obviously, this holiday has some pretty horrific roots to answer for," he says. There are nods all around the table. "Which is why I refuse to celebrate Thanksgiving, and instead I choose to celebrate Peoplesgiving."

"Come again?" Tom shouts from the end of the table.

Benson holds up his wine glass as he looks around the table at all of us. "Some of you know that I haven't always been lucky enough to be surrounded by people who love me. Or even realize it when I was surrounded by people who love me. Right, Jack?"

"I take the fifth," Jack says solemnly, and everyone at the table laughs again.

"Anyway," Benson goes on, "now I'm lucky enough to often find myself at tables eating with people who fill the spaces around them—around me—with love. That's what I want to celebrate on this holiday. Hence: Peoplesgiving."

"Devon Falls really has done a number on you, hasn't it?" Marie says.

"It really has, Momma Lancer." We all let out a long *awww* together as Marie winks at Benson and lifts her glass to him.

"And today," Benson goes on, "I want to celebrate two people who I'm really fucking glad decided to end up here and then end up with each other. Because they add to all that love and other bullshit, you know?" Everyone laughs again as he raises his glass. "To Malachai and Sam," he says loudly. "May the universe help you both if you decide to get married, because I will insist your ceremony take place as a town festival launch complete with a state cow and miniature ballet dancers. Oh, and you both still owe me some HR paperwork."

Tom's laughing so hard I'm a little worried he's going to be sick. "To Malachai and Sam!" he manages to finally shout.

"To Malachai and Sam!" everyone at the table echoes.

I let my eyes travel around the table as I clink glasses with everyone: between Jack and Benson and Marie and Alan, and then over to Sam's mothers and Tom, then to the empty seat that was supposed to be for Colin—at the last minute he decided not to come. Tom and Sam didn't seem surprised by that, but I was disappointed. I hope he comes for our next round of holidays. Then I clink glasses with my mother, who's staring around at everyone like she's had the entire world presented to her on a silver platter.

I understand the feeling.

I turn to Sam, whose arm is wrapped tightly around my shoulder. "I love you, Malachai Flynn," he whispers in my ear.

He first said those words to me over a romantic dinner a few days after the leaf festival, at the same restaurant by the river where we once had our first date—well, I think of that as our first date, anyway. He's said those words so many times since then. But every single time feels new, somehow, a fresh wash of sunshine and warmth passing through my whole body.

"I love you too," I tell him. "Happy Peoplesgiving."

"Happy Peoplesgiving, my darling."

The kiss he leaves on my lips is quiet and soft and perfect, and it tastes better than every single dish the waiter places on the table.

I do what I will always do for Malachai from now on. I tell him everything. —Sam Evers

Jody opts to stay at the winery and carry on the celebrations long after conventional wisdom and good practices with alcohol suggest that anyone should still be celebrating. She and Marie and Alan and my mothers have all become fast friends. Malachai and I decide to say our good-byes before they get into the port.

We wave to Gabe, who's been working the front desk this entire evening. I've seen him occasionally lingering in the doorway of the dining room, casting glances in the direction of our table that look more than a little wistful. More than once I've seen Tom glance back in his direction, and then over at the empty chair Colin was supposed to occupy tonight.

Something is going on with my brother, that's for certain. But Tom's not exactly the strong, silent type. He'll tell me whatever he needs to tell me when he's ready; I'm sure of that.

I drive with Malachai through the quiet streets of Devon Falls, our hands lightly twined together between the front seats of the Rover. Every moment since the first day he came back to me feels like the first day of our lives together, and I cherish every single one of those days. I cherish every one of Malachai's wondrous expressions: none more so than the one that takes over his face when we pull into the driveway of the house we now own together and Malachai sees what is parked there.

He leans so far forward I'm a bit worried he's going to choke himself with his seatbelt. "Sam," he whispers. "What did you do now?"

I could tell him that I've officially become one of those sadists from a commercial who buys a car for their partner without telling them—luckily I'm not; not exactly. I did indeed rent another large Land Rover to place a giant bow on and park here, but it's entirely symbolic. I would never buy Malachai a car without asking for his input. A house? Yes. A car? That felt absurd, somehow.

I could tell him that I'm simply making a gesture in the hopes that he'll let me buy him a car because I detest the idea of him driving back and forth to Burlington in the coming year with that deathtrap he calls a vehicle. But that would also be leaving out crucial information.

So I do what I will always do for Malachai from now on. I tell him everything.

"I sold the condo in New York," I say quickly.

Malachai whirls to look at me. "You did what?" he asks.

"I sold the condo I owned with Christian. The money's set up in a trust for you to use for school, and there's a portion set aside for you to buy a new car for the commute."

Malachai lets out a sound that's somewhere between a laugh and a groan. "Sam, you can't be serious! You've already bought us a house!"

"I know. And if you really don't want us to use the money this way, we don't have to. This is *our* money, and we should decide together what to do with it. But I wanted to find a way to show you how good I feel about this decision." I grasp his hand in mine, pulling it up against my chest. "I'm ready to let go of that chapter of my life. Fully. I said my goodbyes to that space, and I'm making this space my home now. With you. And I'd like to have a car in the driveway that doesn't make me want to cringe every time you step into it."

Malachai laughs as he leans across the car seats and into the place where I've pulled his hand to my chest. "Oh, Sam," he says. "You're incredible. No wonder I never used to be able to talk around you."

"You what?" I don't even have a chance to ask what on earth he's talking about before Malachai swallows any questions I was about to ask with a kiss.

It's a long kiss, one that continues all the way from the car to the house and finds us tripping out of shoes and socks and through the hallway up into the bedroom. "Want you, sir," Malachai whispers as we arrive at the foot of the bed.

He always knows when to say that word to me.

The light of the moon etches its way through the curtains as I whisper soft orders in his ear, telling him just how to ready himself, just how to prepare his body for me. The slight, small gasps he makes when I enter him are burned deeply into my brain now, part of our life together, and they are noises I know I will never, ever tire of.

Nothing is between us as I lose myself inside of him, my body shaking hard in the wake of the lightning storm Malachai always manages to unleash within me. "I love you," I whisper into the darkness of the room as the two of us come together at exactly the same moment. "I love you so very much, my darling."

He falls asleep buried in my arms, soft snores echoing in the silence of the space. I hold him tightly against me, studying him and taking the time to be grateful for every single thing he's gifted me. The moonlight makes its way through the movement of the curtains, hovering on objects and spaces as it drifts.

It stops, for just a moment, on a picture of me and Christian; the same picture I turned upside down not all that long ago. It's back as it once was, in its rightful place on full display. Next to it is a picture of me and Malachai, one taken by Benson and Jack's wedding photographer. We're dancing in the picture, arm in arm, and I'm leaning over to kiss the top of Malachai's head. Jack gifted me the picture in a frame a few weeks ago. "To old and new memories," he said as I unwrapped it.

The two pictures look good side by side. As if they're both exactly where they're meant to be.

"To old memories," I whisper to the picture of Christian. I swear, the picture glints in the light at just that moment.

I hold Malachai as tightly as I can and let myself swim in the sweet sensation of the rise and fall of his chest against mine.

"And to all the new memories we've only just begun to make," I whisper.

Malachai smiles sleepily in the moonlight, and all is right with the world.

THE END

Thank you for reading *Forbidden in the Falls.* WANT MORE Sam and Malachai? Grab their bonus scene at this link: https://ti nyurl.com/forbiddenbonus

Curious about Benson and Jack? Their book is *Fauxmance in the Falls*, book one in the Devon Falls series.

Curious about Gabe, Tom, and Colin? Their book, *Fanboy in the Falls*, is the next story in the Devon Falls series!

Turn the page for more titles from J.E. Birk!

More Books by J.E. Birk

Find all of J.E.'s books at www.jebirk.com.

Curious about Adam, Embry, and Jeb? Their book is *ILYBSM*, the first book in the ILYBSM series.

Want more Vermont-y kisses and happy endings from J.E. Birk? Check out *Booklover* and *Counterpoint*. (Benson makes his first appearance in *Counterpoint*.)

If you're looking for a darker, angstier read, you may enjoy *The Worst Bad Thing*. Please heed the content warnings in the author's note.

Happy reading, everyone!

About the Author

J.E. Birk was raised in Vermont and is now adulting in Colorado with intermittent success. She is a long-time lover of stories, and she writes and reads in worlds where imperfect characters find their happily ever after. Snag free bonus content and stay up-to-date on J.E. Birk's news and releases by signing up for her newsletter at www.jebirk.com.